HEATHCLIFF

CAT AND MOUSE GAMES

TOR

A TOM DOHERTY ASSOCIATES BOOK
NEW YORK

This is a work of fiction. All the characters and events portrayed in this book are fictitious, and any resemblance to real people or events is purely coincidental.

HEATHCLIFF®: CAT AND MOUSE GAMES

Originally published by Marvel Comics in magazine form as HEATHCLIFF #2, #3, #4, #6, #10, #11, #24, and #32

Copyright © 1985, 1986, 1987, 1988, 1989, 1990 by Geo. Gately

HEATHCLIFF and all prominent characters appearing herein and the distinctive names and likenesses thereof are trademarks of Geo. Gately.

All rights reserved, including the right to reproduce this book, or portions thereof, in any form.

A Tor Book
Published by Tom Doherty Associates, Inc.
49 West 24th Street
New York, N.Y. 10010

ISBN: 0-812-50988-9

First printing: August 1990

Printed in the United States of America

0 9 8 7 6 5 4 3 2 1

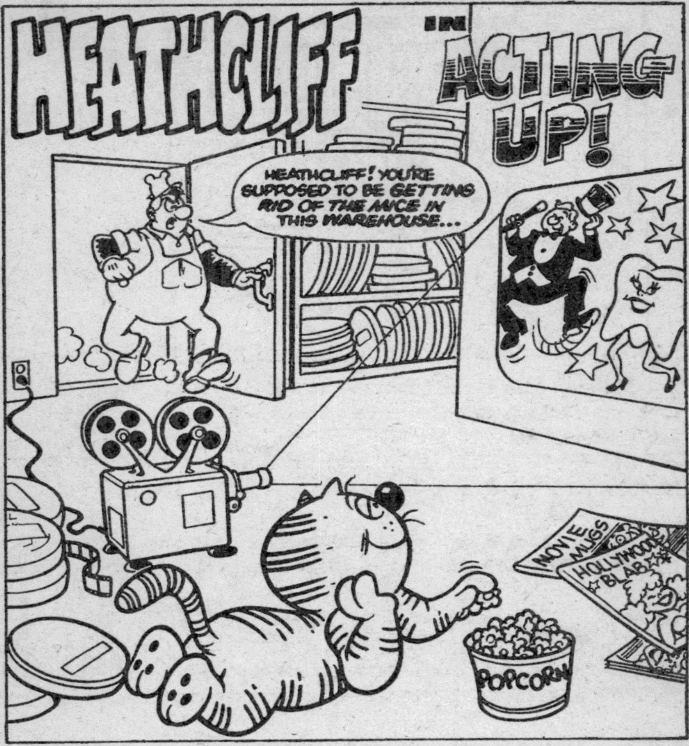
HEATHCLIFF
IN
ACTING UP!
HEATHCLIFF! YOU'RE SUPPOSED TO BE GETTING RID OF THE MICE IN THIS WAREHOUSE...
MOVIE MUGS
HOLLYWOOD BLAB
POPCORN

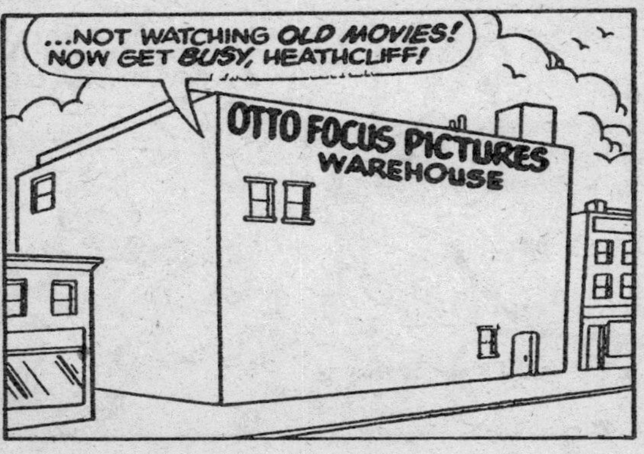
...NOT WATCHING OLD MOVIES! NOW GET BUSY, HEATHCLIFF!
OTTO FOCUS PICTURES
WAREHOUSE

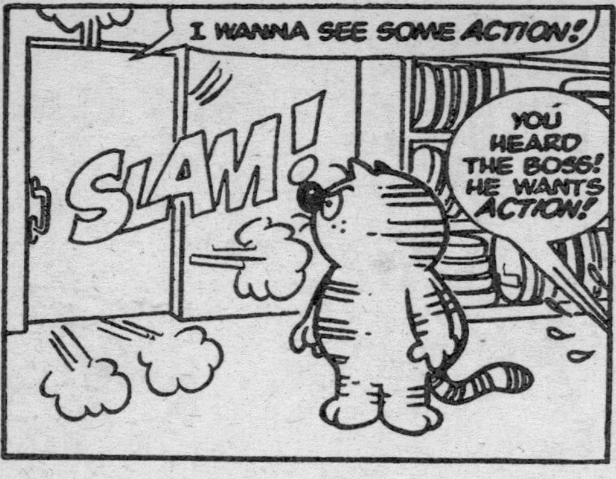
I WANNA SEE SOME ACTION!
SLAM!
YOU HEARD THE BOSS! HE WANTS ACTION!

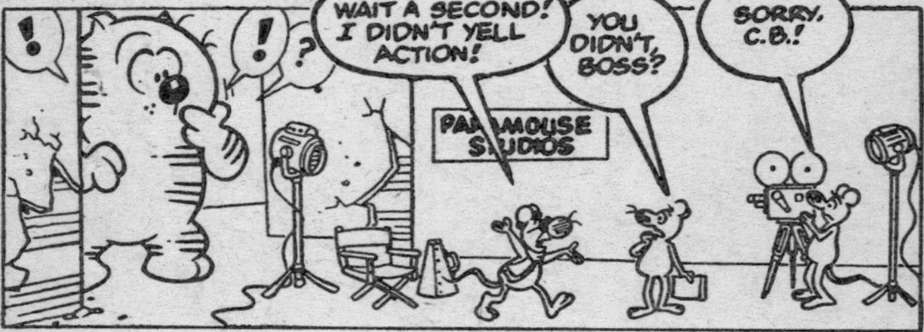
!
!
?
WAIT A SECOND! I DIDN'T YELL ACTION!
YOU DIDN'T, BOSS?
SORRY, C.B.!

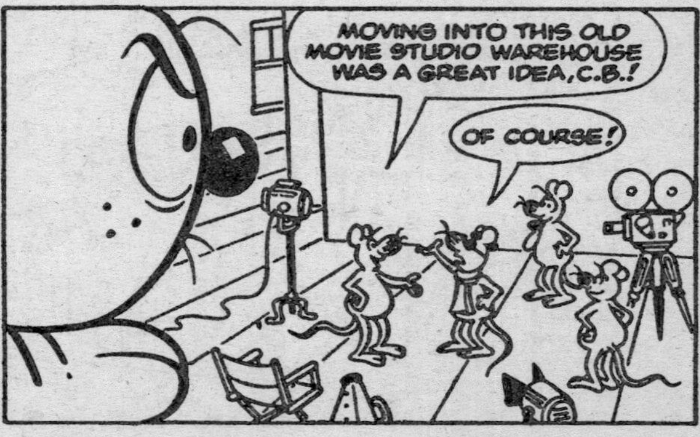
MOVING INTO THIS OLD MOVIE STUDIO WAREHOUSE WAS A GREAT IDEA, C.B.!
OF COURSE!

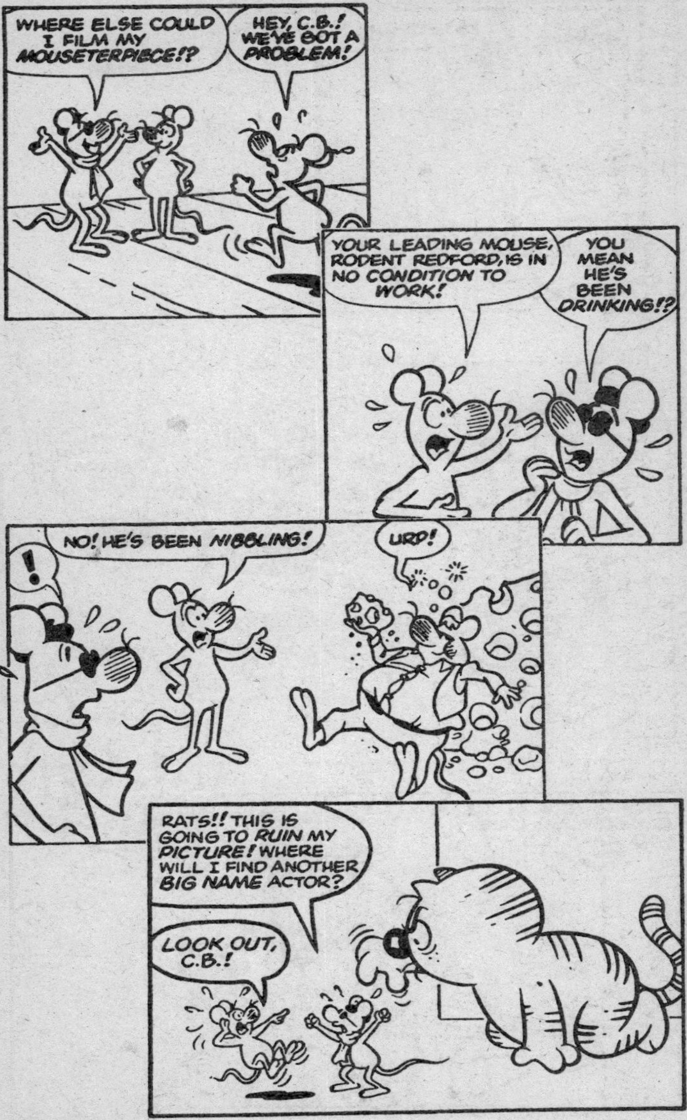
WHERE ELSE COULD I FILM MY MOUSETERPIECE!?
HEY, C.B.! WE'VE GOT A PROBLEM!
YOUR LEADING MOUSE, RODENT REDFORD, IS IN NO CONDITION TO WORK!
YOU MEAN HE'S BEEN DRINKING!?
!
NO! HE'S BEEN NIBBLING!
URP!
RATS!! THIS IS GOING TO RUIN MY PICTURE! WHERE WILL I FIND ANOTHER BIG NAME ACTOR?
LOOK OUT, C.B.!

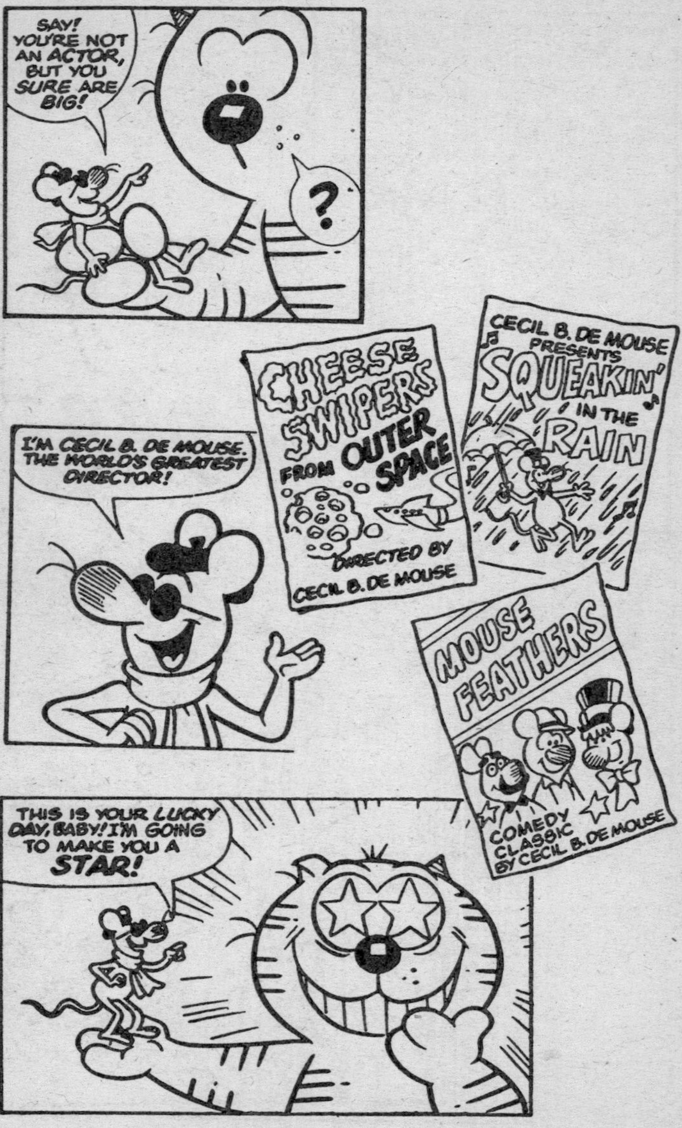
SAY! YOU'RE NOT AN ACTOR, BUT YOU SURE ARE BIG!
?
I'M CECIL B. DE MOUSE. THE WORLD'S GREATEST DIRECTOR!
CHEESE SWIPERS FROM OUTER SPACE
DIRECTED BY CECIL B. DE MOUSE
CECIL B. DE MOUSE PRESENTS
SQUEAKIN' IN THE RAIN
MOUSE FEATHERS
COMEDY CLASSIC BY CECIL B. DE MOUSE
THIS IS YOUR LUCKY DAY, BABY! I'M GOING TO MAKE YOU A STAR!

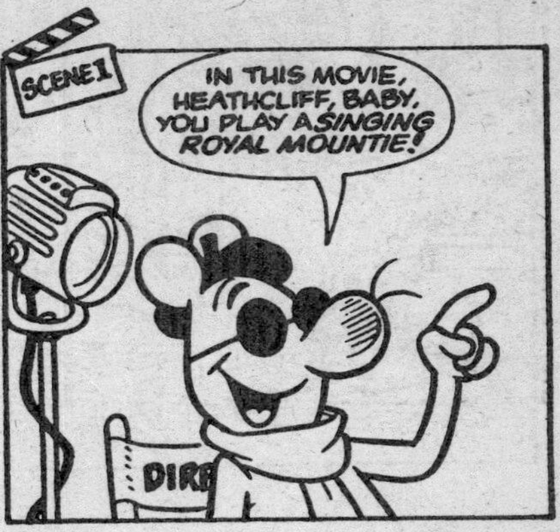
SCENE 1
IN THIS MOVIE, HEATHCLIFF, BABY, YOU PLAY A *SINGING ROYAL MOUNTIE!*

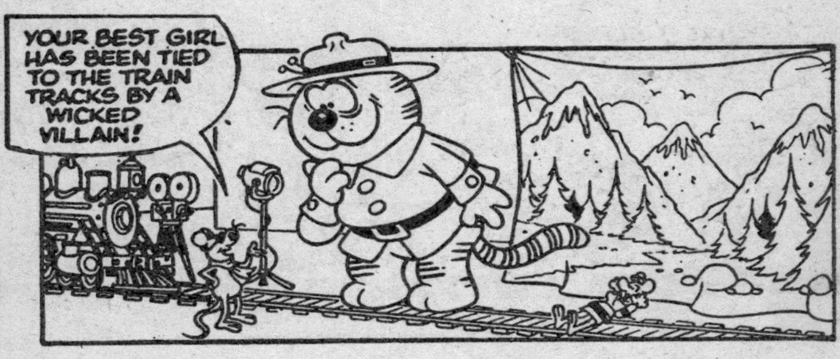
YOUR BEST GIRL HAS BEEN TIED TO THE TRAIN TRACKS BY A WICKED VILLAIN!

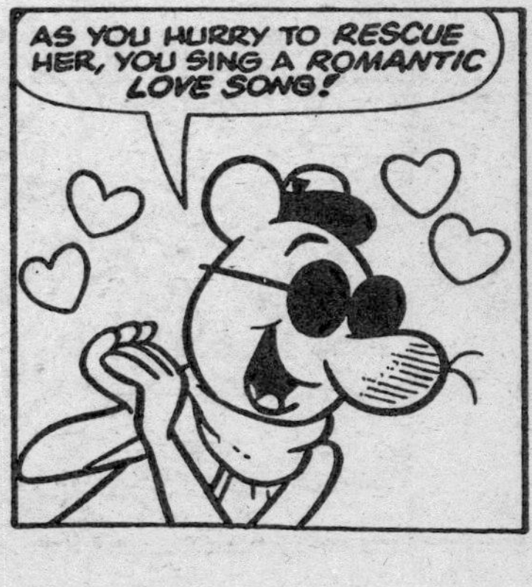
AS YOU HURRY TO *RESCUE* HER, YOU SING A *ROMANTIC LOVE SONG!*

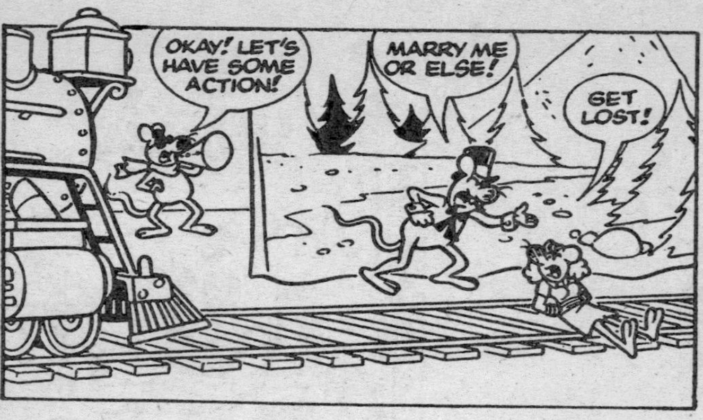
OKAY! LET'S HAVE SOME ACTION!
MARRY ME OR ELSE!
GET LOST!

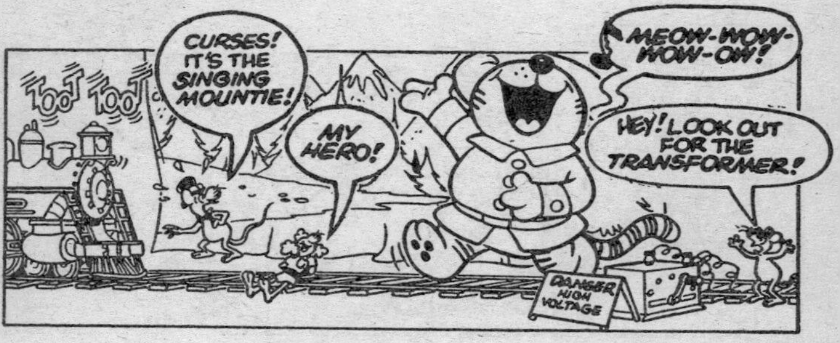
TOOT TOOT
CURSES! IT'S THE SINGING MOUNTIE!
MEOW-WOW-WOW-OW!
MY HERO!
HEY! LOOK OUT FOR THE TRANSFORMER!
DANGER HIGH VOLTAGE

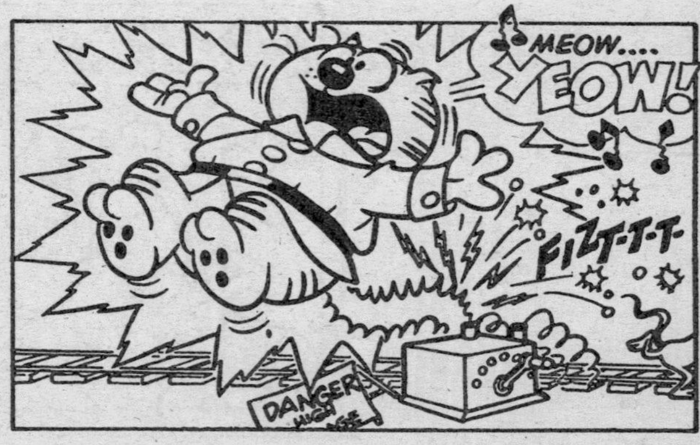
MEOW.... YEOW!
FIZT-T-T-
DANGER

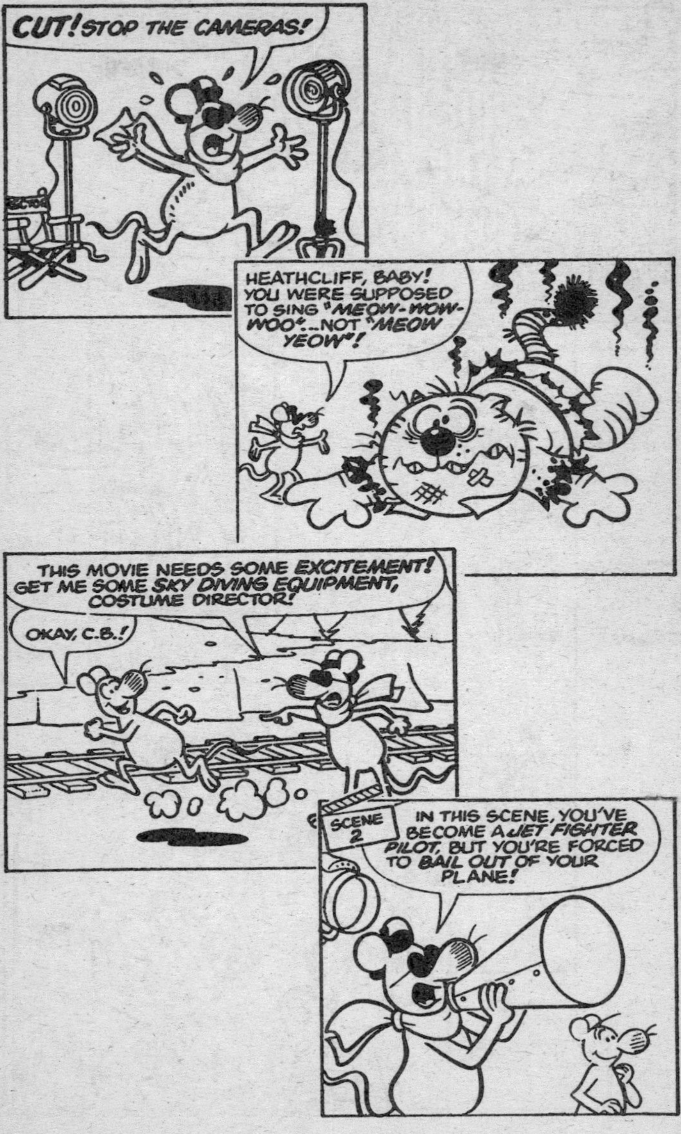
CUT! STOP THE CAMERAS!
HEATHCLIFF, BABY! YOU WERE SUPPOSED TO SING "MEOW-WOW-WOO"...NOT "MEOW YEOW"!
THIS MOVIE NEEDS SOME EXCITEMENT! GET ME SOME SKY DIVING EQUIPMENT, COSTUME DIRECTOR!
OKAY, C.B.!
SCENE 2
IN THIS SCENE, YOU'VE BECOME A JET FIGHTER PILOT, BUT YOU'RE FORCED TO BAIL OUT OF YOUR PLANE!

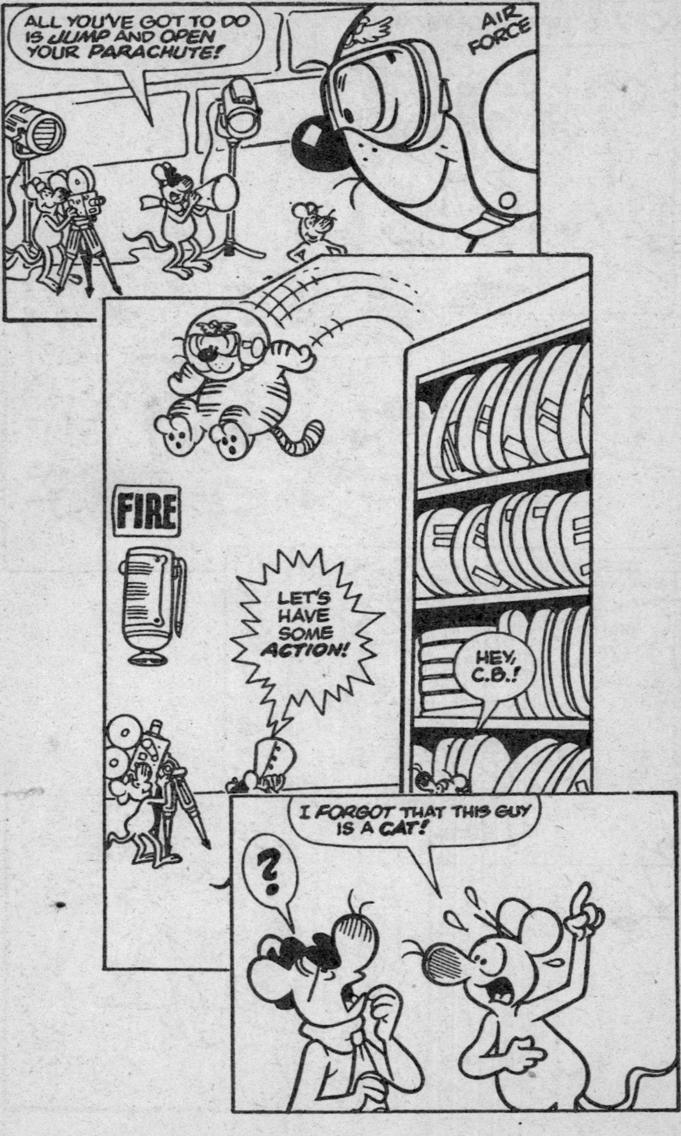
ALL YOU'VE GOT TO DO IS JUMP AND OPEN YOUR PARACHUTE!
AIR FORCE
FIRE
LET'S HAVE SOME ACTION!
HEY, C.B.!
?
I FORGOT THAT THIS GUY IS A CAT!

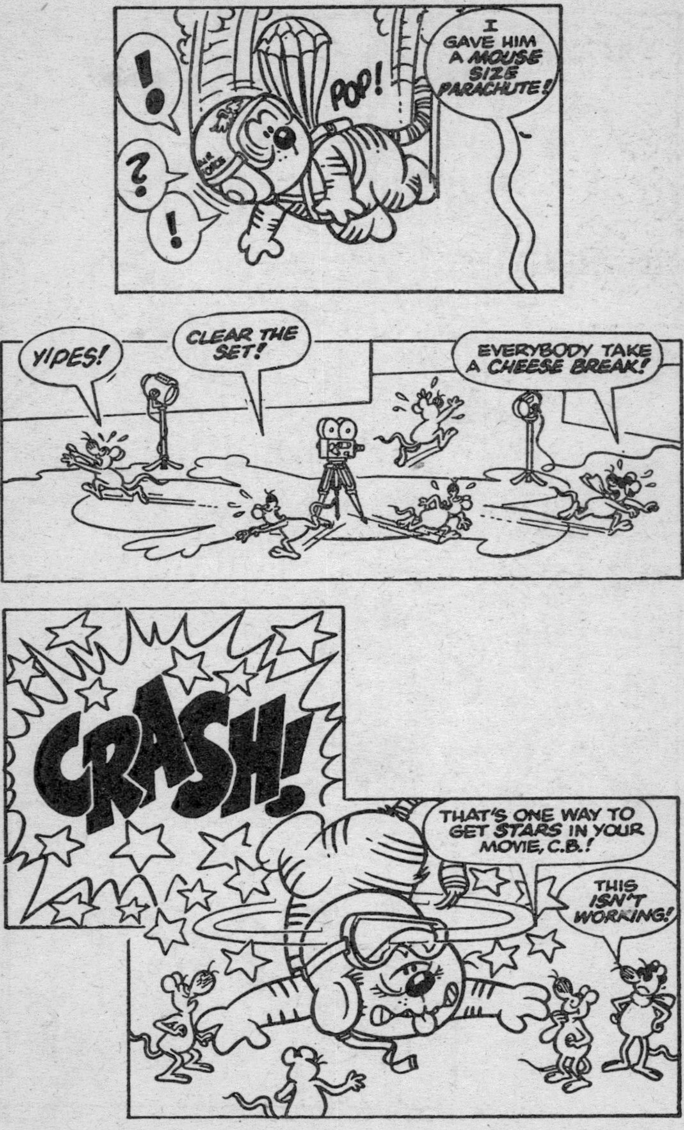

!
?
!
POP!
I GAVE HIM A MOUSE SIZE PARACHUTE!
YIPES!
CLEAR THE SET!
EVERYBODY TAKE A CHEESE BREAK!
CRASH!
THAT'S ONE WAY TO GET STARS IN YOUR MOVIE, C.B.!
THIS ISN'T WORKING!

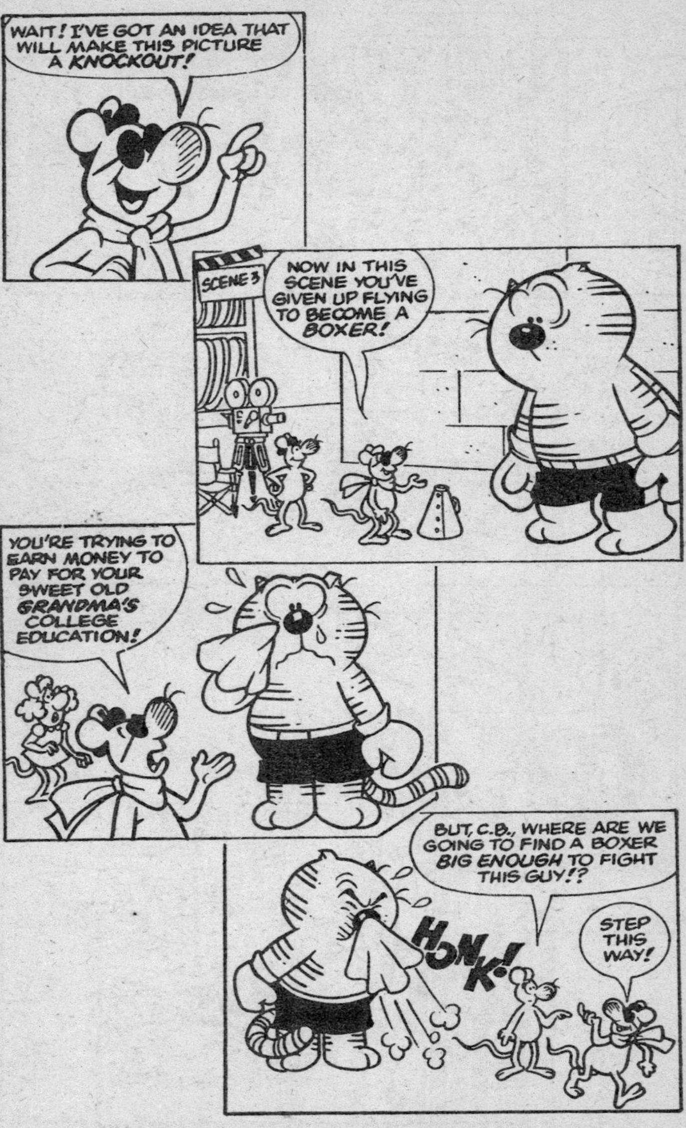
WAIT! I'VE GOT AN IDEA THAT WILL MAKE THIS PICTURE A KNOCKOUT!
SCENE 3
NOW IN THIS SCENE YOU'VE GIVEN UP FLYING TO BECOME A BOXER!
YOU'RE TRYING TO EARN MONEY TO PAY FOR YOUR SWEET OLD GRANDMA'S COLLEGE EDUCATION!
HONK!
BUT, C.B., WHERE ARE WE GOING TO FIND A BOXER BIG ENOUGH TO FIGHT THIS GUY!?
STEP THIS WAY!

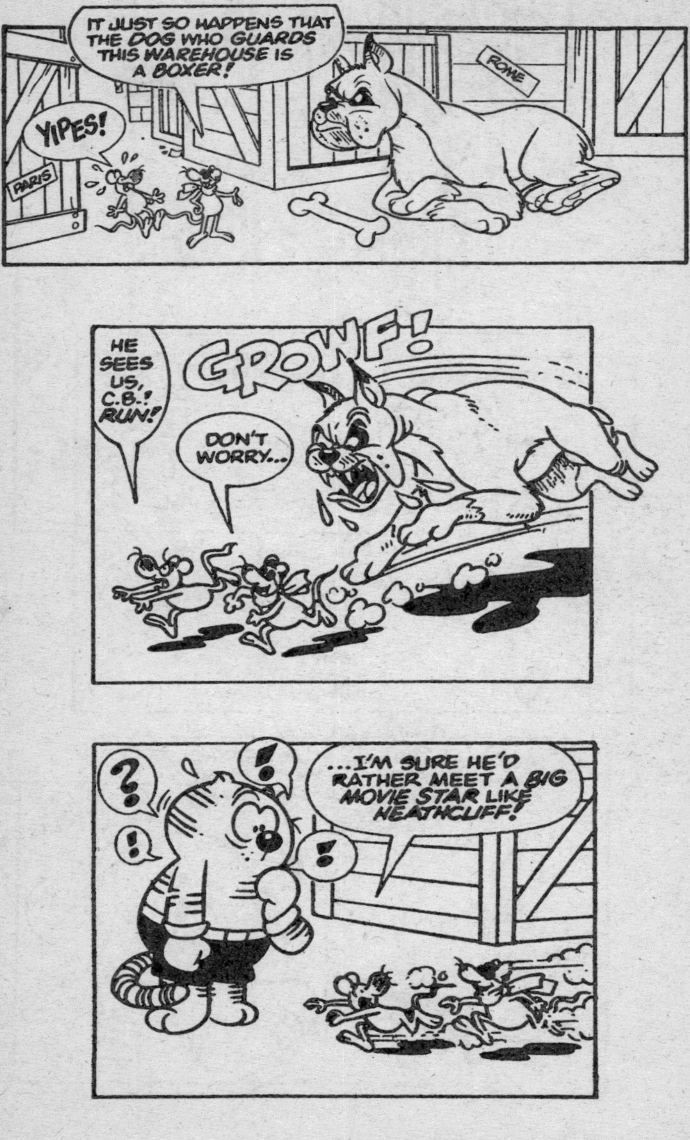
IT JUST SO HAPPENS THAT THE *DOG* WHO *GUARDS* THIS *WAREHOUSE* IS A *BOXER!*
ROME
YIPES!
PARIS
GROWF!
HE SEES US, C.B.! *RUN!*
DON'T WORRY...
?
!
!
!
...I'M SURE HE'D RATHER MEET A *BIG MOVIE STAR* LIKE *HEATHCLIFF!*

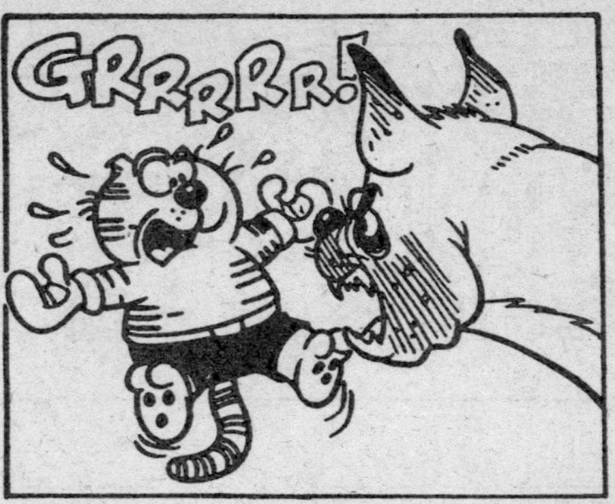
GRRRRR!

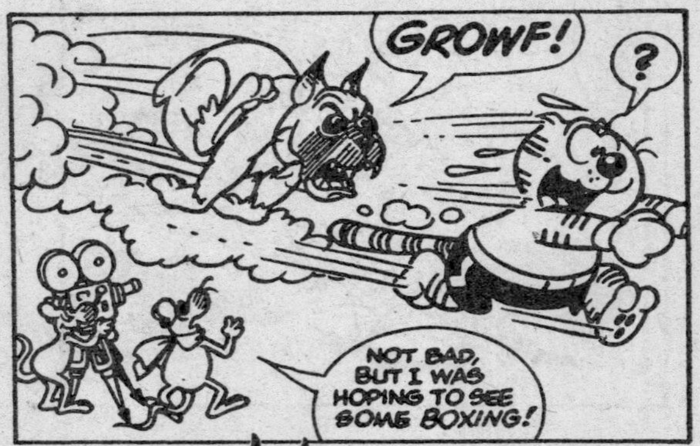
GROWF!
?
NOT BAD, BUT I WAS HOPING TO SEE SOME BOXING!

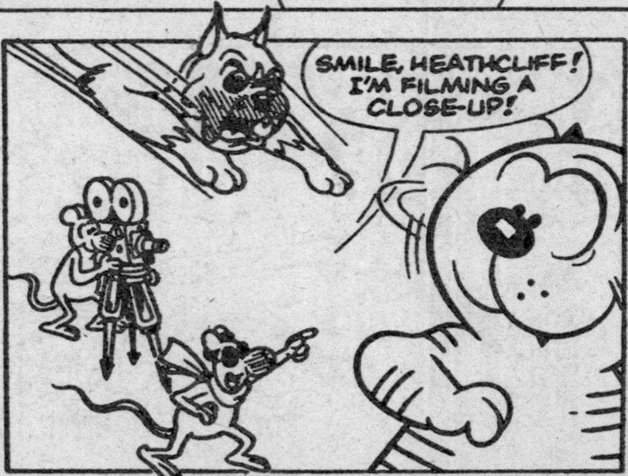
SMILE, HEATHCLIFF! I'M FILMING A CLOSE-UP!

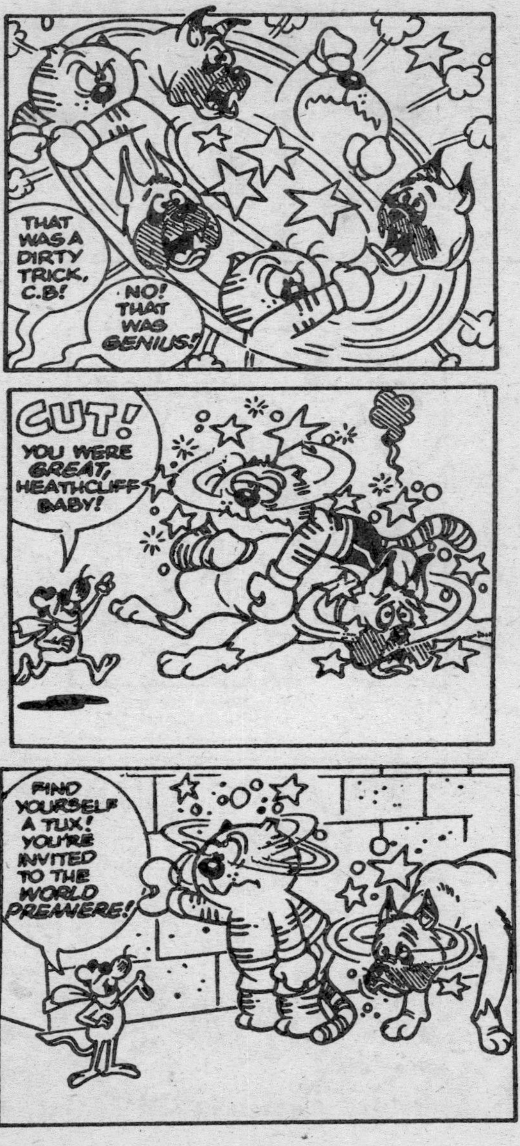
THAT WAS A DIRTY TRICK, C.B!
NO! THAT WAS GENIUS!
CUT! YOU WERE GREAT, HEATHCLIFF BABY!
FIND YOURSELF A TUX! YOU'RE INVITED TO THE WORLD PREMIERE!

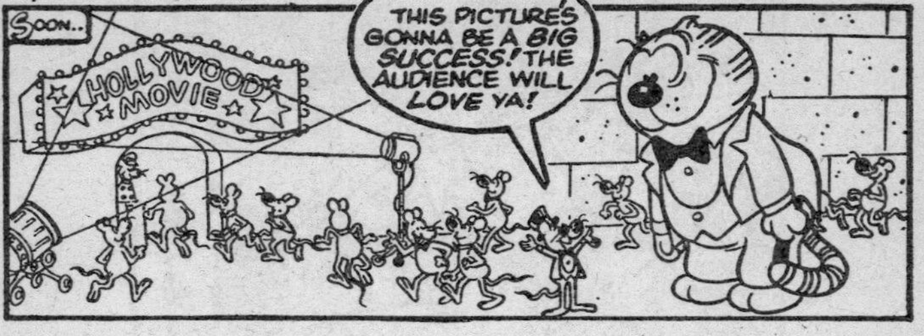
SOON..
HOLLYWOOD MOVIE
THIS PICTURE'S GONNA BE A BIG SUCCESS! THE AUDIENCE WILL LOVE YA!

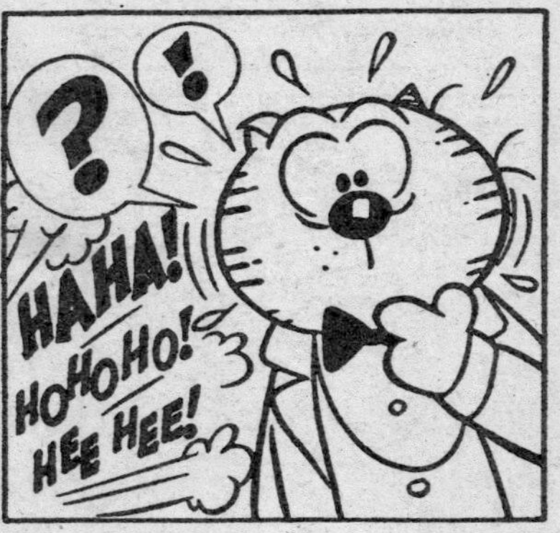
?
!
HAHA!
HOHOHO!
HEE HEE!

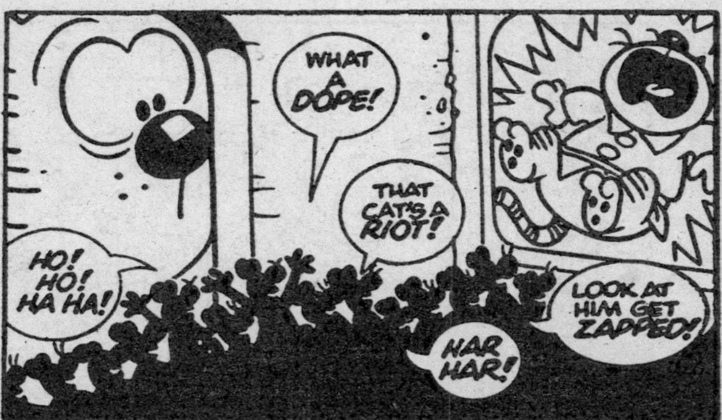
HO! HO! HA HA!
WHAT A DOPE!
THAT CAT'S A RIOT!
HAR HAR!
LOOK AT HIM GET ZAPPED!

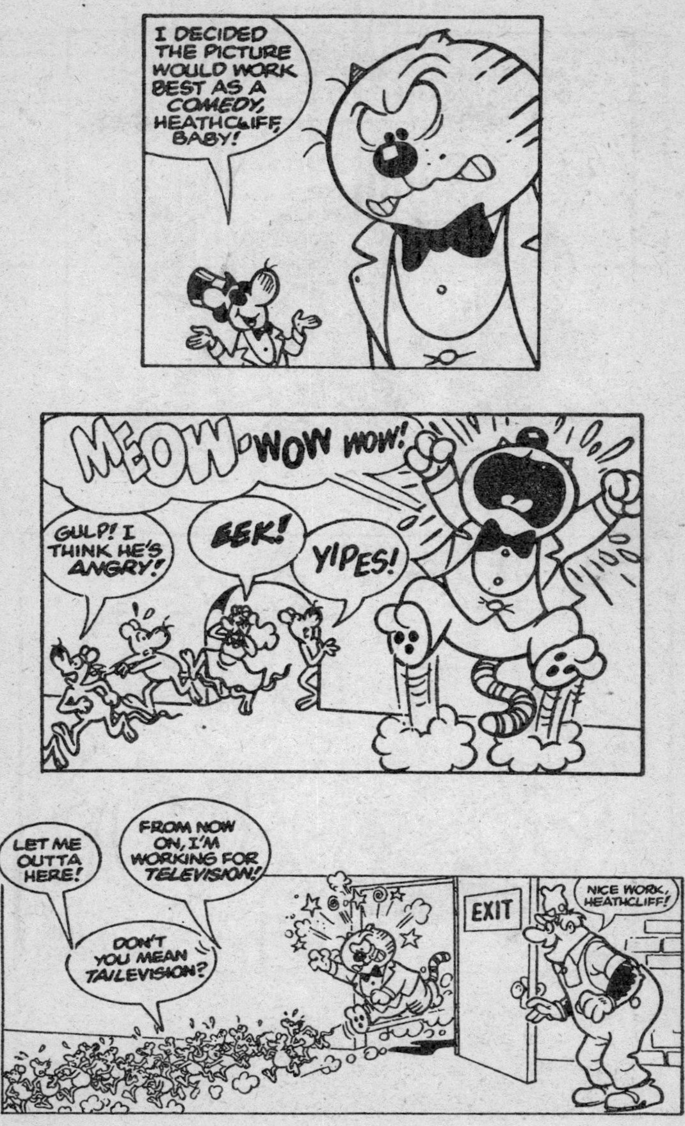
I DECIDED THE PICTURE WOULD WORK BEST AS A COMEDY, HEATHCLIFF, BABY!
MEOW-WOW WOW!
GULP! I THINK HE'S ANGRY!
EEK!
YIPES!
LET ME OUTTA HERE!
FROM NOW ON, I'M WORKING FOR TELEVISION!
DON'T YOU MEAN TAILEVISION?
EXIT
NICE WORK, HEATHCLIFF!

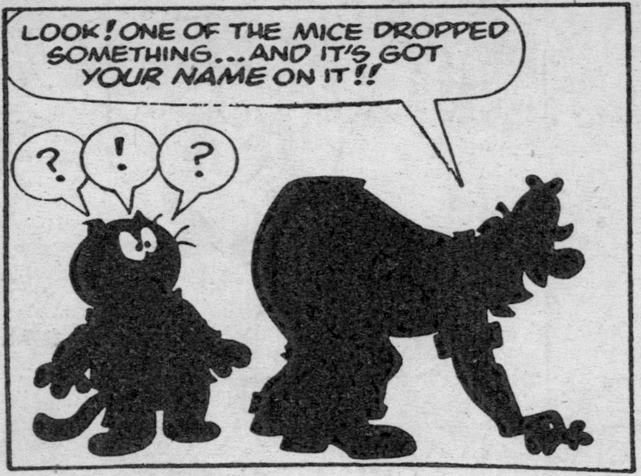
LOOK! ONE OF THE MICE DROPPED SOMETHING...AND IT'S GOT YOUR NAME ON IT!!
?
!
?

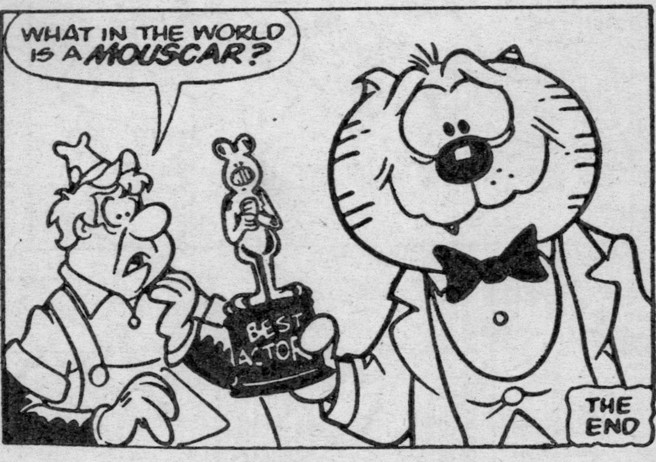
WHAT IN THE WORLD IS A MOUSCAR?
BEST ACTOR
THE END

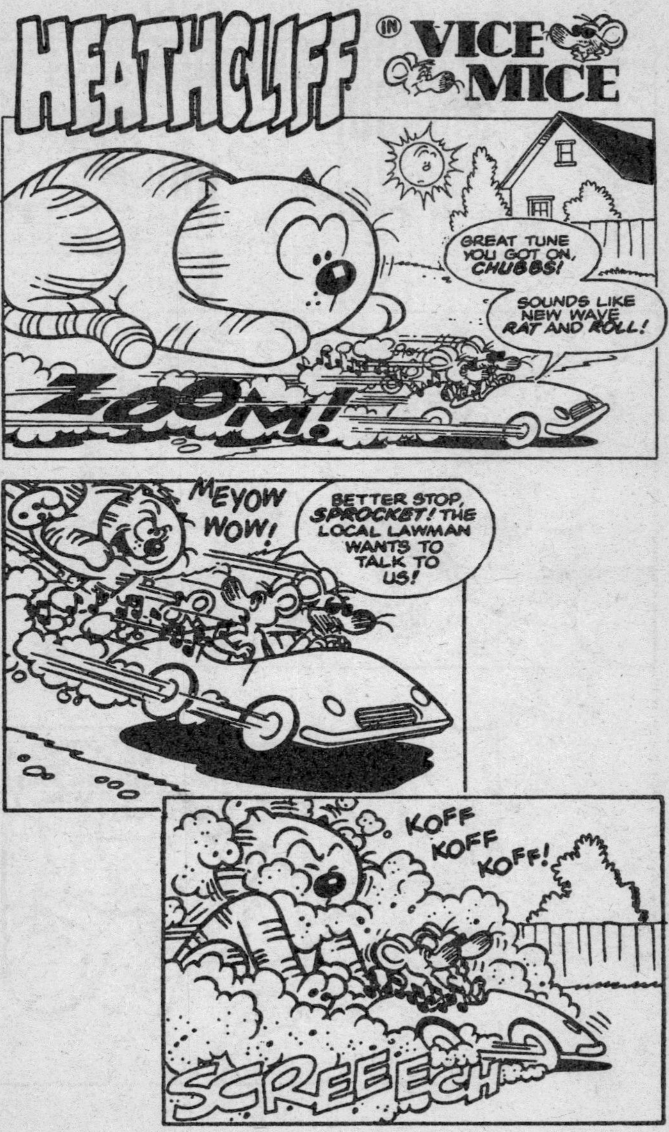
HEATHCLIFF
IN
VICE MICE
GREAT TUNE YOU GOT ON, CHUBBS!
SOUNDS LIKE NEW WAVE RAT AND ROLL!
ZOOM!
MEYOW WOW!
BETTER STOP, SPROCKET! THE LOCAL LAWMAN WANTS TO TALK TO US!
KOFF KOFF KOFF!
SCREEECH

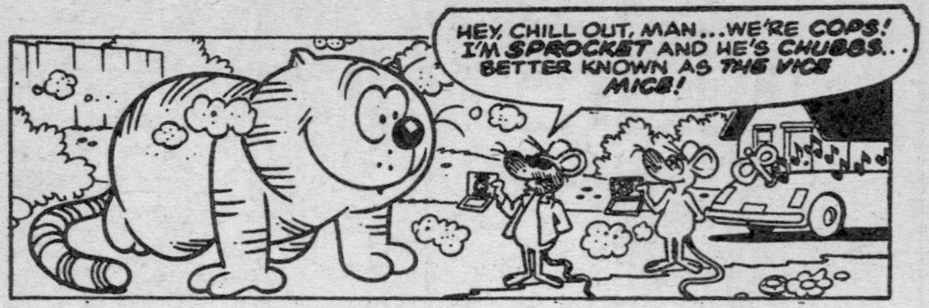
HEY, CHILL OUT, MAN...WE'RE COPS! I'M SPROCKET AND HE'S CHUBBS... BETTER KNOWN AS THE VICE MICE!

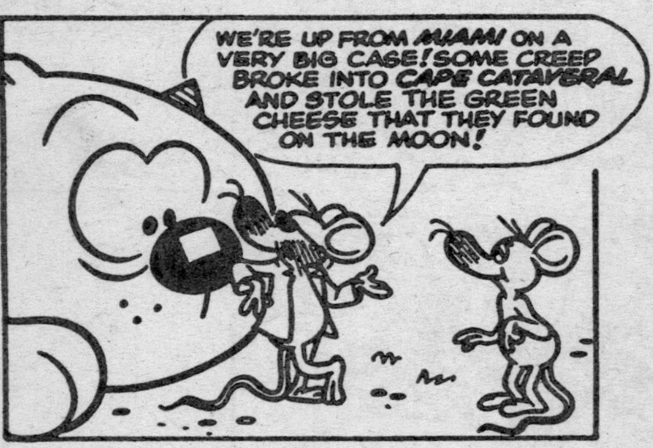
WE'RE UP FROM MIAMI ON A VERY BIG CASE! SOME CREEP BROKE INTO CAPE CATAVERAL AND STOLE THE GREEN CHEESE THAT THEY FOUND ON THE MOON!

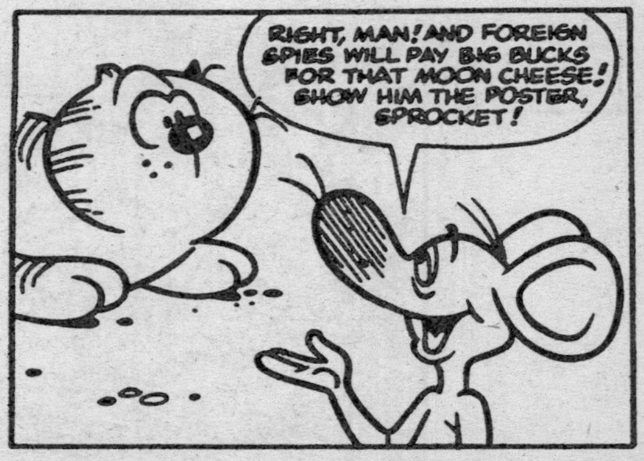
RIGHT, MAN! AND FOREIGN SPIES WILL PAY BIG BUCKS FOR THAT MOON CHEESE! SHOW HIM THE POSTER, SPROCKET!

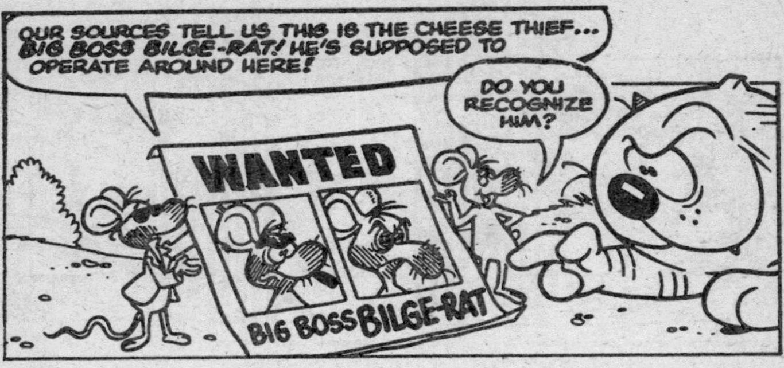
OUR SOURCES TELL US THIS IS THE CHEESE THIEF... BIG BOSS BILGE-RAT! HE'S SUPPOSED TO OPERATE AROUND HERE!
DO YOU RECOGNIZE HIM?
WANTED
BIG BOSS BILGE-RAT

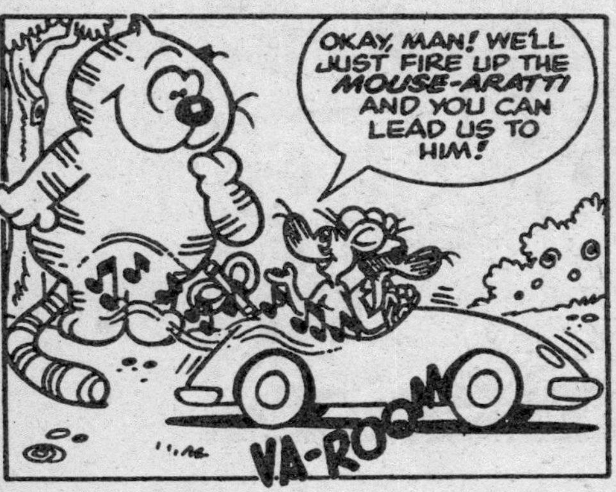
OKAY, MAN! WE'LL JUST FIRE UP THE MOUSE-ARATTI AND YOU CAN LEAD US TO HIM!
VA-ROOM

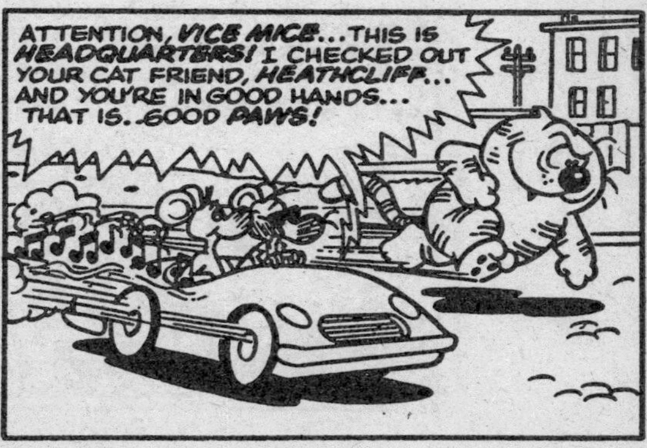
ATTENTION, VICE MICE...THIS IS HEADQUARTERS! I CHECKED OUT YOUR CAT FRIEND, HEATHCLIFF... AND YOU'RE IN GOOD HANDS... THAT IS..GOOD PAWS!

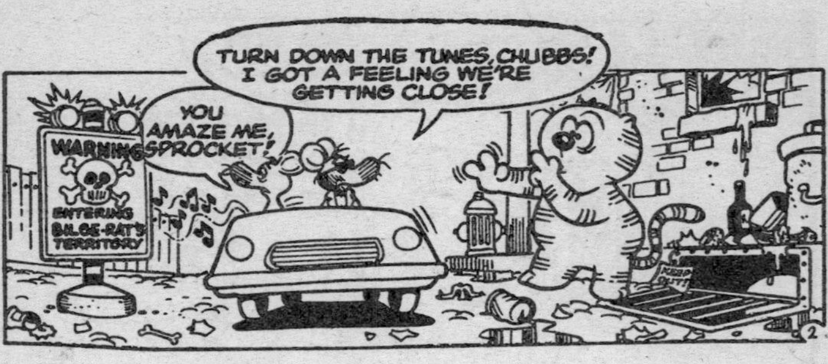
TURN DOWN THE TUNES, CHUBBS! I GOT A FEELING WE'RE GETTING CLOSE!
YOU AMAZE ME, SPROCKET!
WARNING
ENTERING BILGE-RAT'S TERRITORY
KEEP OUT!
2

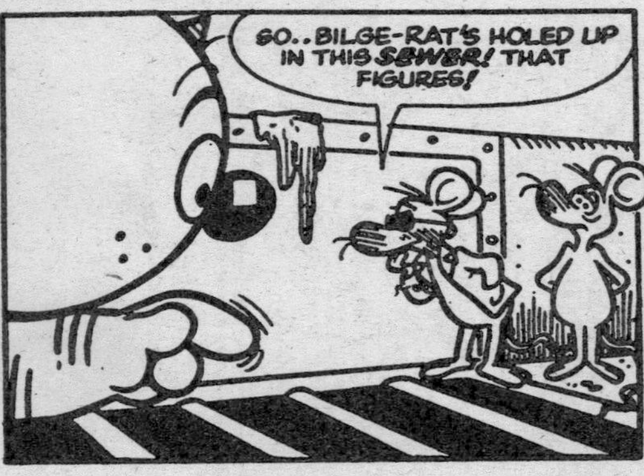
SO.. BILGE-RAT'S HOLED UP IN THIS SEWER! THAT FIGURES!

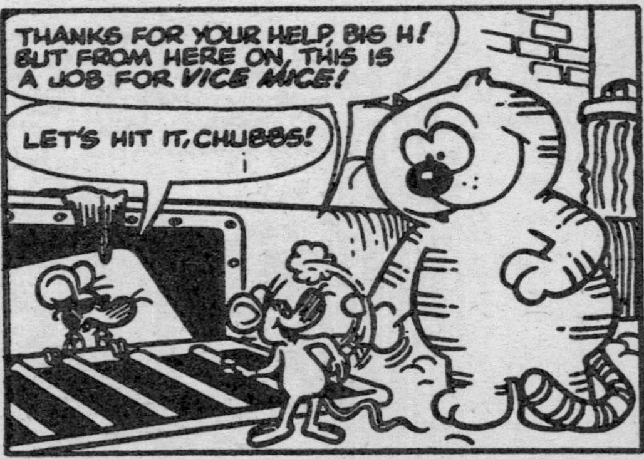
THANKS FOR YOUR HELP, BIG H! BUT FROM HERE ON, THIS IS A JOB FOR VICE MICE!
LET'S HIT IT, CHUBBS!

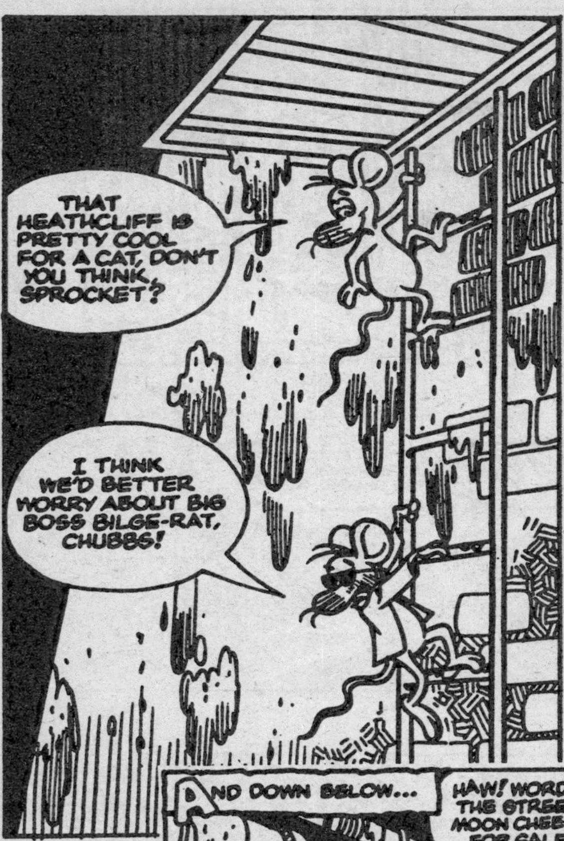
THAT HEATHCLIFF IS PRETTY COOL FOR A CAT, DON'T YOU THINK, SPROCKET?
I THINK WE'D BETTER WORRY ABOUT BIG BOSS BILGE-RAT, CHUBBS!
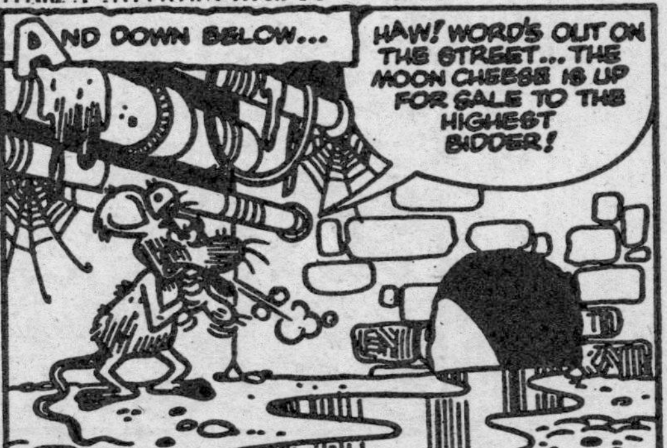
AND DOWN BELOW...
HAW! WORD'S OUT ON THE STREET... THE MOON CHEESE IS UP FOR SALE TO THE HIGHEST BIDDER!

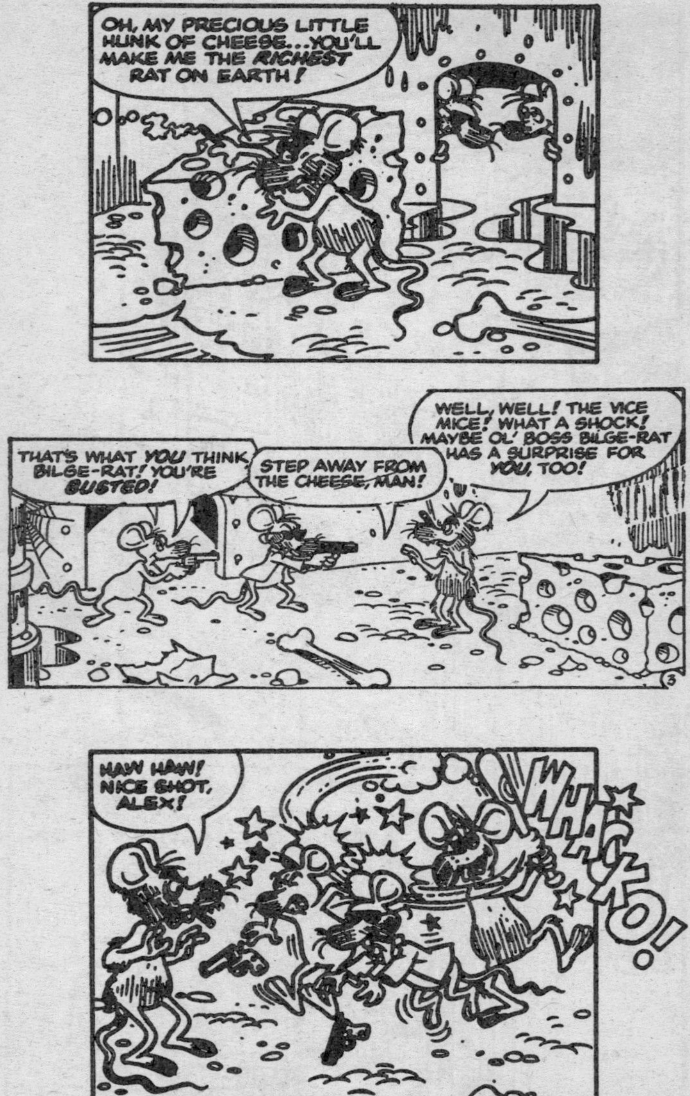
OH, MY PRECIOUS LITTLE HUNK OF CHEESE...YOU'LL MAKE ME THE RICHEST RAT ON EARTH!
THAT'S WHAT YOU THINK, BILGE-RAT! YOU'RE BUSTED!
STEP AWAY FROM THE CHEESE, MAN!
WELL, WELL! THE VICE MICE! WHAT A SHOCK! MAYBE OL' BOSS BILGE-RAT HAS A SURPRISE FOR YOU, TOO!
HAW HAW! NICE SHOT, ALEX!
WHAKO!

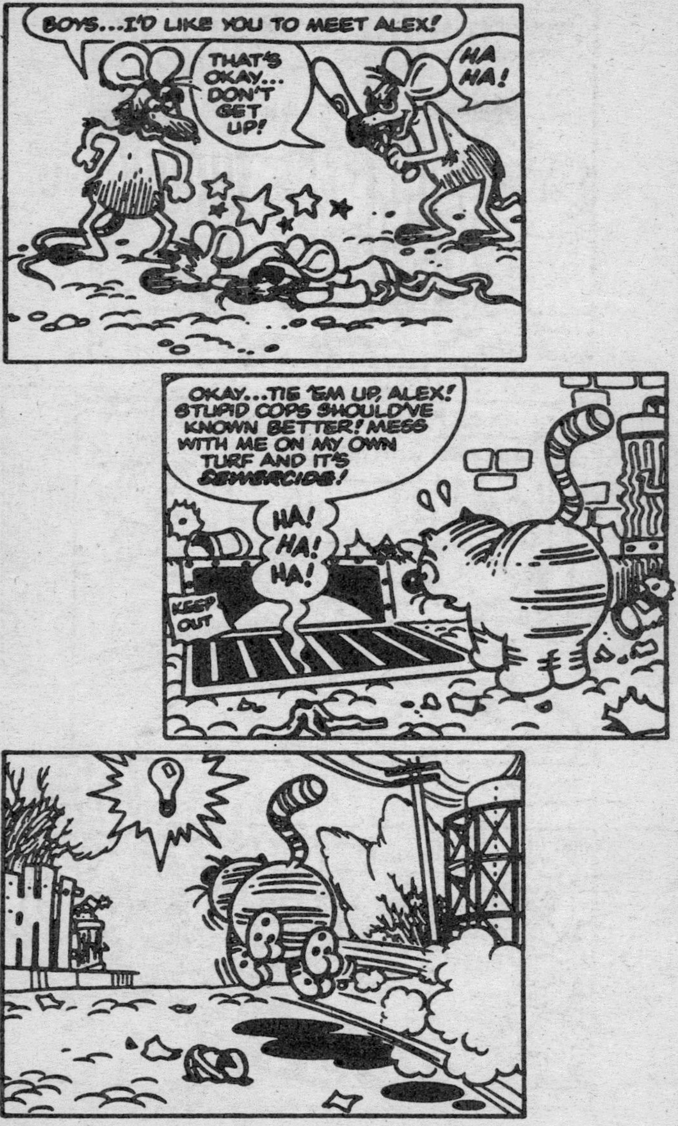
BOYS...I'D LIKE YOU TO MEET ALEX!
THAT'S OKAY... DON'T GET UP!
HA HA!
OKAY...TIE 'EM UP, ALEX! STUPID COPS SHOULD'VE KNOWN BETTER! MESS WITH ME ON MY OWN TURF AND IT'S SEWERCIDE!
HA! HA! HA!
KEEP OUT

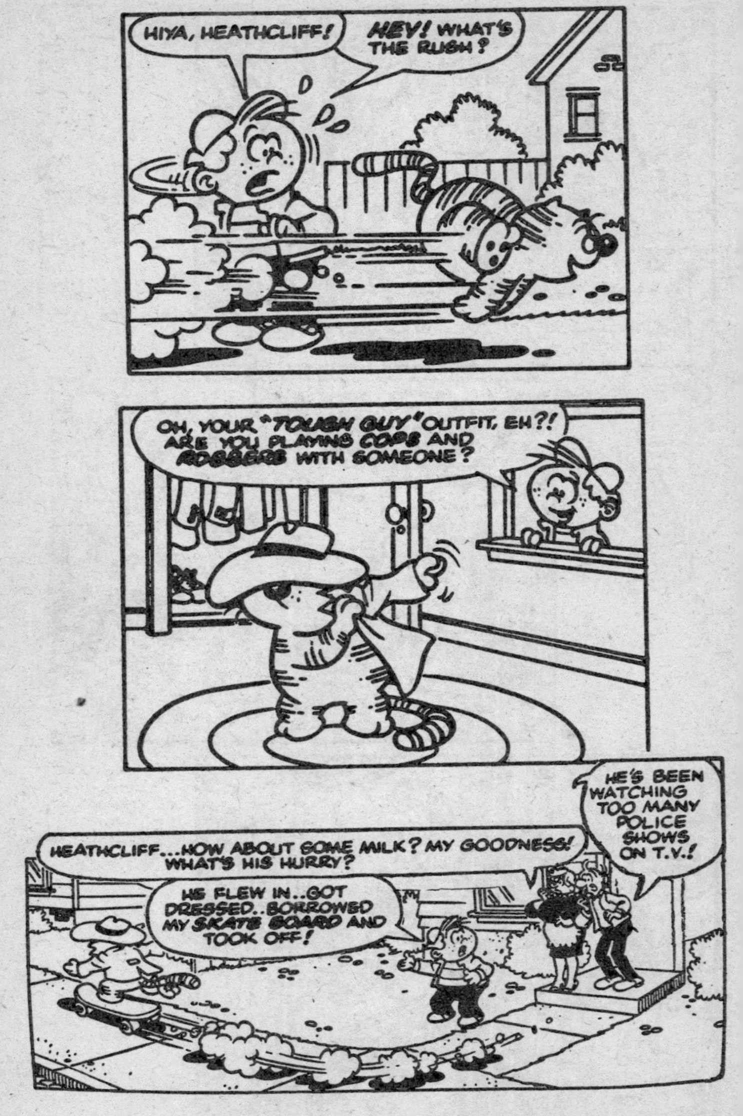
HIYA, HEATHCLIFF!
HEY! WHAT'S THE RUSH?
OH, YOUR "TOUGH GUY" OUTFIT, EH?! ARE YOU PLAYING COPS AND ROBBERS WITH SOMEONE?
HEATHCLIFF...HOW ABOUT SOME MILK? MY GOODNESS! WHAT'S HIS HURRY?
HE'S BEEN WATCHING TOO MANY POLICE SHOWS ON T.V.!
HE FLEW IN..GOT DRESSED..BORROWED MY SKATE BOARD AND TOOK OFF!

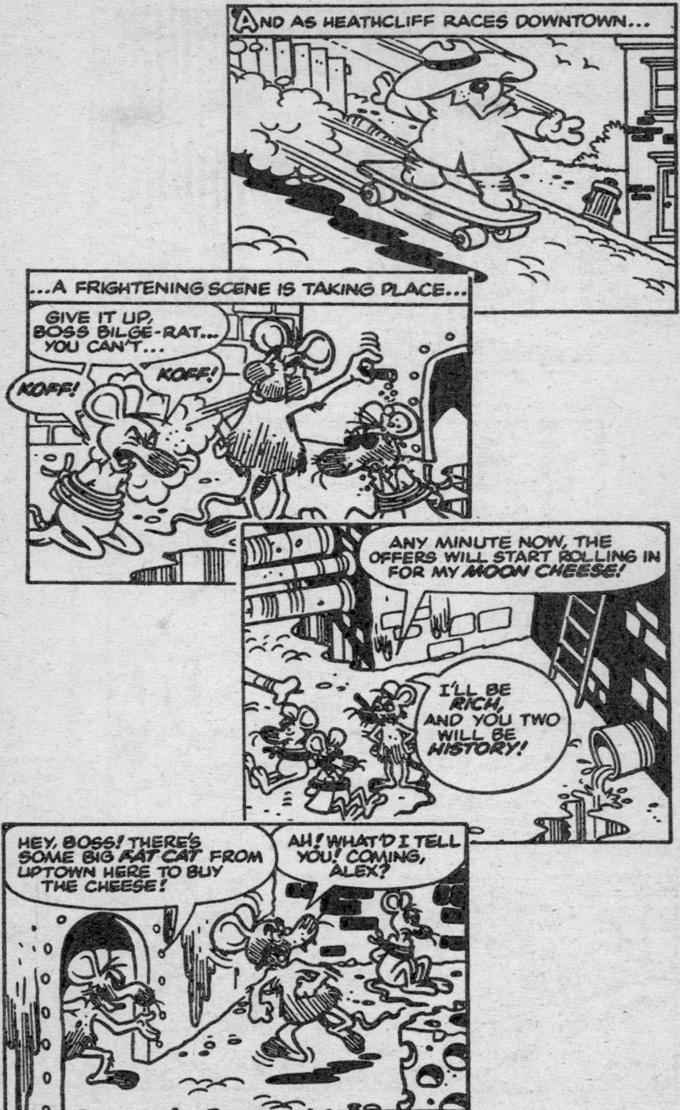
AND AS HEATHCLIFF RACES DOWNTOWN...
...A FRIGHTENING SCENE IS TAKING PLACE...
GIVE IT UP, BOSS BILGE-RAT... YOU CAN'T...
KOFF!
KOFF!
ANY MINUTE NOW, THE OFFERS WILL START ROLLING IN FOR MY MOON CHEESE!
I'LL BE RICH, AND YOU TWO WILL BE HISTORY!
HEY, BOSS! THERE'S SOME BIG FAT CAT FROM UPTOWN HERE TO BUY THE CHEESE!
AH! WHAT'D I TELL YOU! COMING, ALEX?

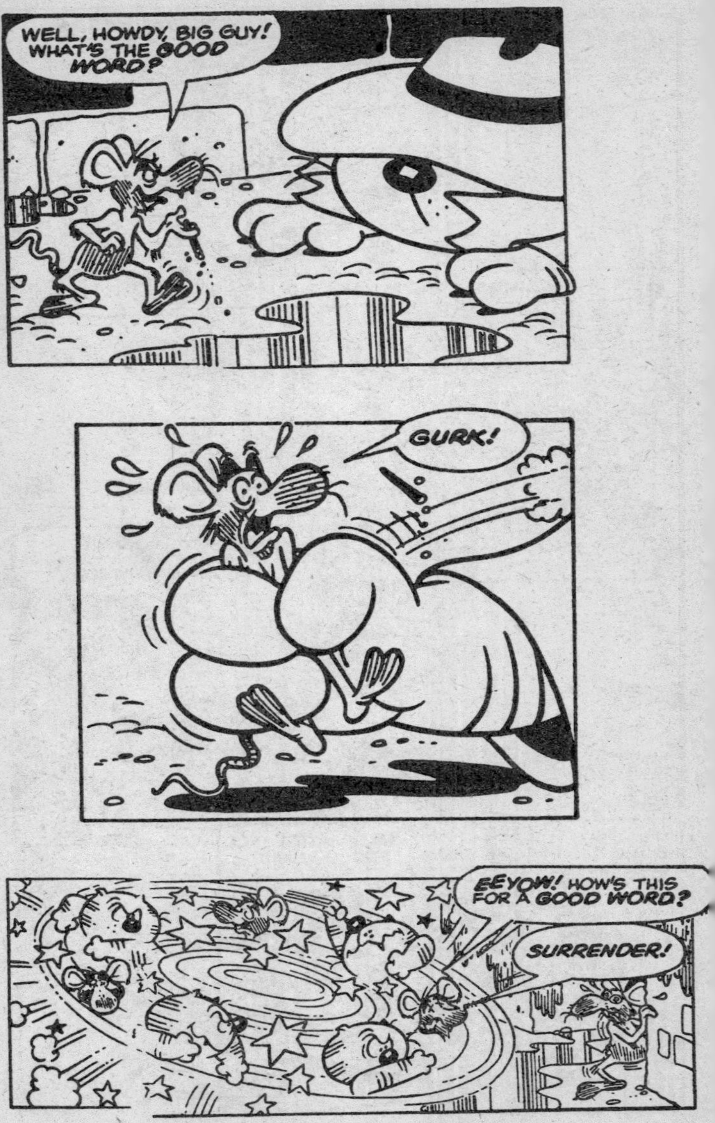
WELL, HOWDY, BIG GUY! WHAT'S THE GOOD WORD?
GURK!
EEYOW! HOW'S THIS FOR A GOOD WORD?
SURRENDER!

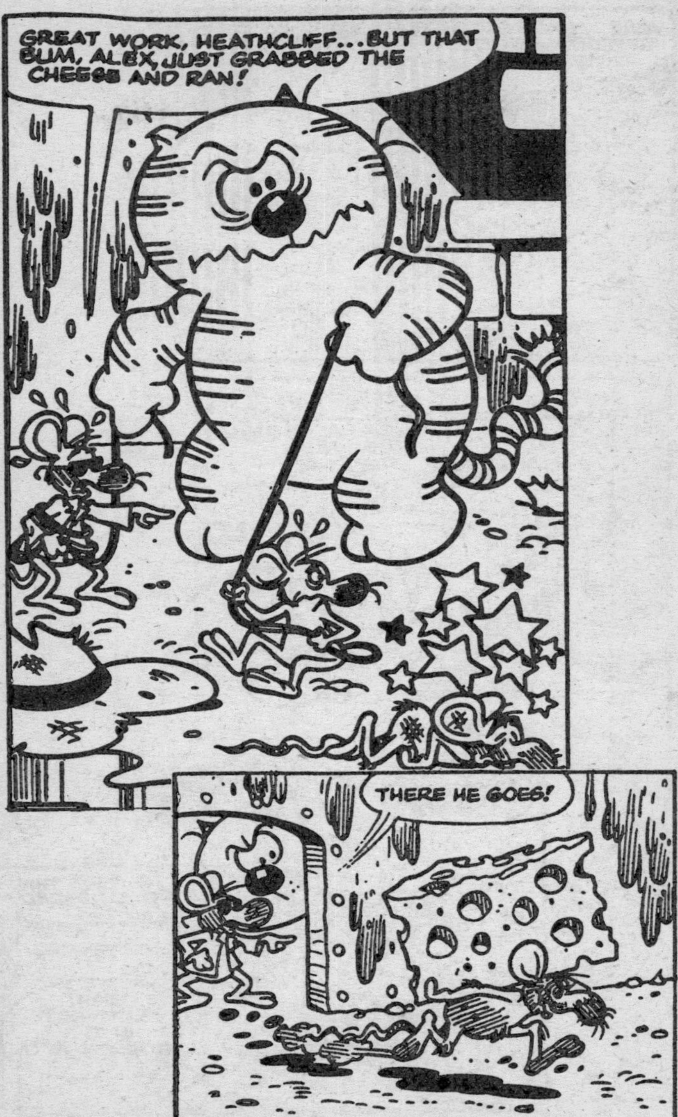
GREAT WORK, HEATHCLIFF...BUT THAT BUM, ALEX, JUST GRABBED THE CHEESE AND RAN!
THERE HE GOES!

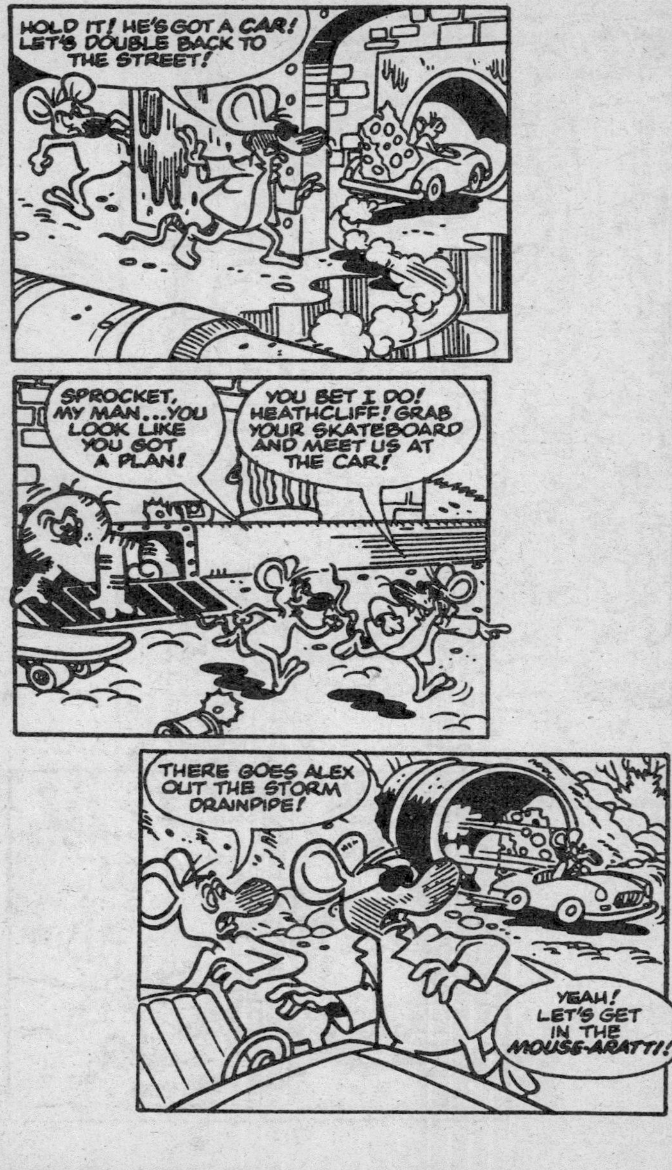
HOLD IT! HE'S GOT A CAR! LET'S DOUBLE BACK TO THE STREET!
SPROCKET, MY MAN...YOU LOOK LIKE YOU GOT A PLAN!
YOU BET I DO! HEATHCLIFF! GRAB YOUR SKATEBOARD AND MEET US AT THE CAR!
THERE GOES ALEX OUT THE STORM DRAINPIPE!
YEAH! LET'S GET IN THE MOUSE-ARATTI!

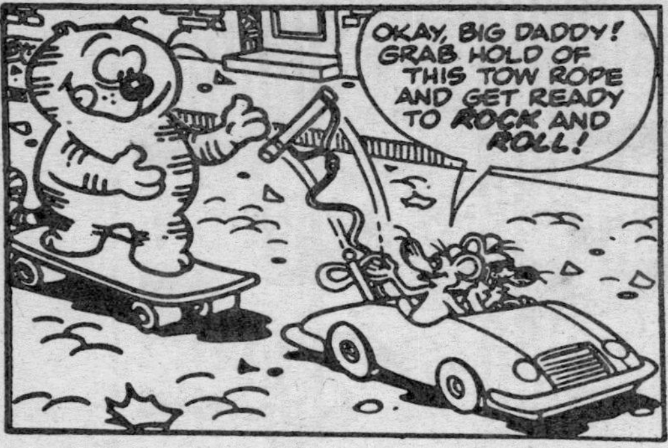
OKAY, BIG DADDY! GRAB HOLD OF THIS TOW ROPE AND GET READY TO ROCK AND ROLL!

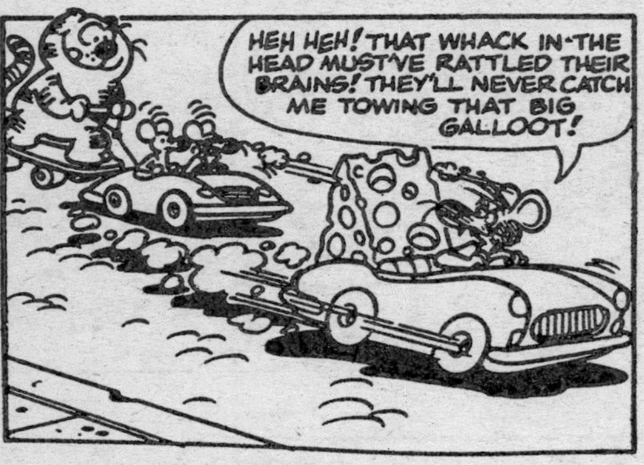
HEH HEH! THAT WHACK IN-THE HEAD MUST'VE RATTLED THEIR BRAINS! THEY'LL NEVER CATCH ME TOWING THAT BIG GALLOOT!

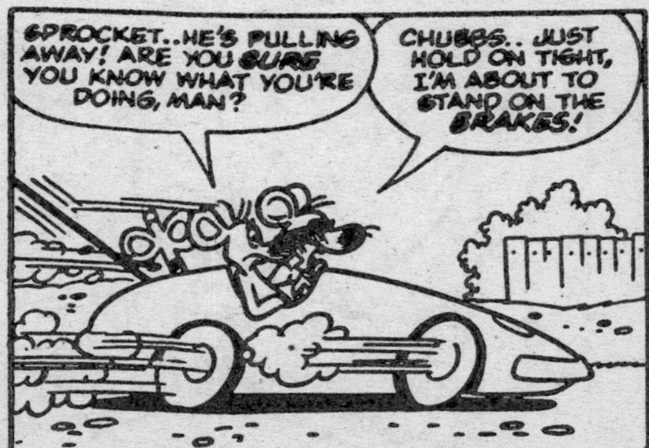
SPROCKET..HE'S PULLING AWAY! ARE YOU SURE YOU KNOW WHAT YOU'RE DOING, MAN?
CHUBBS.. JUST HOLD ON TIGHT, I'M ABOUT TO STAND ON THE BRAKES!

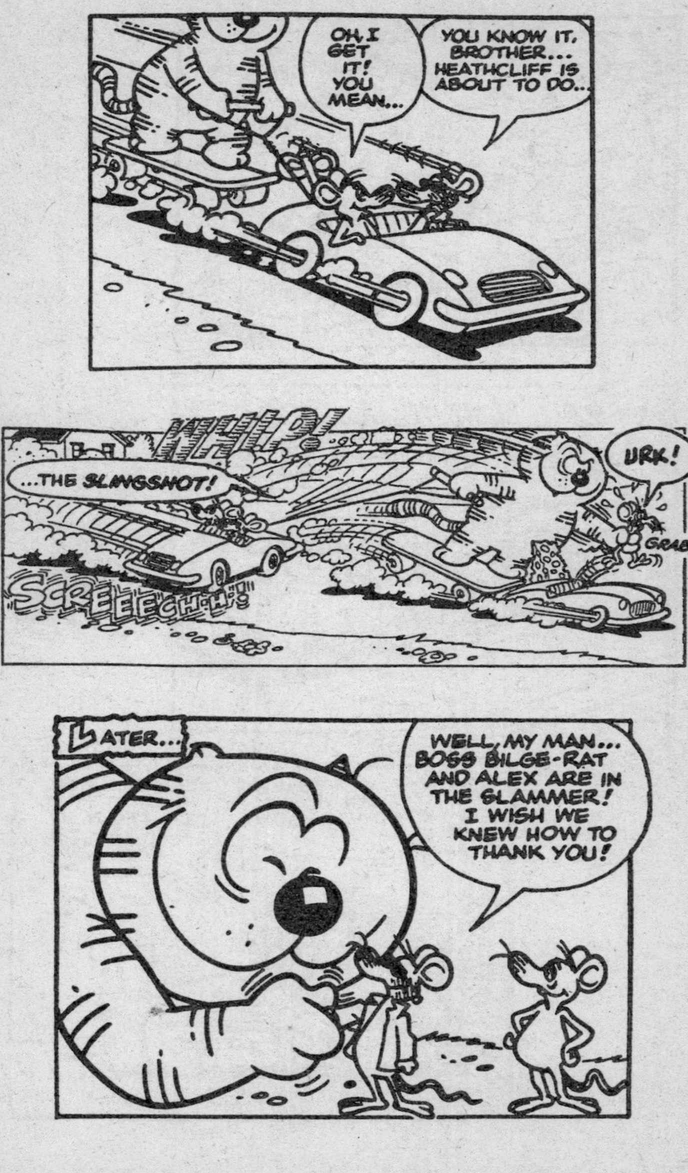
OH, I GET IT! YOU MEAN...
YOU KNOW IT, BROTHER... HEATHCLIFF IS ABOUT TO DO...
WHIP!
...THE SLINGSHOT!
URK!
GRAB!
SCREEECH-H-!
LATER...
WELL, MY MAN... BOSS BILGE-RAT AND ALEX ARE IN THE SLAMMER! I WISH WE KNEW HOW TO THANK YOU!

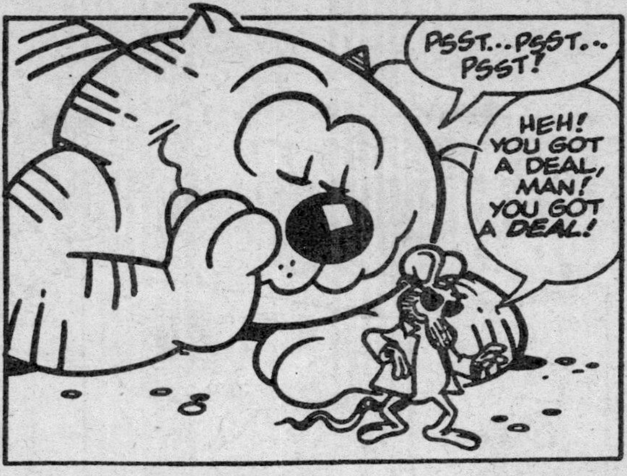
PSST...PSST...
PSST!
HEH! YOU GOT A DEAL, MAN! YOU GOT A DEAL!

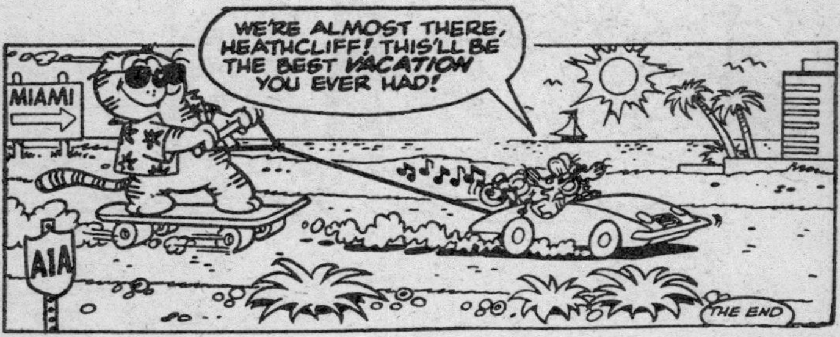
WE'RE ALMOST THERE, HEATHCLIFF! THIS'LL BE THE BEST VACATION YOU EVER HAD!
MIAMI
AIA
THE END

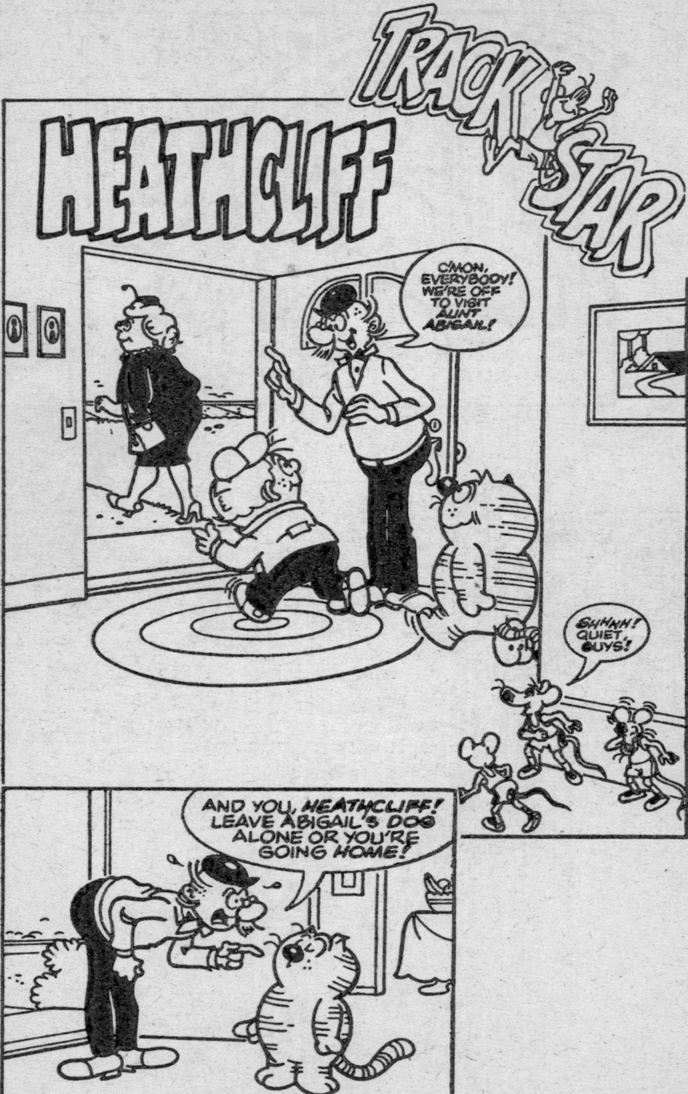
HEATHCLIFF
TRACK STAR
C'MON, EVERYBODY! WE'RE OFF TO VISIT AUNT ABIGAIL!
SHHHH! QUIET, GUYS!
AND YOU, HEATHCLIFF! LEAVE ABIGAIL'S DOG ALONE OR YOU'RE GOING HOME!

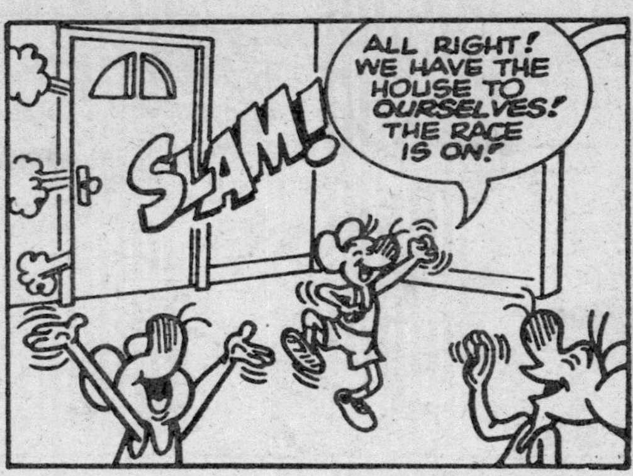
SLAM!
ALL RIGHT! WE HAVE THE HOUSE TO OURSELVES! THE RACE IS ON!

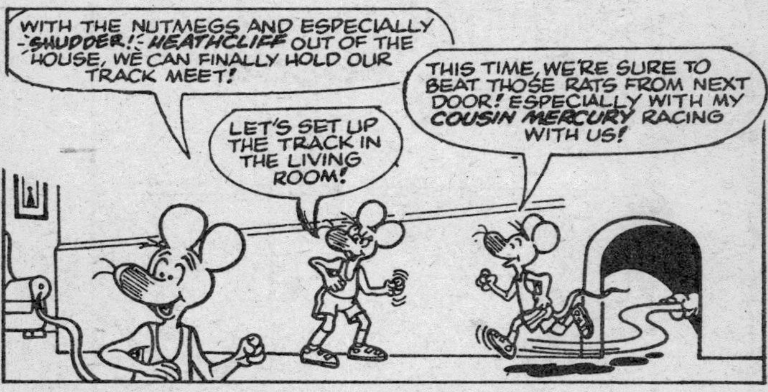
WITH THE NUTMEGS AND ESPECIALLY -SHUDDER!- HEATHCLIFF OUT OF THE HOUSE, WE CAN FINALLY HOLD OUR TRACK MEET!
LET'S SET UP THE TRACK IN THE LIVING ROOM!
THIS TIME, WE'RE SURE TO BEAT THOSE RATS FROM NEXT DOOR! ESPECIALLY WITH MY COUSIN MERCURY RACING WITH US!

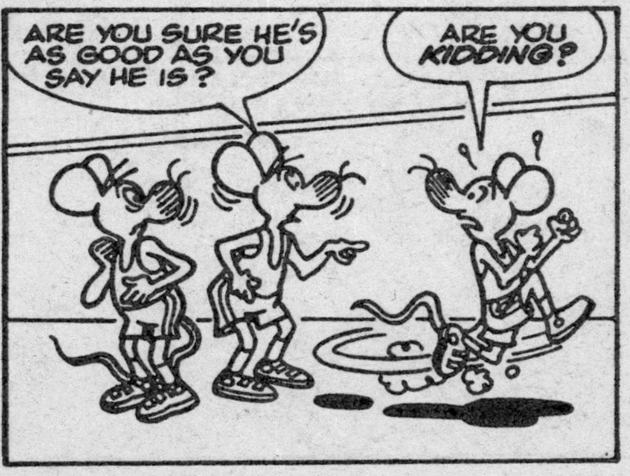
ARE YOU SURE HE'S AS GOOD AS YOU SAY HE IS?
ARE YOU KIDDING?

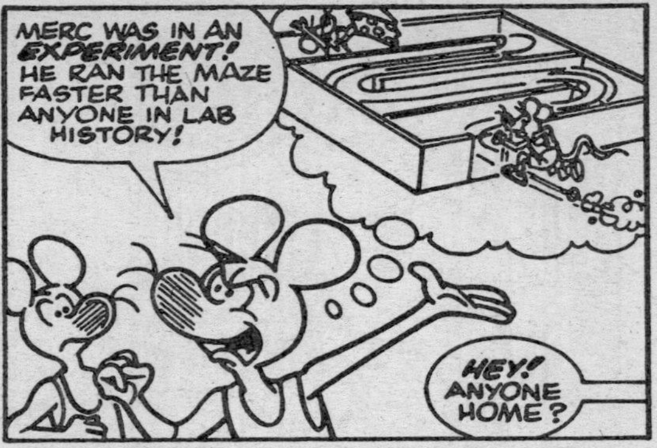
MERC WAS IN AN EXPERIMENT! HE RAN THE MAZE FASTER THAN ANYONE IN LAB HISTORY!
HEY! ANYONE HOME?

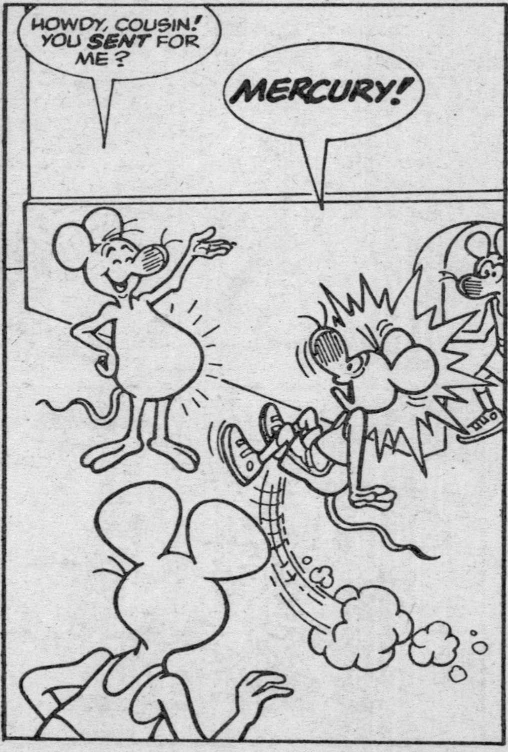
HOWDY, COUSIN! YOU SENT FOR ME?
MERCURY!

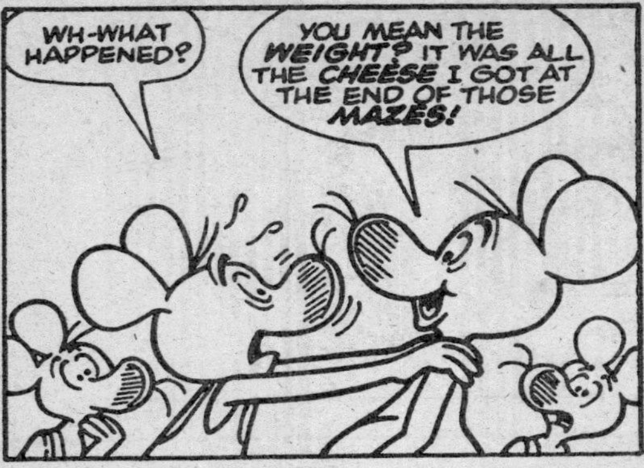
WH-WHAT HAPPENED?
YOU MEAN THE WEIGHT? IT WAS ALL THE CHEESE I GOT AT THE END OF THOSE MAZES!

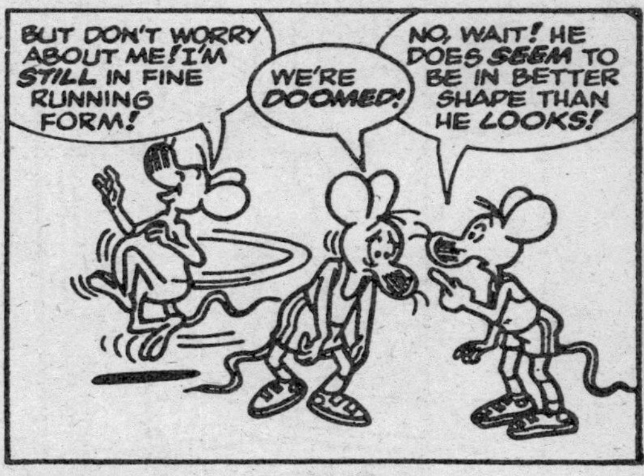
BUT DON'T WORRY ABOUT ME! I'M STILL IN FINE RUNNING FORM!
WE'RE DOOMED!
NO, WAIT! HE DOES SEEM TO BE IN BETTER SHAPE THAN HE LOOKS!

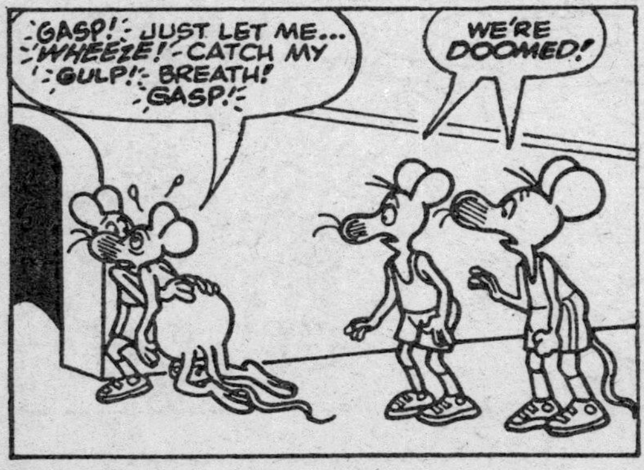
GASP! JUST LET ME... WHEEZE! CATCH MY GULP! BREATH! GASP!
WE'RE DOOMED!

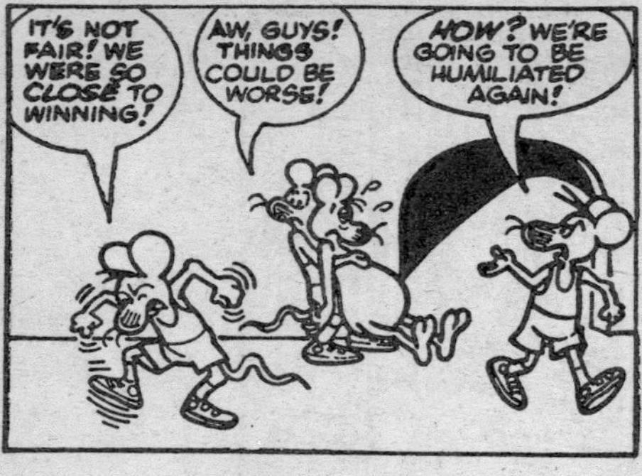
IT'S NOT FAIR! WE WERE SO CLOSE TO WINNING!
AW, GUYS! THINGS COULD BE WORSE!
HOW? WE'RE GOING TO BE HUMILIATED AGAIN!

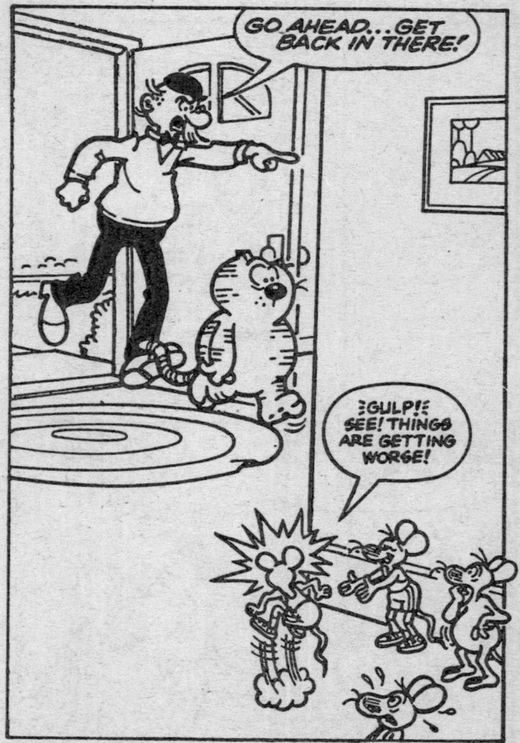
GO AHEAD... GET BACK IN THERE!
GULP! SEE! THINGS ARE GETTING WORSE!

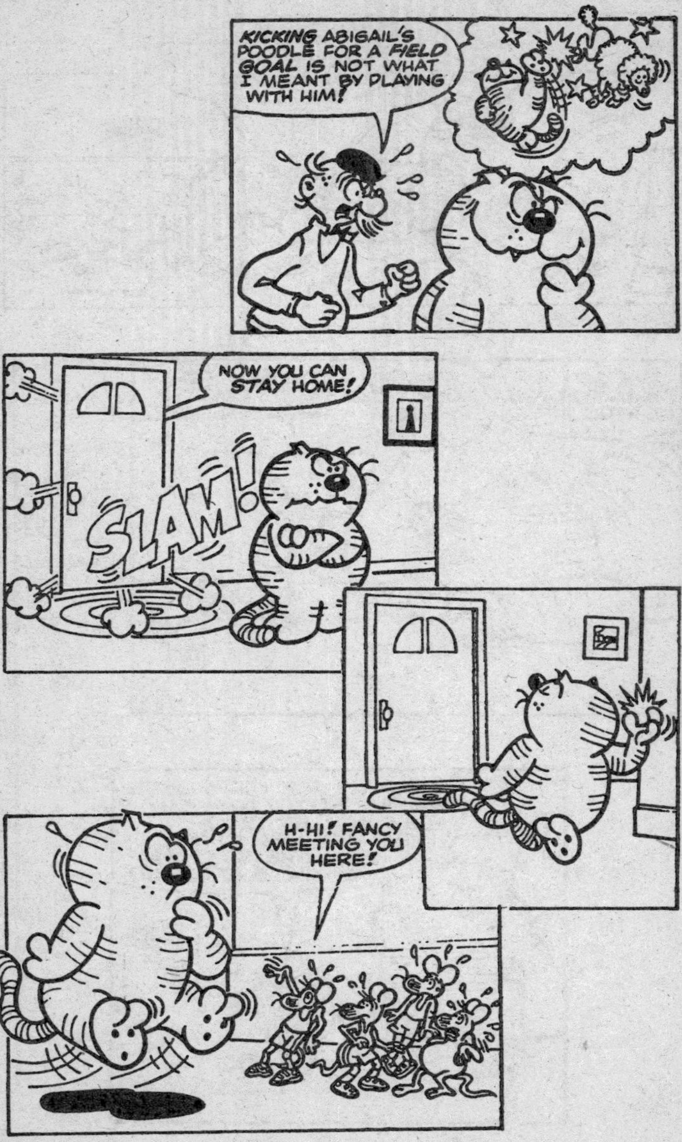
KICKING ABIGAIL'S POODLE FOR A FIELD GOAL IS NOT WHAT I MEANT BY PLAYING WITH HIM!
NOW YOU CAN STAY HOME!
SLAM!
H-HI! FANCY MEETING YOU HERE!

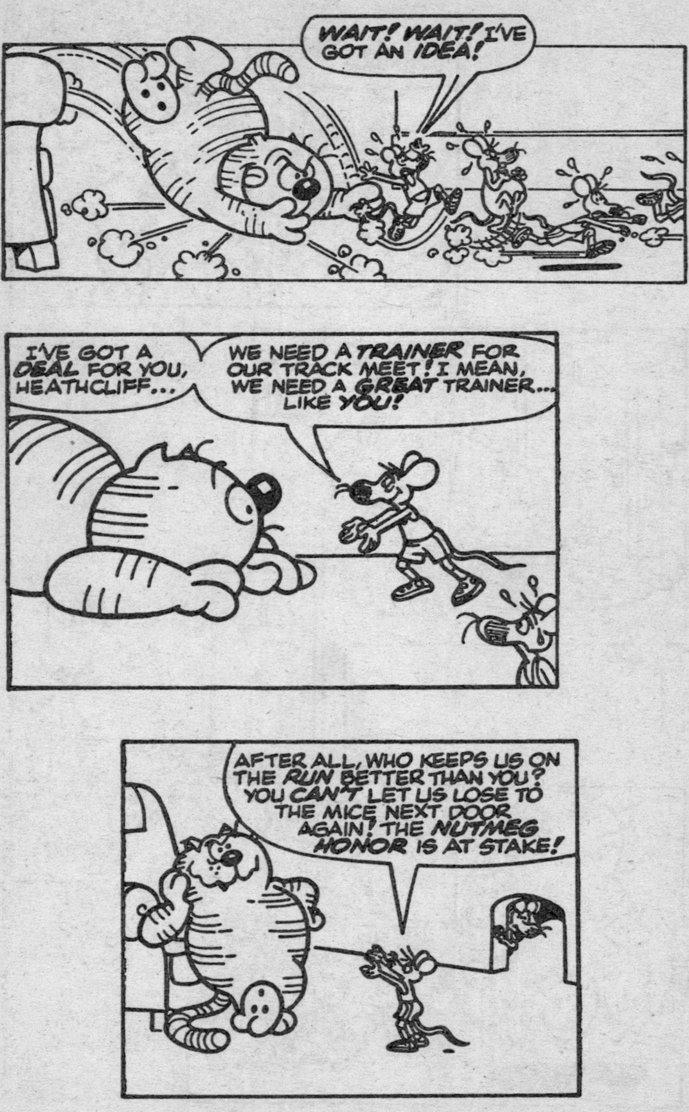
WAIT! WAIT! I'VE GOT AN IDEA!
I'VE GOT A DEAL FOR YOU, HEATHCLIFF...
WE NEED A TRAINER FOR OUR TRACK MEET! I MEAN, WE NEED A GREAT TRAINER... LIKE YOU!
AFTER ALL, WHO KEEPS US ON THE RUN BETTER THAN YOU? YOU CAN'T LET US LOSE TO THE MICE NEXT DOOR AGAIN! THE NUTMEG HONOR IS AT STAKE!

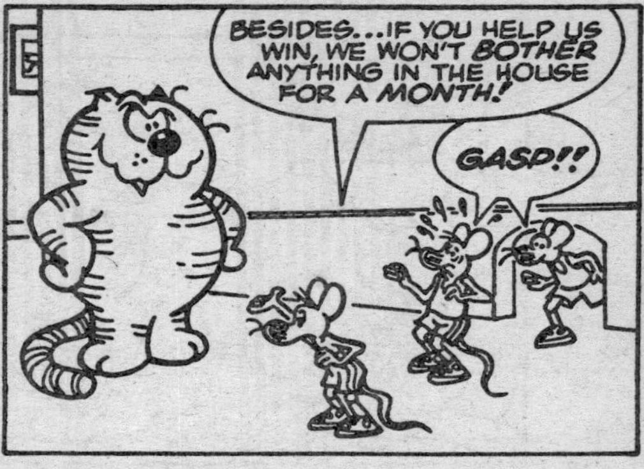
BESIDES...IF YOU HELP US WIN, WE WON'T BOTHER ANYTHING IN THE HOUSE FOR A MONTH!
GASP!!

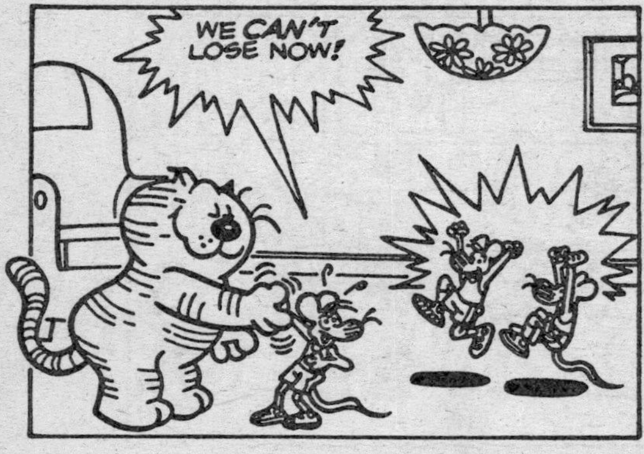
WE CAN'T LOSE NOW!

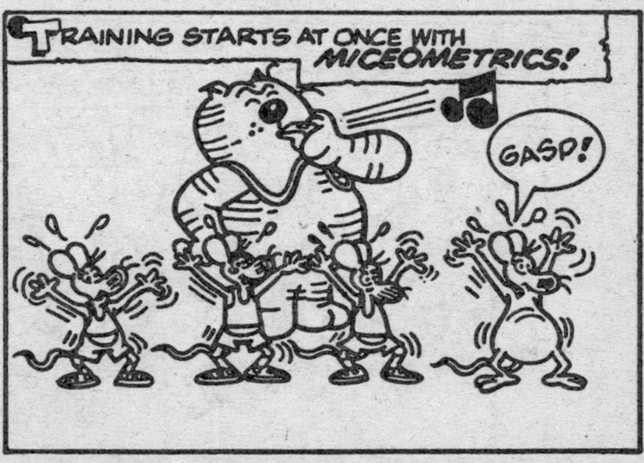
TRAINING STARTS AT ONCE WITH MICEOMETRICS!
GASP!

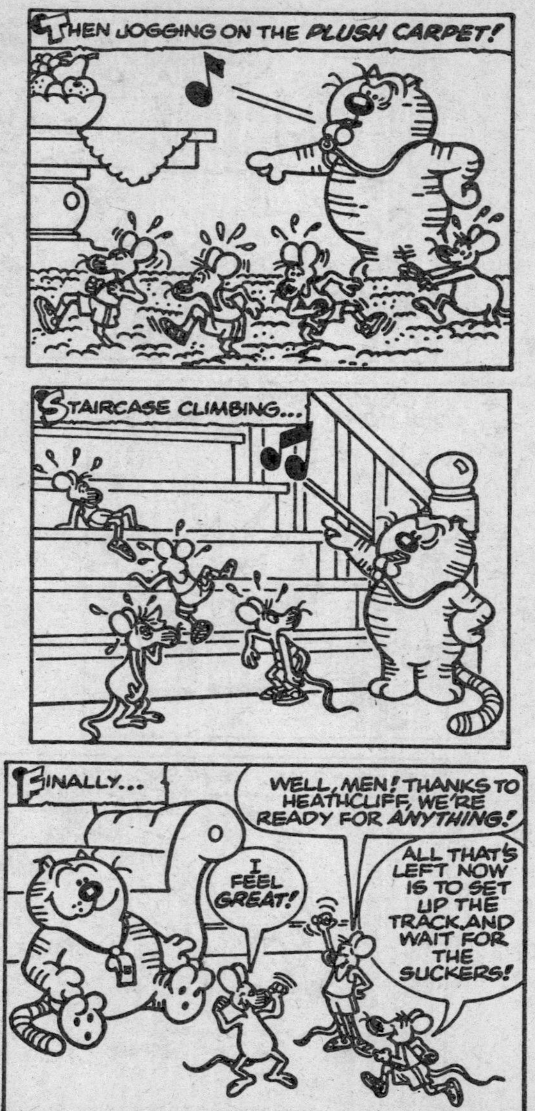
THEN JOGGING ON THE PLUSH CARPET!
STAIRCASE CLIMBING...
FINALLY...
WELL, MEN! THANKS TO HEATHCLIFF, WE'RE READY FOR ANYTHING!
I FEEL GREAT!
ALL THAT'S LEFT NOW IS TO SET UP THE TRACK AND WAIT FOR THE SUCKERS!

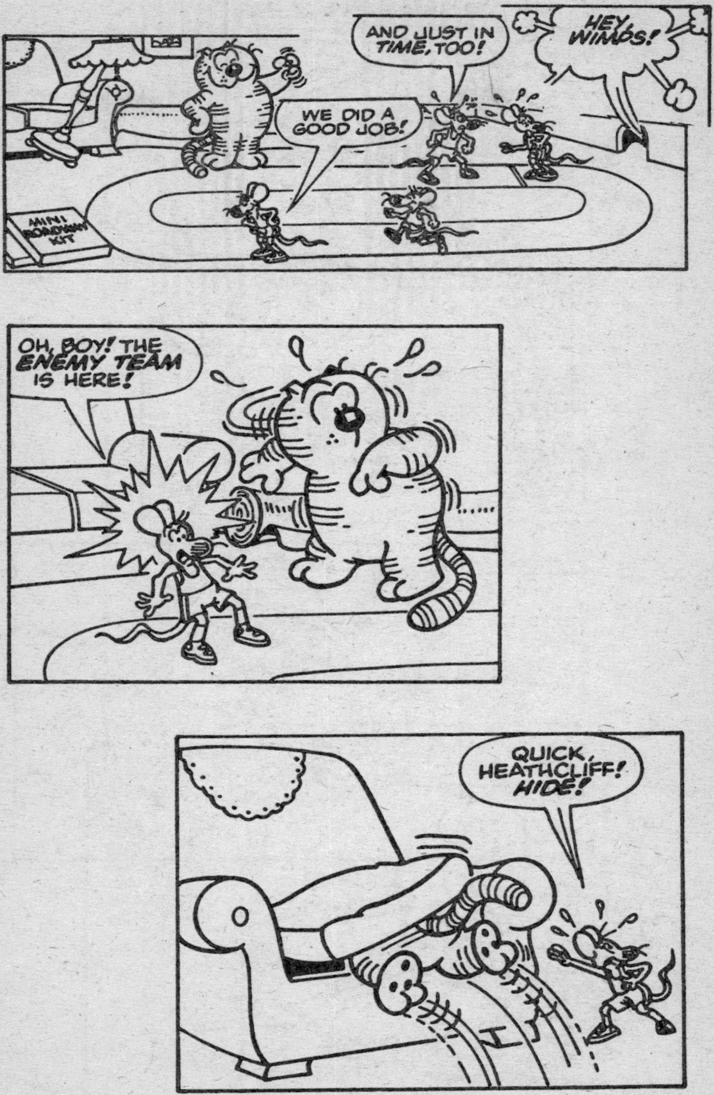
MINI ROADWAY KIT
WE DID A GOOD JOB!
AND JUST IN TIME, TOO!
HEY, WIMPS!
OH, BOY! THE ENEMY TEAM IS HERE!
QUICK, HEATHCLIFF! HIDE!

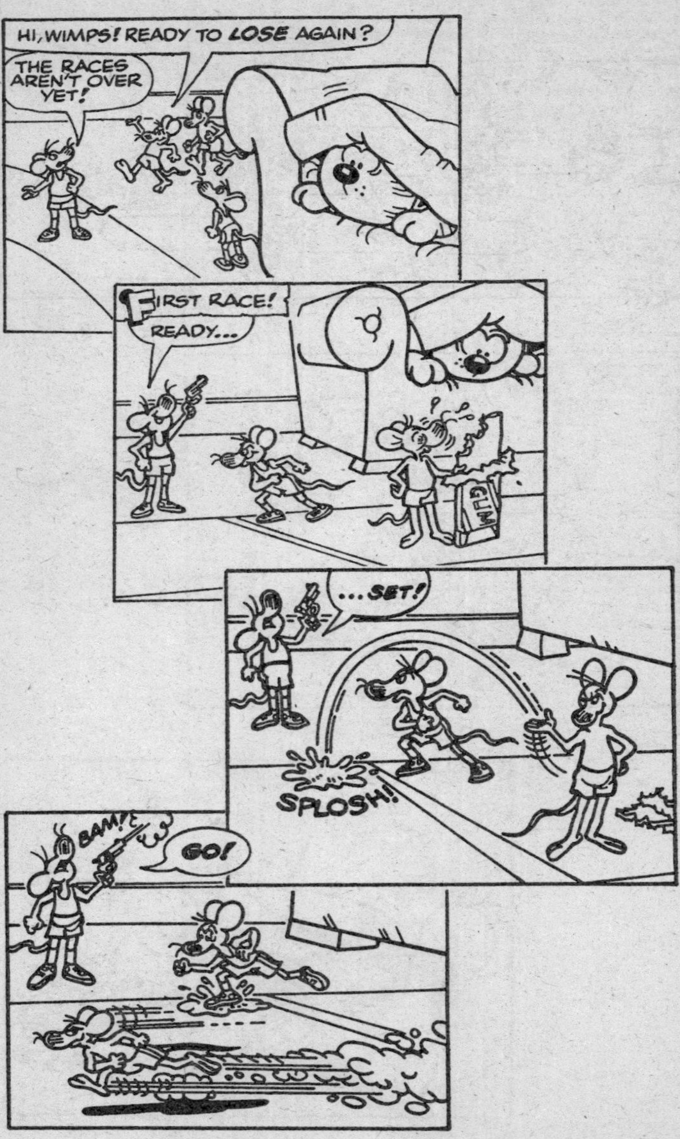
HI, WIMPS! READY TO LOSE AGAIN?
THE RACES AREN'T OVER YET!
FIRST RACE!
READY...
GUM
...SET!
SPLOSH!
BAM!
GO!

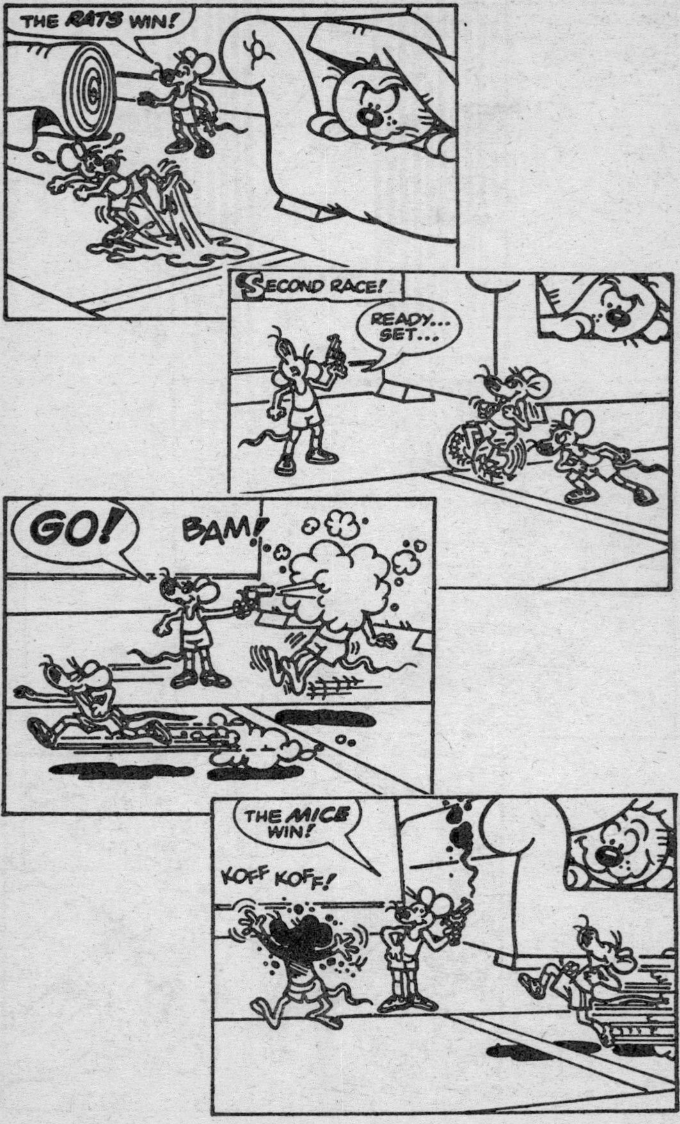
THE RATS WIN!
SECOND RACE!
READY... SET...
GO!
BAM!
THE MICE WIN!
KOFF KOFF!

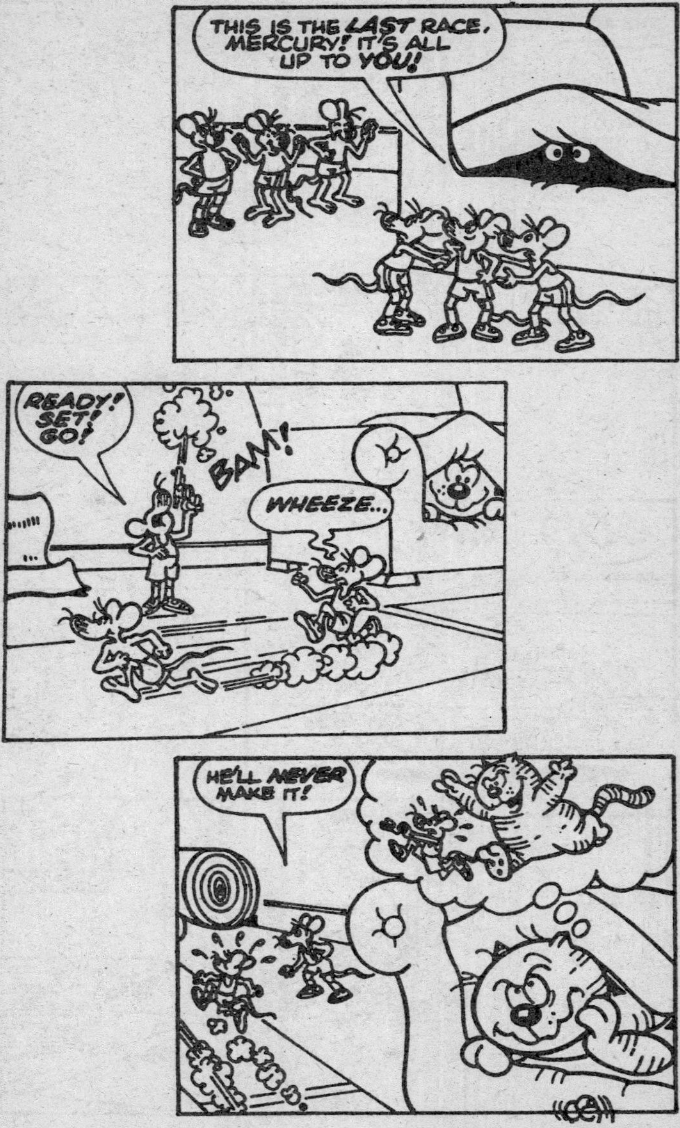
THIS IS THE LAST RACE, MERCURY! IT'S ALL UP TO YOU!
READY! SET! GO!
BAM!
WHEEZE...
HE'LL NEVER MAKE IT!

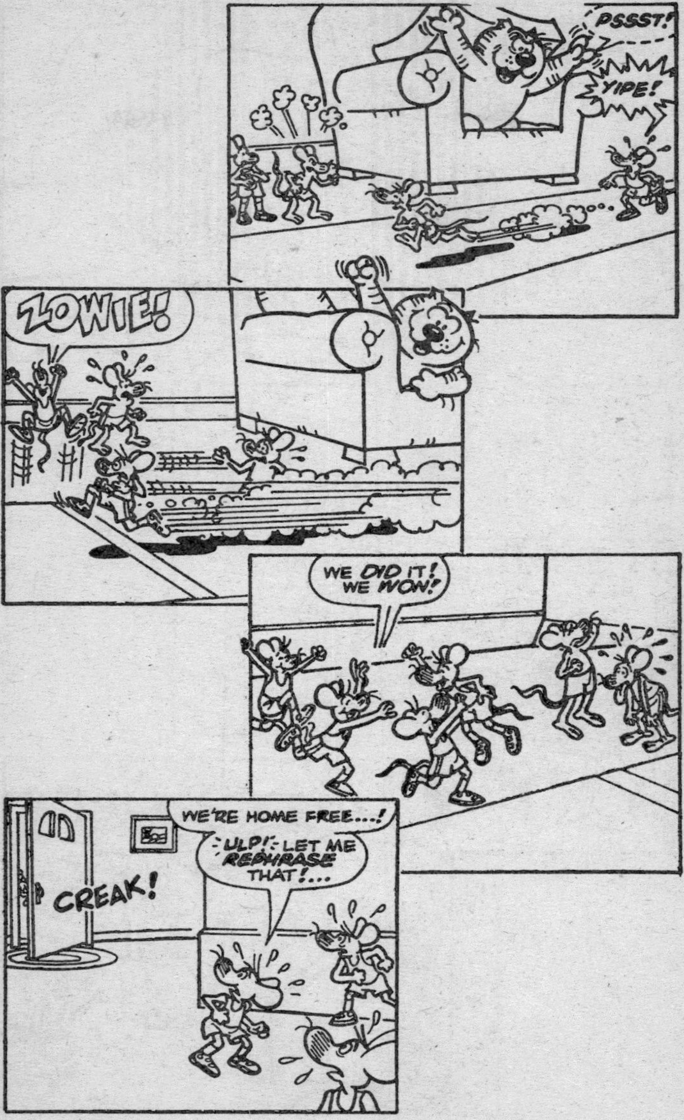
PSSST!
YIPE!
ZOWIE!
WE DID IT! WE WON!
CREAK!
WE'RE HOME FREE...!
ULP! LET ME REPHRASE THAT!...

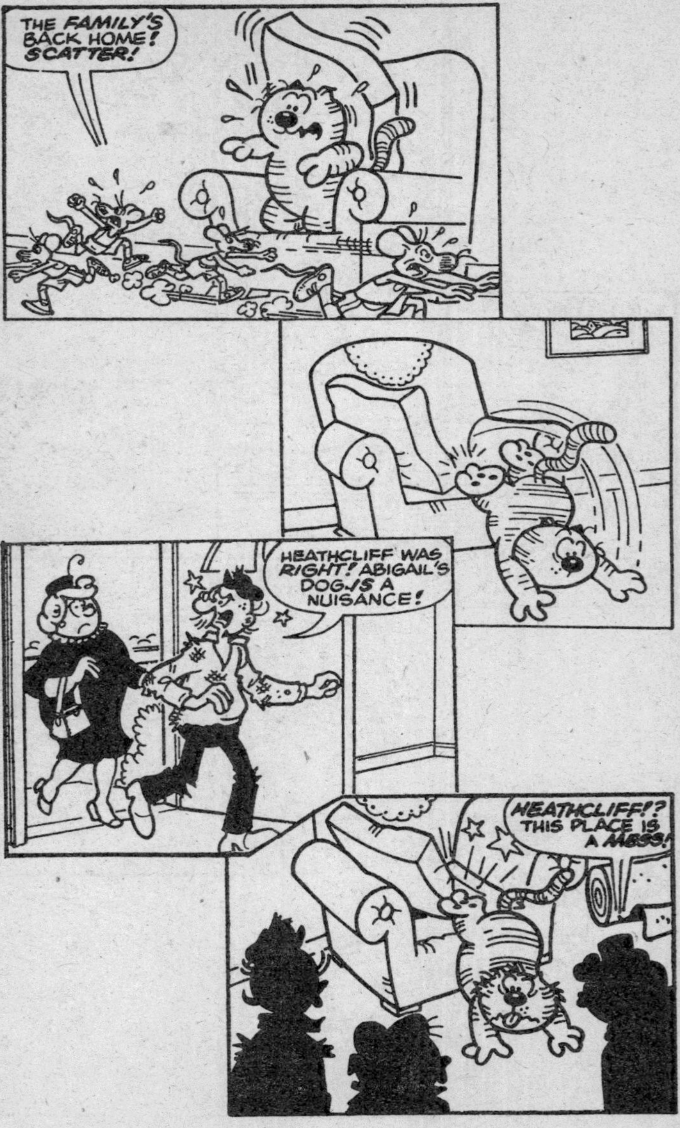
THE FAMILY'S BACK HOME! SCATTER!
HEATHCLIFF WAS RIGHT! ABIGAIL'S DOG IS A NUISANCE!
HEATHCLIFF!? THIS PLACE IS A MESS!

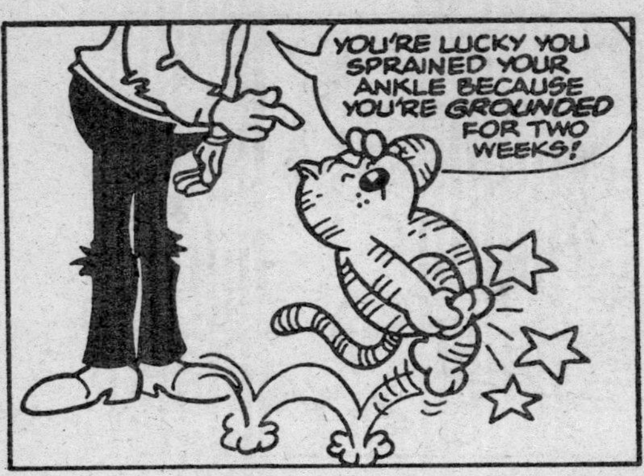
YOU'RE LUCKY YOU SPRAINED YOUR ANKLE BECAUSE YOU'RE GROUNDED FOR TWO WEEKS!

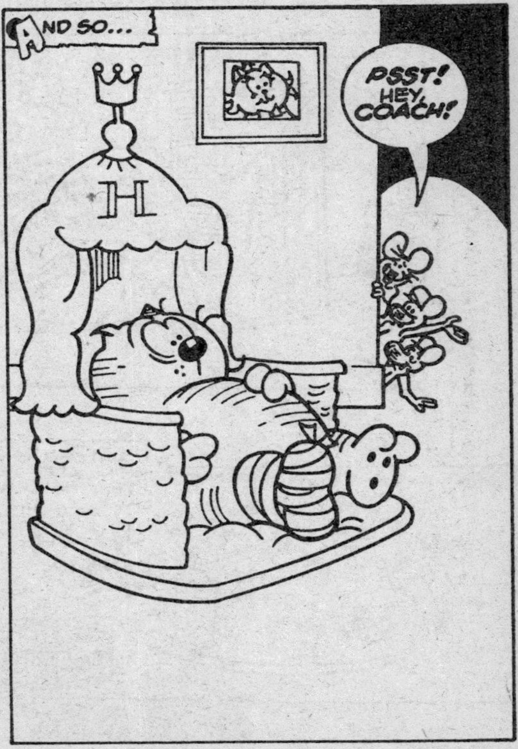
AND SO...
PSST! HEY, COACH!

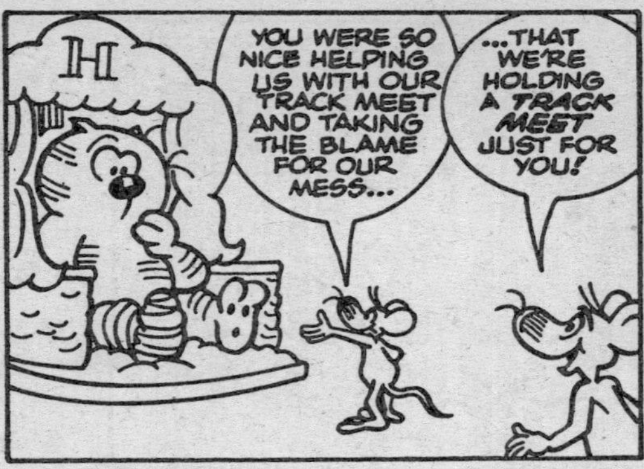
H
YOU WERE SO NICE HELPING US WITH OUR TRACK MEET AND TAKING THE BLAME FOR OUR MESS...
...THAT WE'RE HOLDING A *TRACK MEET* JUST FOR YOU!

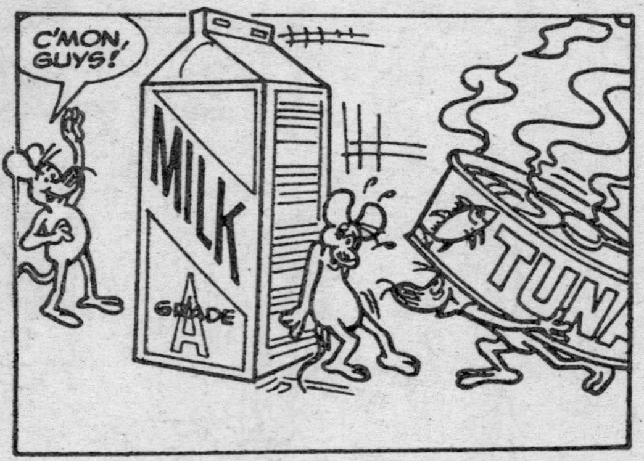
C'MON, GUYS!
MILK
GRADE
A
TUNA

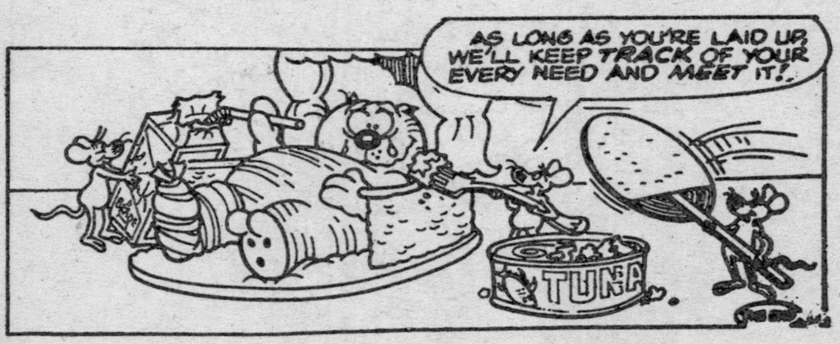
AS LONG AS YOU'RE LAID UP, WE'LL KEEP *TRACK* OF YOUR EVERY NEED AND *MEET* IT!
TUNA

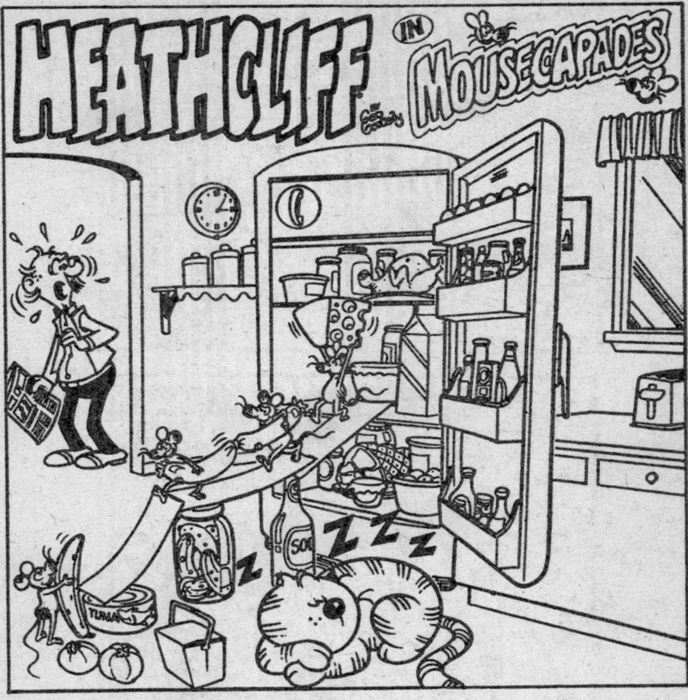
HEATHCLIFF
IN
MOUSECAPADES
TUNA
SOU
Z Z Z
Z
Z

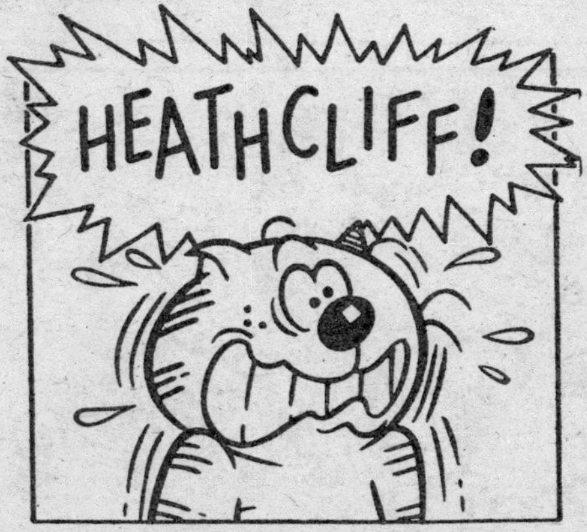
HEATHCLIFF!

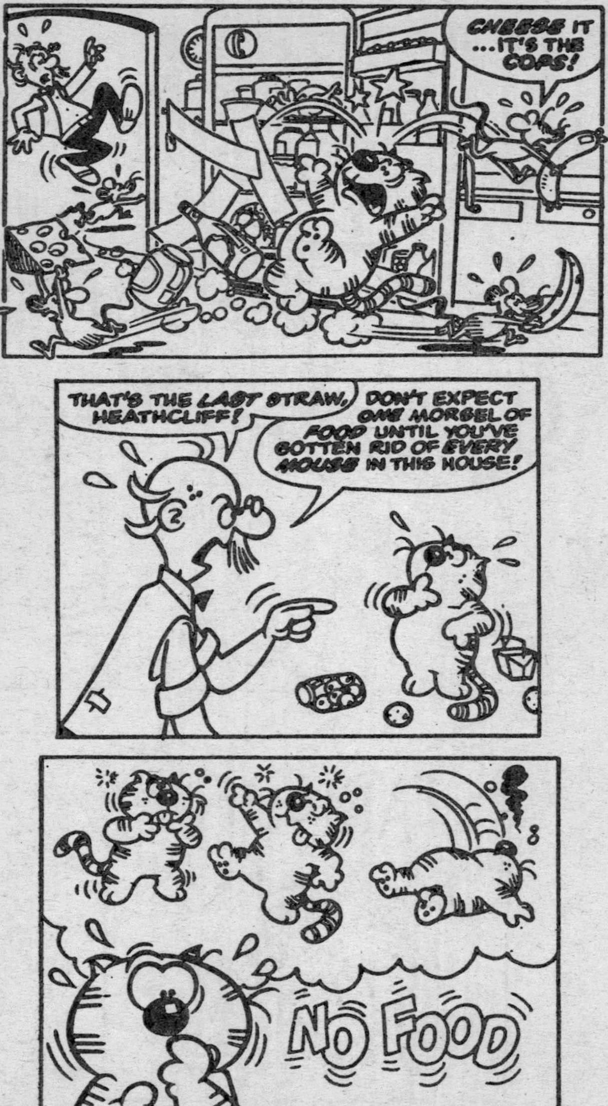
CHEESE IT ...IT'S THE COPS!
THAT'S THE LAST STRAW, HEATHCLIFF!
DON'T EXPECT ONE MORSEL OF FOOD UNTIL YOU'VE GOTTEN RID OF EVERY MOUSE IN THIS HOUSE!
NO FOOD

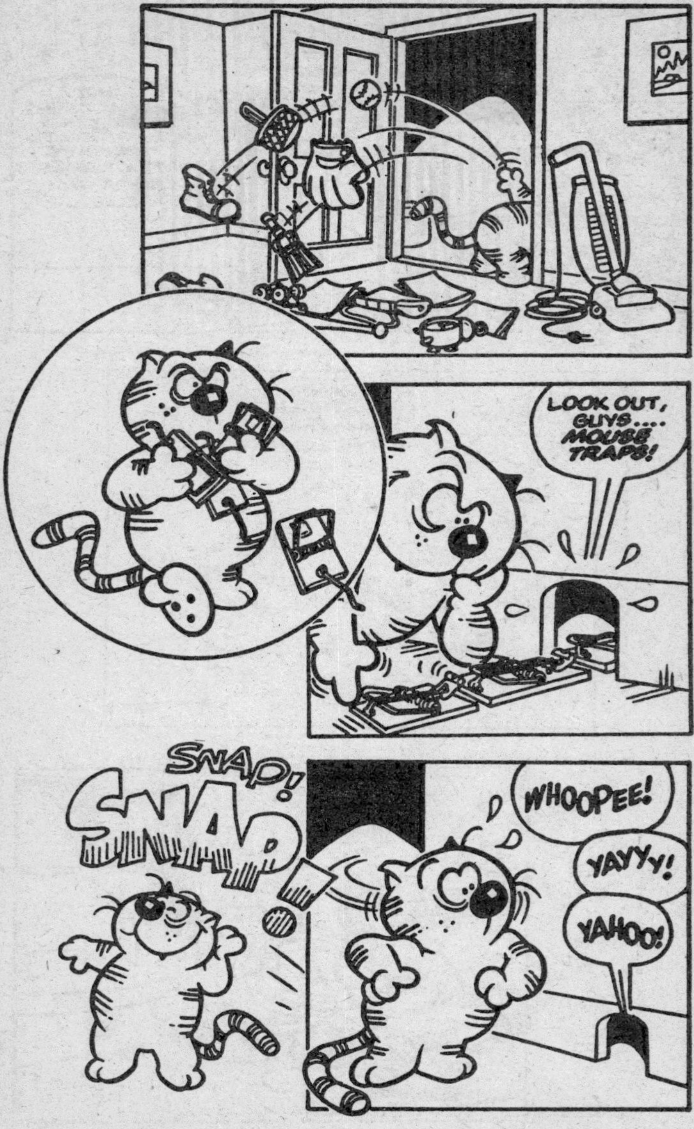
LOOK OUT, GUYS.... MOUSE TRAPS!
SNAP!
SNAP
WHOOPEE!
YAYYY!
YAHOO!

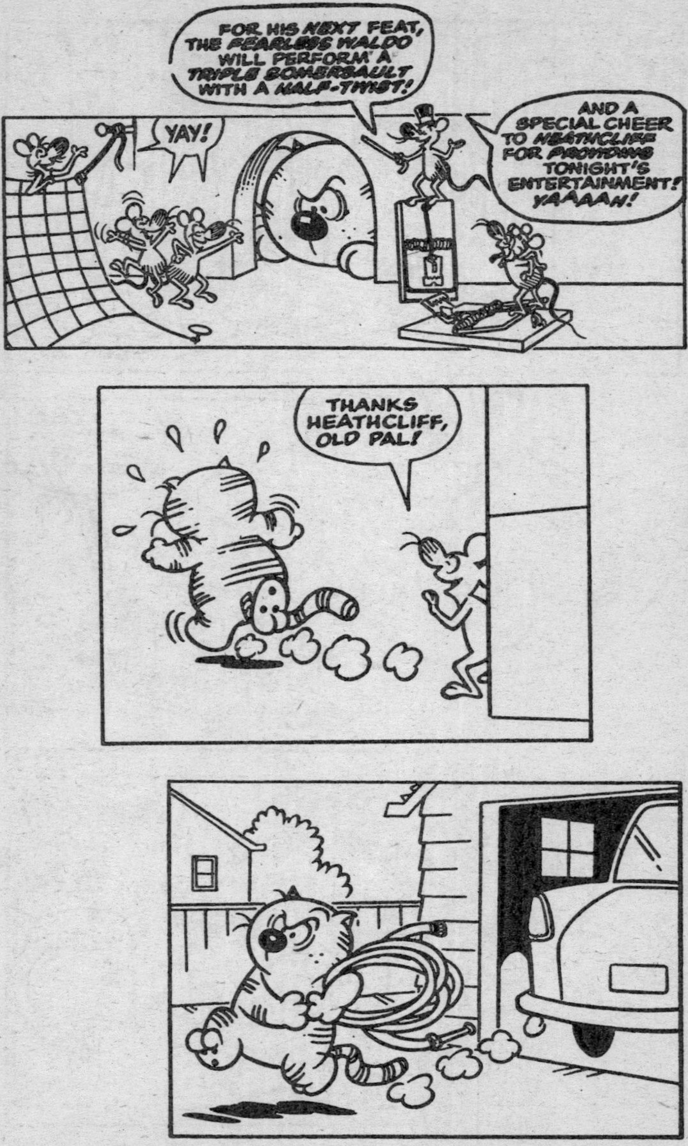
FOR HIS NEXT FEAT, THE FEARLESS WALDO WILL PERFORM A TRIPLE SOMERSAULT WITH A HALF-TWIST!
YAY!
AND A SPECIAL CHEER TO HEATHCLIFF FOR PROVIDING TONIGHT'S ENTERTAINMENT! YAAAAH!
THANKS HEATHCLIFF, OLD PAL!

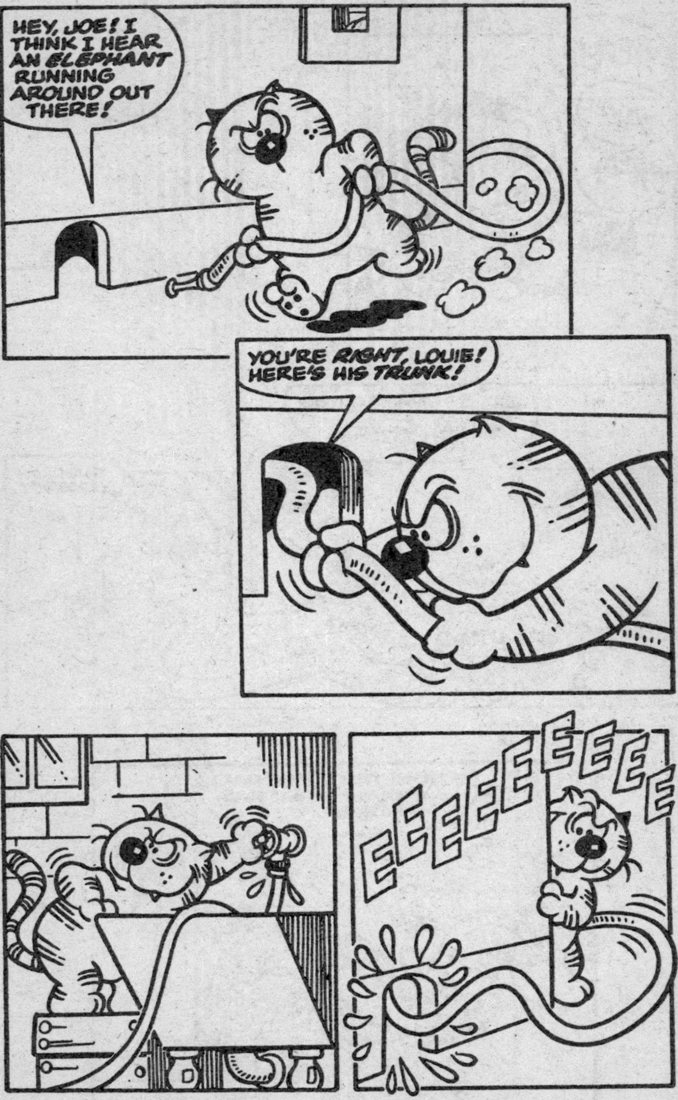
HEY, JOE! I THINK I HEAR AN ELEPHANT RUNNING AROUND OUT THERE!
YOU'RE RIGHT, LOUIE! HERE'S HIS TRUNK!
EEEEEEEEEEEE

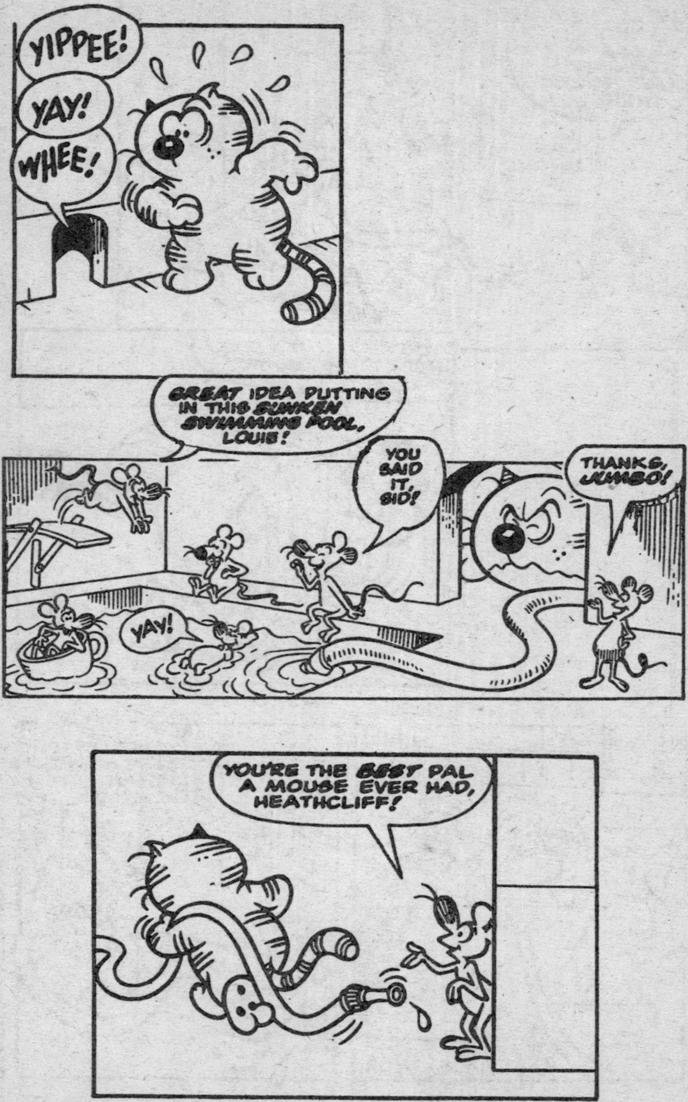
YIPPEE!
YAY!
WHEE!
GREAT IDEA PUTTING IN THIS SUNKEN SWIMMING POOL, LOUIE!
YOU SAID IT, SID!
THANKS, JUMBO!
YAY!
YOU'RE THE BEST PAL A MOUSE EVER HAD, HEATHCLIFF!

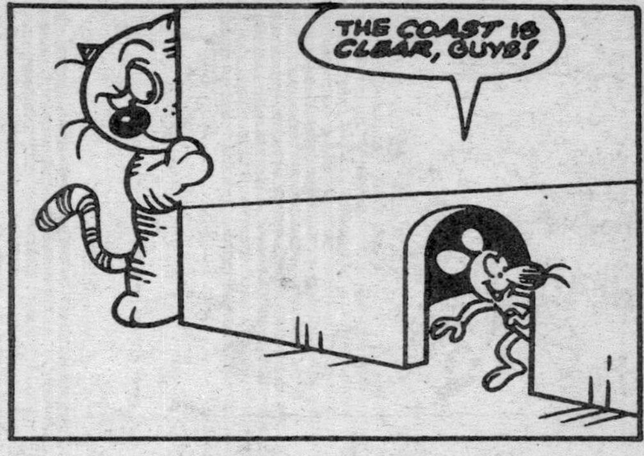
THE COAST IS CLEAR, GUYS!

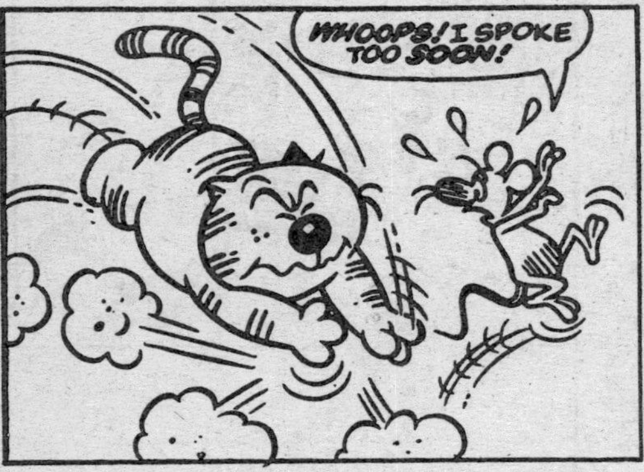
WHOOPS! I SPOKE TOO SOON!

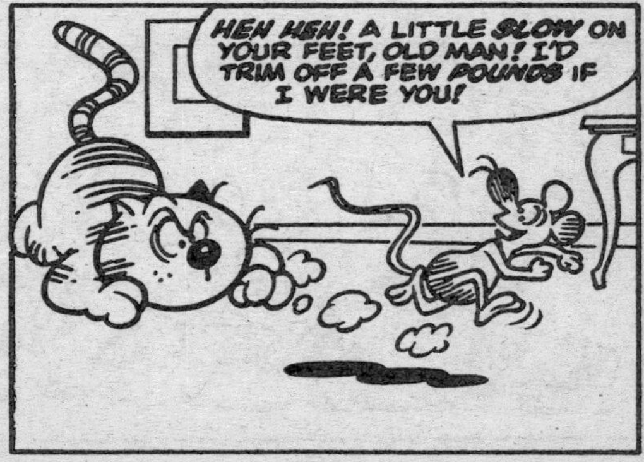
HEH HEH! A LITTLE SLOW ON YOUR FEET, OLD MAN! I'D TRIM OFF A FEW POUNDS IF I WERE YOU!

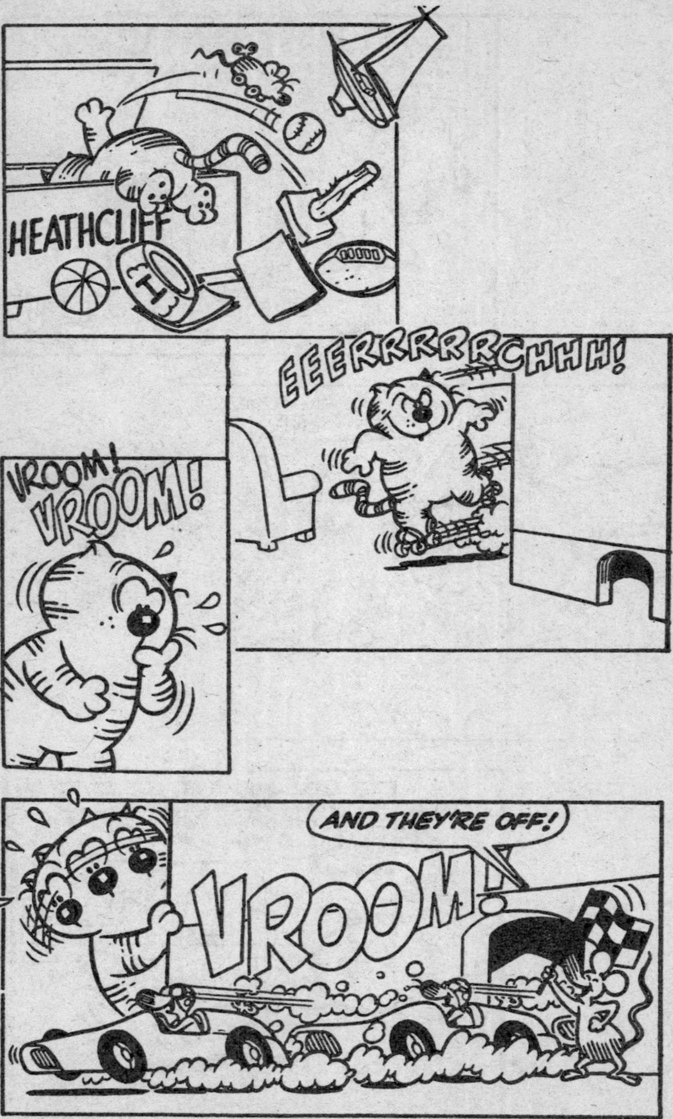

HEATHCLIFF
EEERRRRRCHHH!
VROOM!
VROOM!
AND THEY'RE OFF!
VROOM!

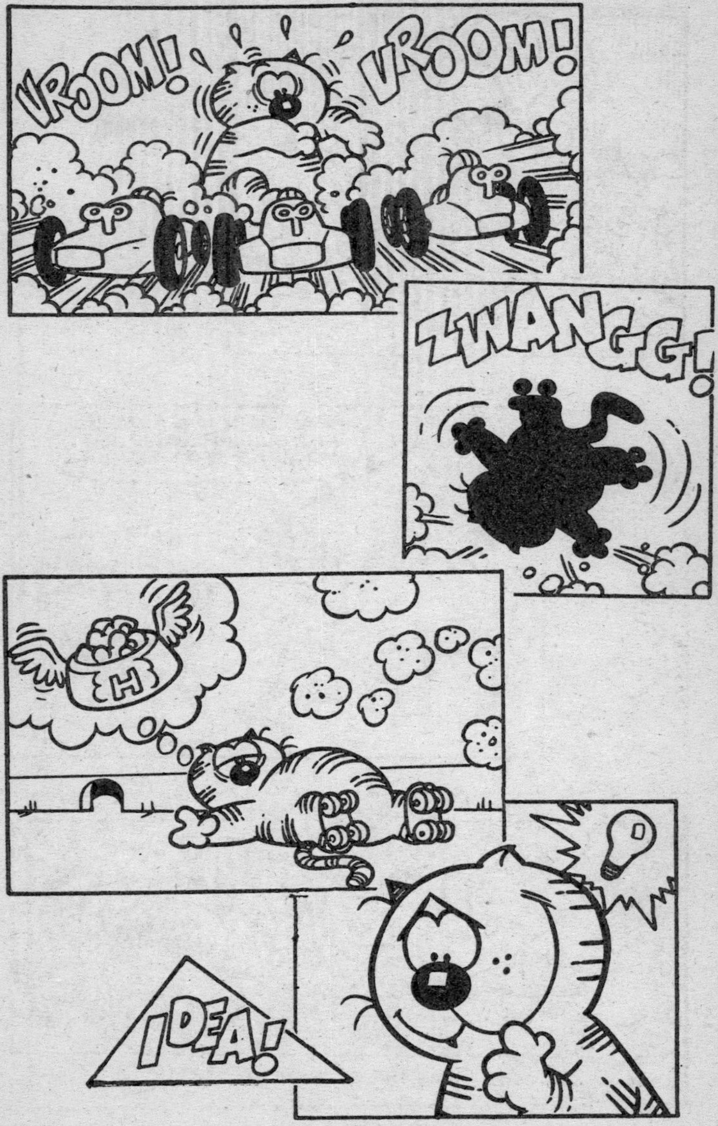
VROOM!
VROOM!
ZWANGG!
IDEA!

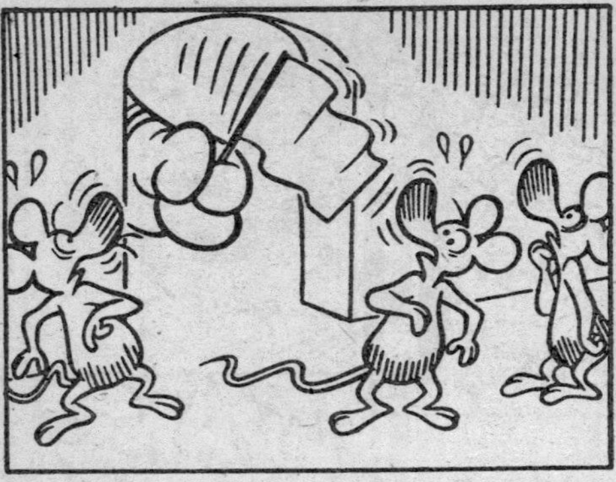

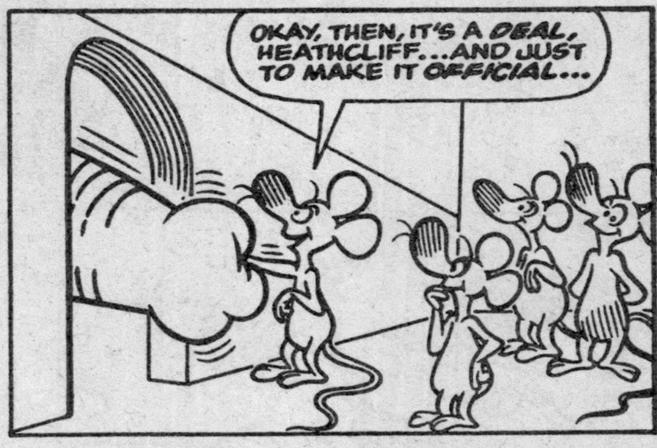
OKAY, THEN, IT'S A DEAL, HEATHCLIFF...AND JUST TO MAKE IT OFFICIAL...

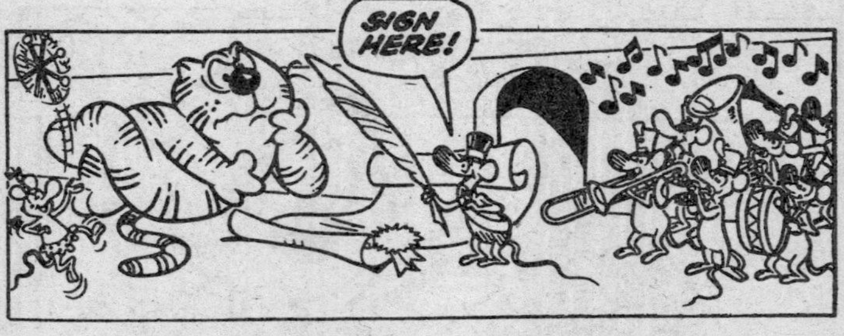
SIGN HERE!

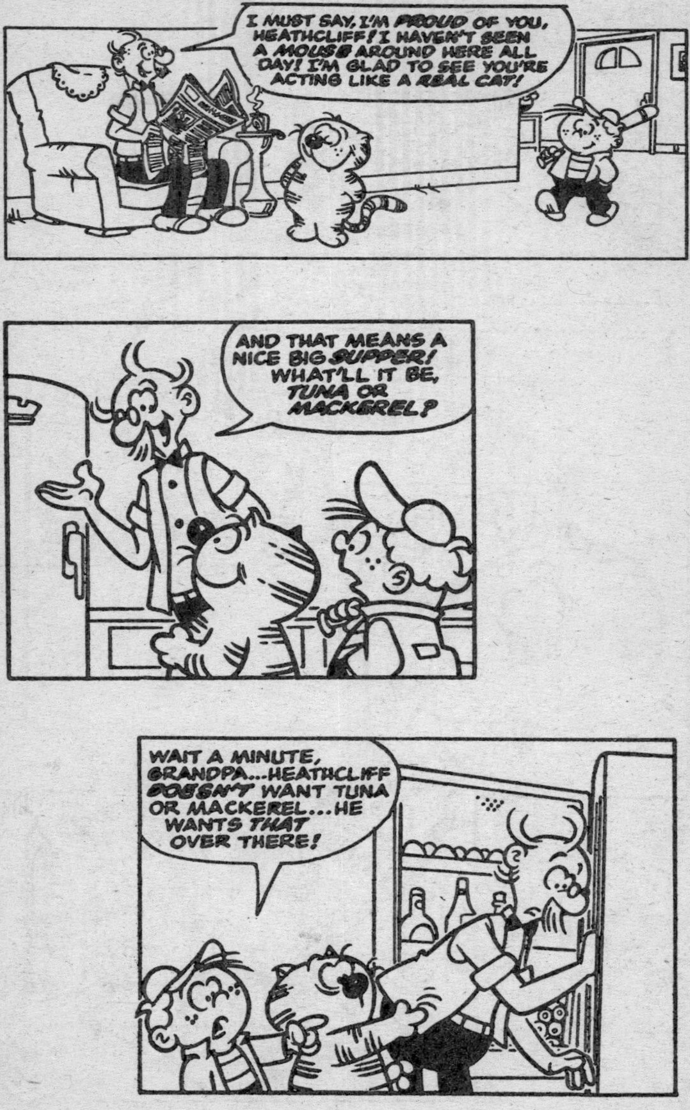
I MUST SAY, I'M PROUD OF YOU, HEATHCLIFF! I HAVEN'T SEEN A MOUSE AROUND HERE ALL DAY! I'M GLAD TO SEE YOU'RE ACTING LIKE A REAL CAT!
AND THAT MEANS A NICE BIG SUPPER! WHAT'LL IT BE, TUNA OR MACKEREL?
WAIT A MINUTE, GRANDPA...HEATHCLIFF DOESN'T WANT TUNA OR MACKEREL...HE WANTS THAT OVER THERE!

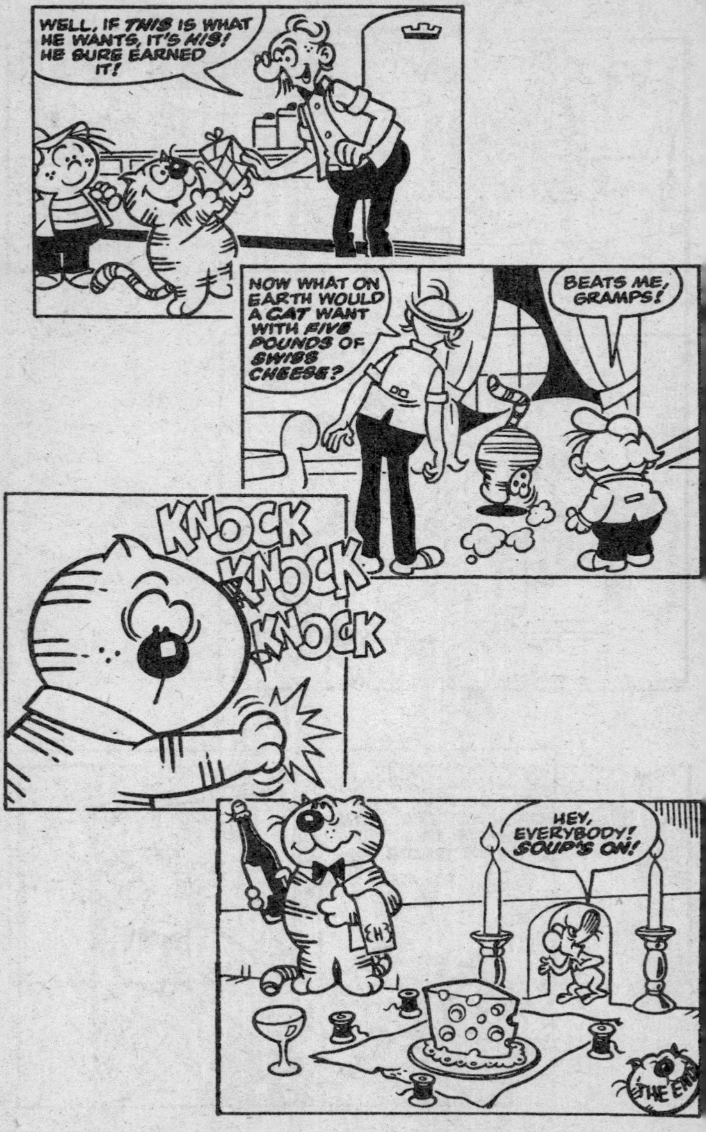
WELL, IF THIS IS WHAT HE WANTS, IT'S HIS! HE SURE EARNED IT!
NOW WHAT ON EARTH WOULD A CAT WANT WITH FIVE POUNDS OF SWISS CHEESE?
BEATS ME, GRAMPS!
KNOCK KNOCK KNOCK
HEY, EVERYBODY! SOUP'S ON!
THE END

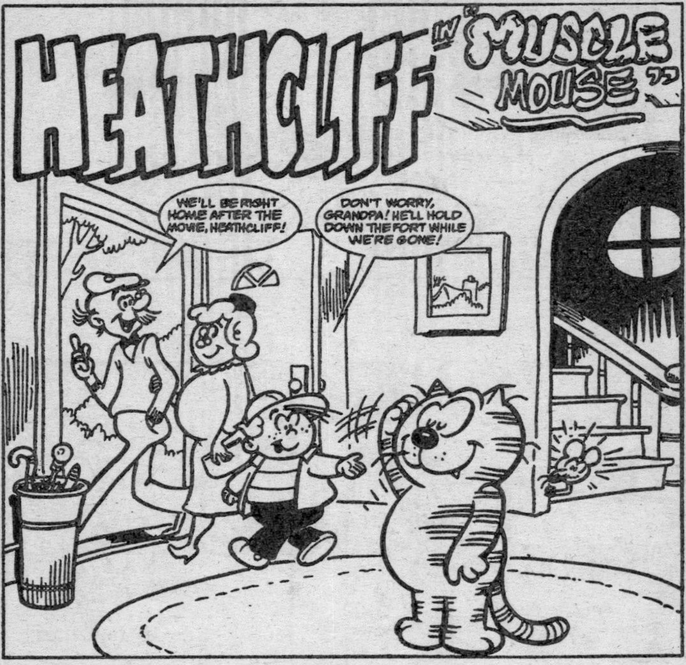
HEATHCLIFF
IN "MUSCLE MOUSE"
WE'LL BE RIGHT HOME AFTER THE MOVIE, HEATHCLIFF!
DON'T WORRY, GRANDPA! HE'LL HOLD DOWN THE FORT WHILE WE'RE GONE!

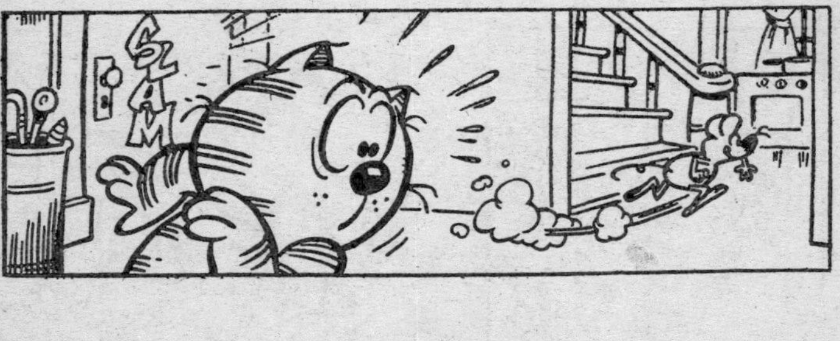
SLAM

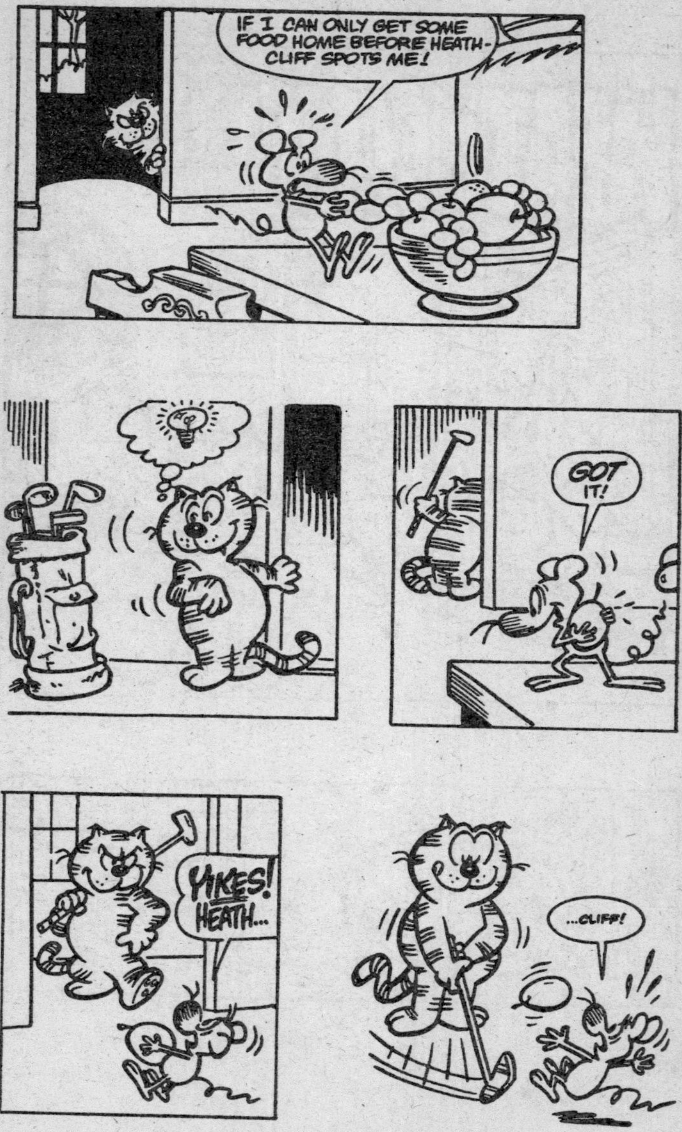
IF I CAN ONLY GET SOME FOOD HOME BEFORE HEATH-CLIFF SPOTS ME!
GOT IT!
YIKES! HEATH...
...CLIFF!

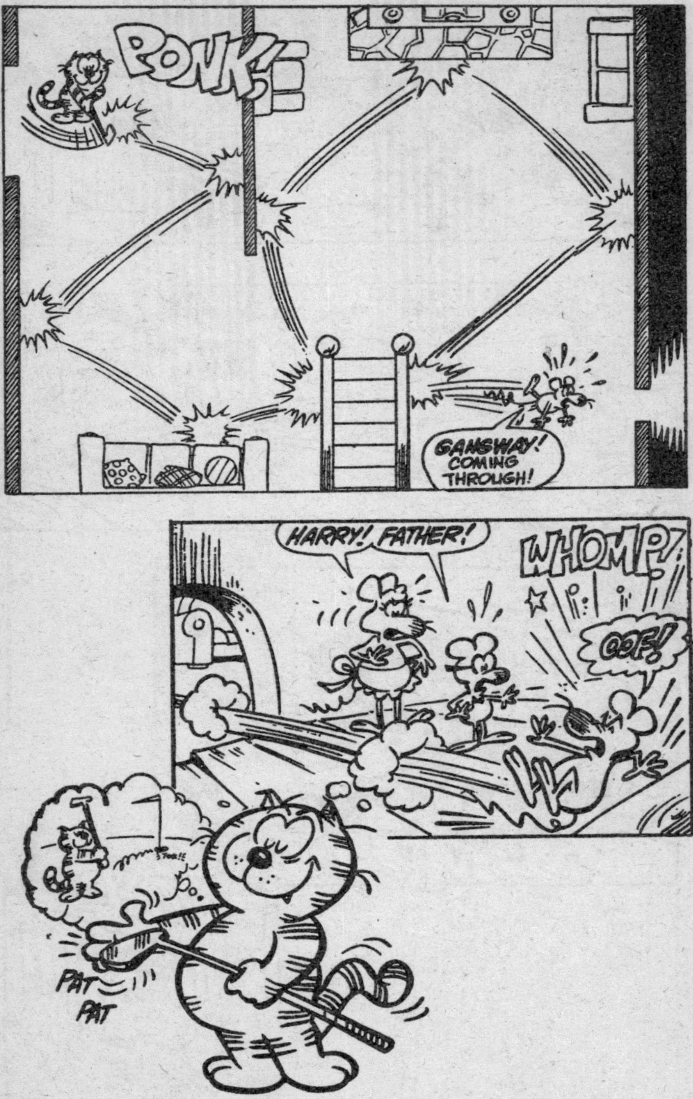
PONK!
GANGWAY! COMING THROUGH!
HARRY! FATHER!
WHOMP!
OOF!
PAT PAT

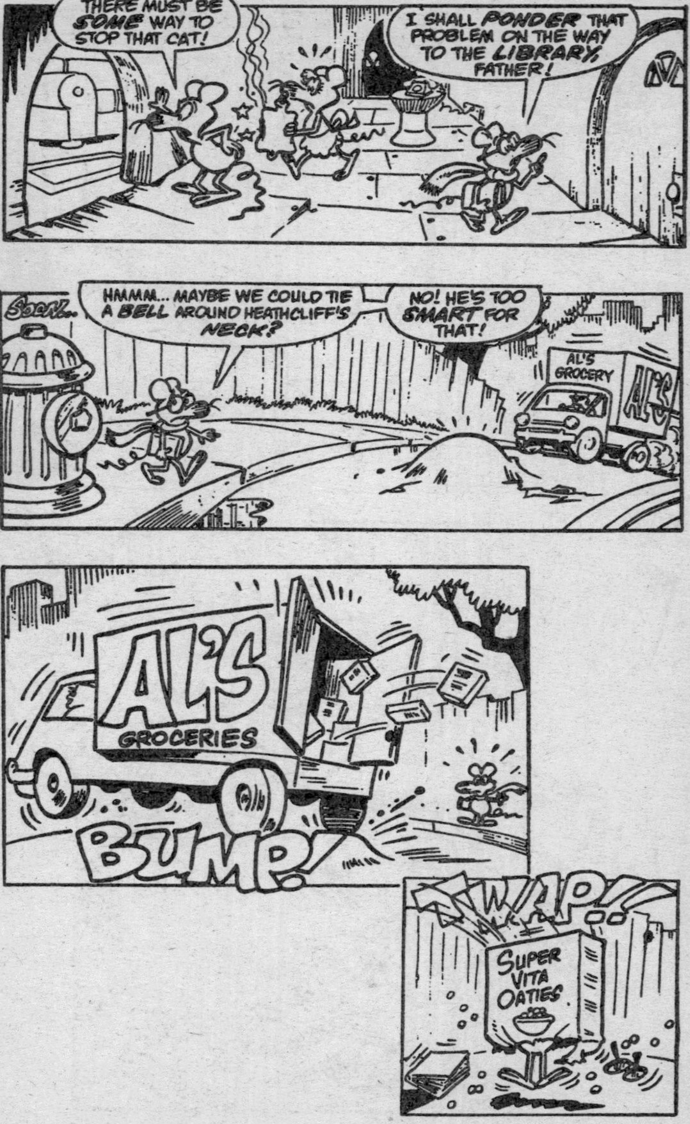
THERE MUST BE SOME WAY TO STOP THAT CAT!
I SHALL PONDER THAT PROBLEM ON THE WAY TO THE LIBRARY, FATHER!
Soon...
HMMM... MAYBE WE COULD TIE A BELL AROUND HEATHCLIFF'S NECK?
NO! HE'S TOO SMART FOR THAT!
AL'S GROCERY
AL'S
AL'S GROCERIES
BUMP!
SWAP!..
SUPER VITA OATIES

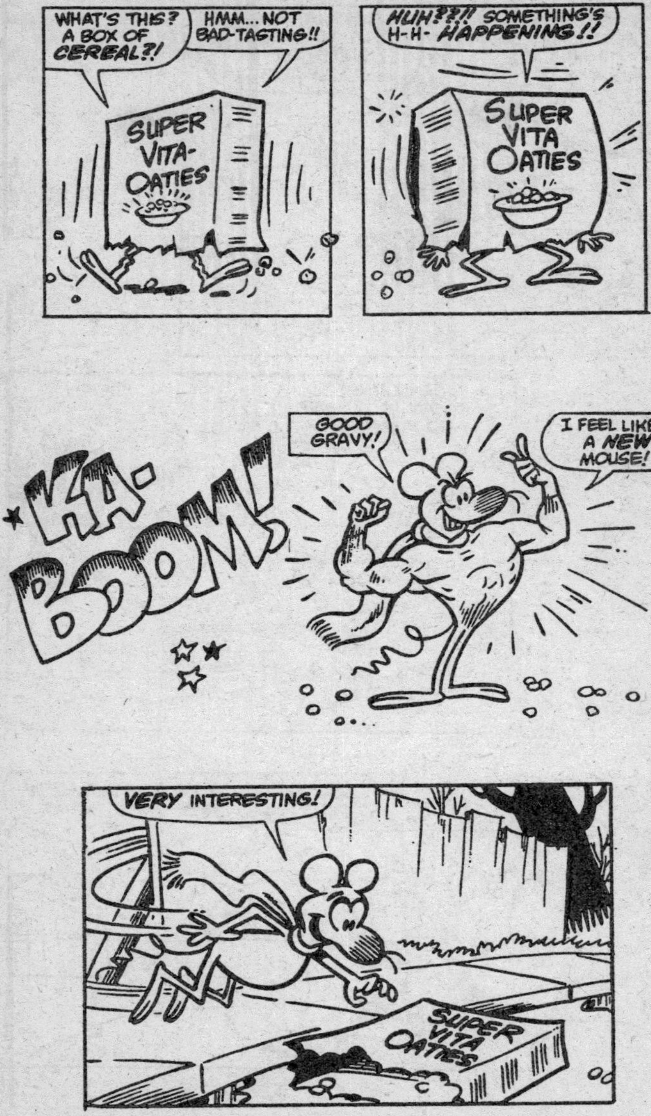
WHAT'S THIS? A BOX OF CEREAL?!
HMM... NOT BAD-TASTING!!
SUPER VITA-OATIES
HUH??!! SOMETHING'S H-H- HAPPENING!!
SUPER VITA OATIES
KA-BOOM!
GOOD GRAVY!
I FEEL LIKE A NEW MOUSE!
VERY INTERESTING!
SUPER VITA OATIES

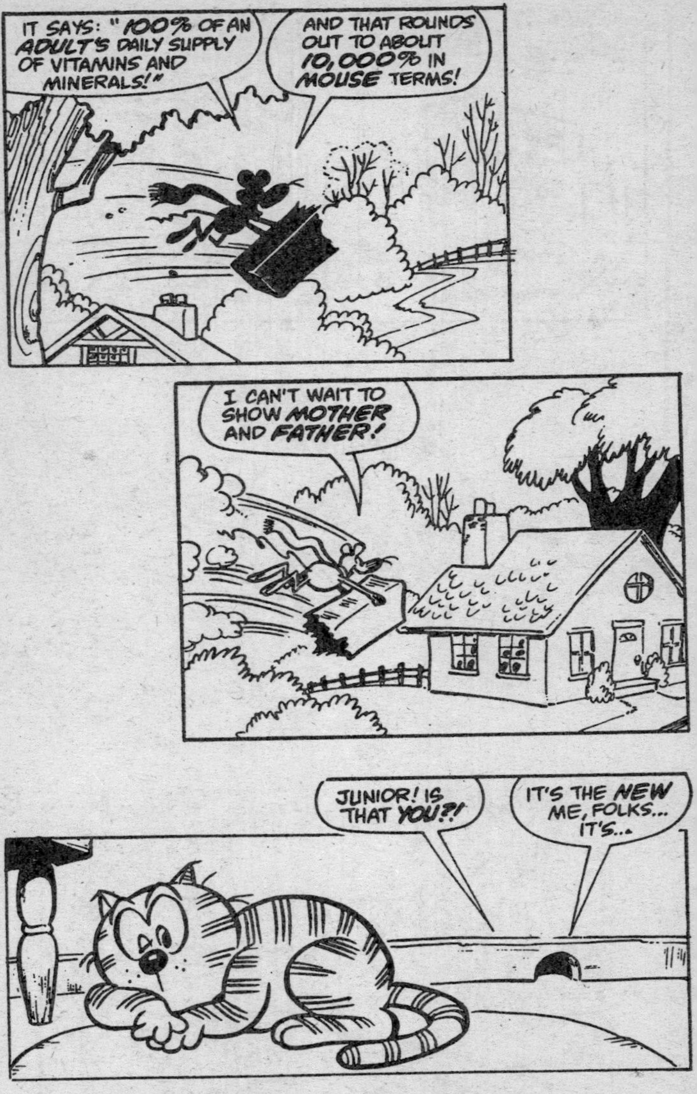
IT SAYS: "100% OF AN ADULT'S DAILY SUPPLY OF VITAMINS AND MINERALS!"
AND THAT ROUNDS OUT TO ABOUT 10,000% IN MOUSE TERMS!
I CAN'T WAIT TO SHOW MOTHER AND FATHER!
JUNIOR! IS THAT YOU?!
IT'S THE NEW ME, FOLKS... IT'S...

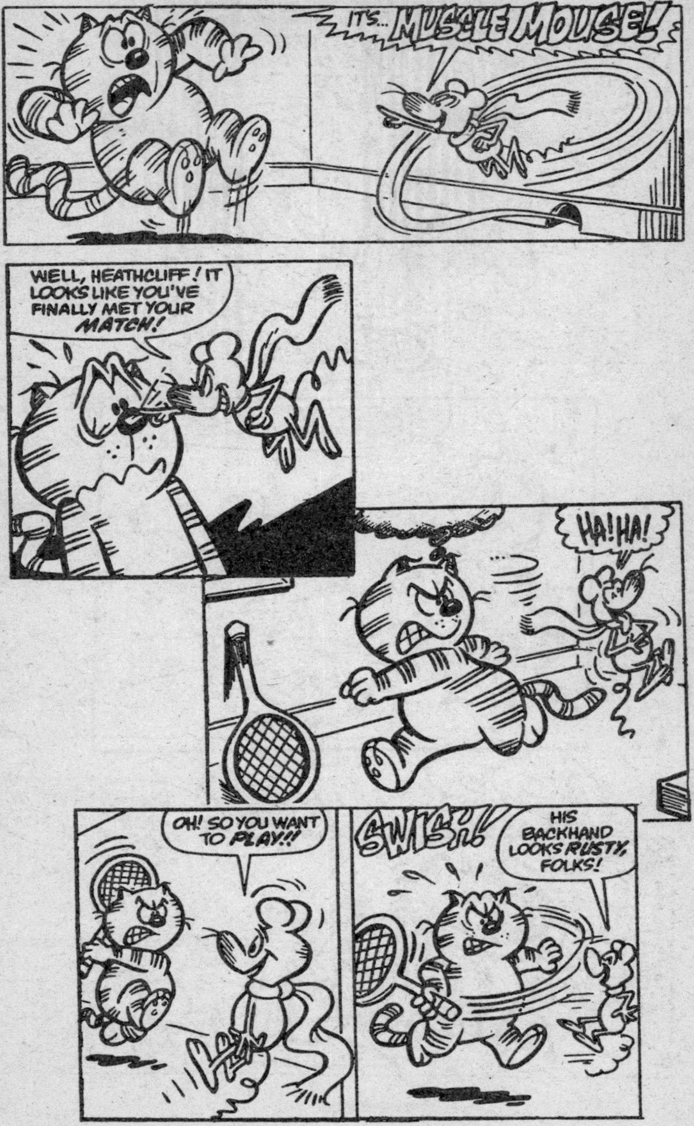
IT'S... MUSCLE MOUSE!
WELL, HEATHCLIFF! IT LOOKS LIKE YOU'VE FINALLY MET YOUR MATCH!
HA! HA!
OH! SO YOU WANT TO PLAY!!
SWISH!
HIS BACKHAND LOOKS RUSTY, FOLKS!

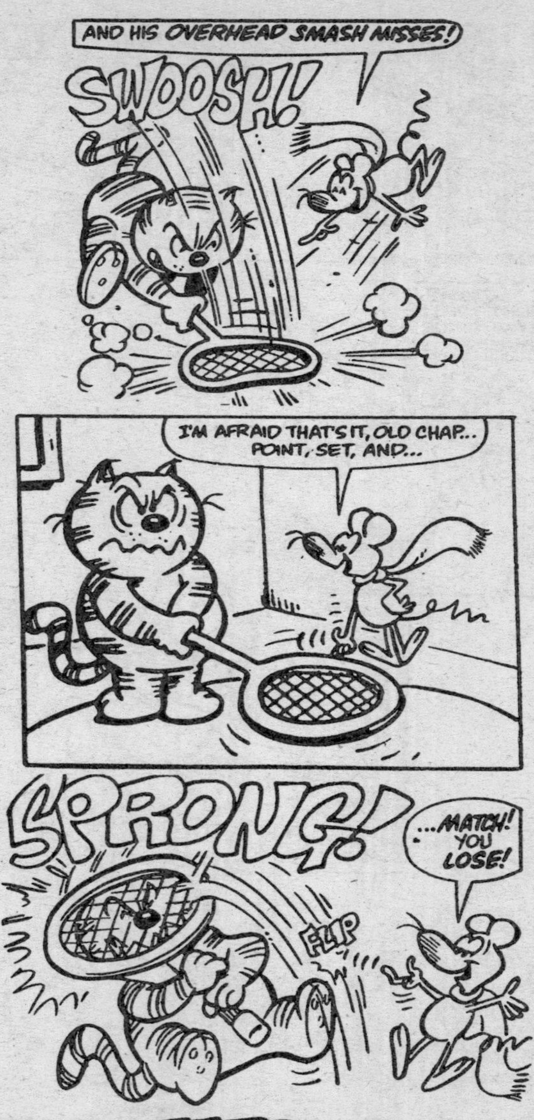
AND HIS OVERHEAD SMASH MISSES!
SWOOSH!
I'M AFRAID THAT'S IT, OLD CHAP... POINT, SET, AND...
SPRONG!
...MATCH! YOU LOSE!
FLIP

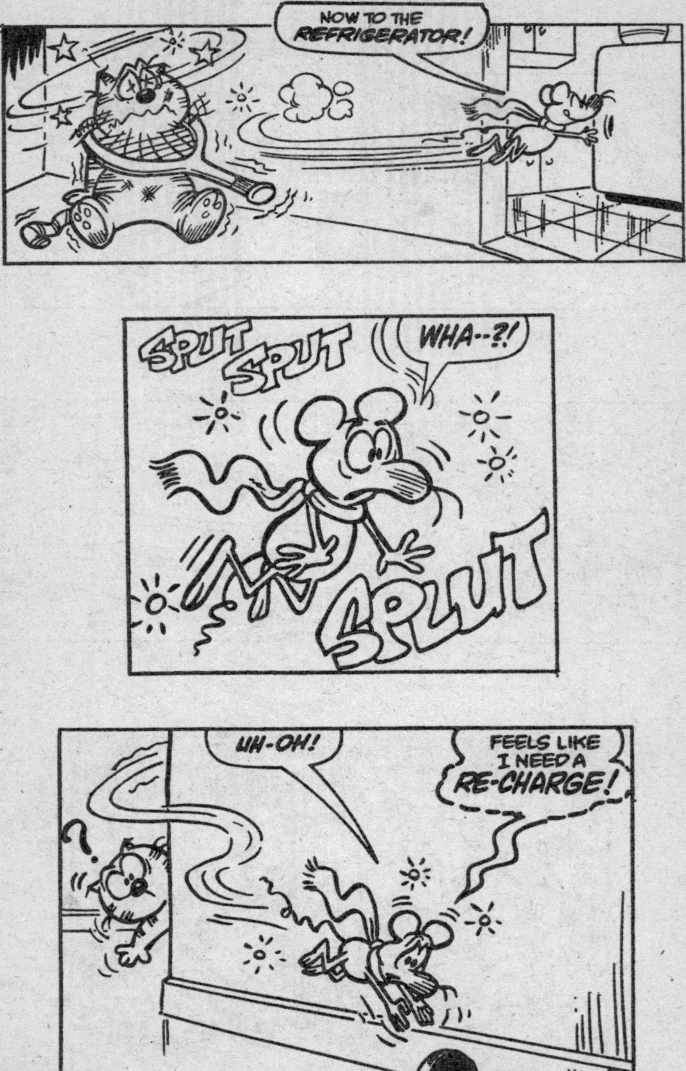
NOW TO THE REFRIGERATOR!
SPUT SPUT
WHA--?!
SPLUT
UH-OH!
FEELS LIKE I NEED A RE-CHARGE!

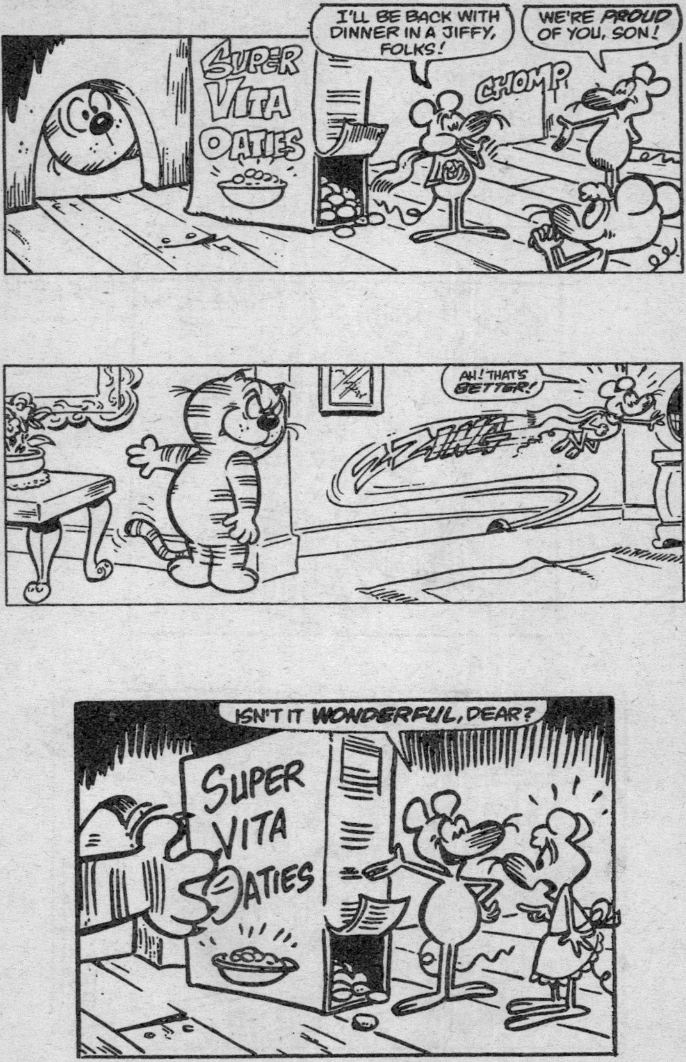
SUPER VITA OATIES
I'LL BE BACK WITH DINNER IN A JIFFY, FOLKS!
CHOMP
WE'RE PROUD OF YOU, SON!
AH! THAT'S BETTER!
ISN'T IT WONDERFUL, DEAR?
SUPER VITA OATIES

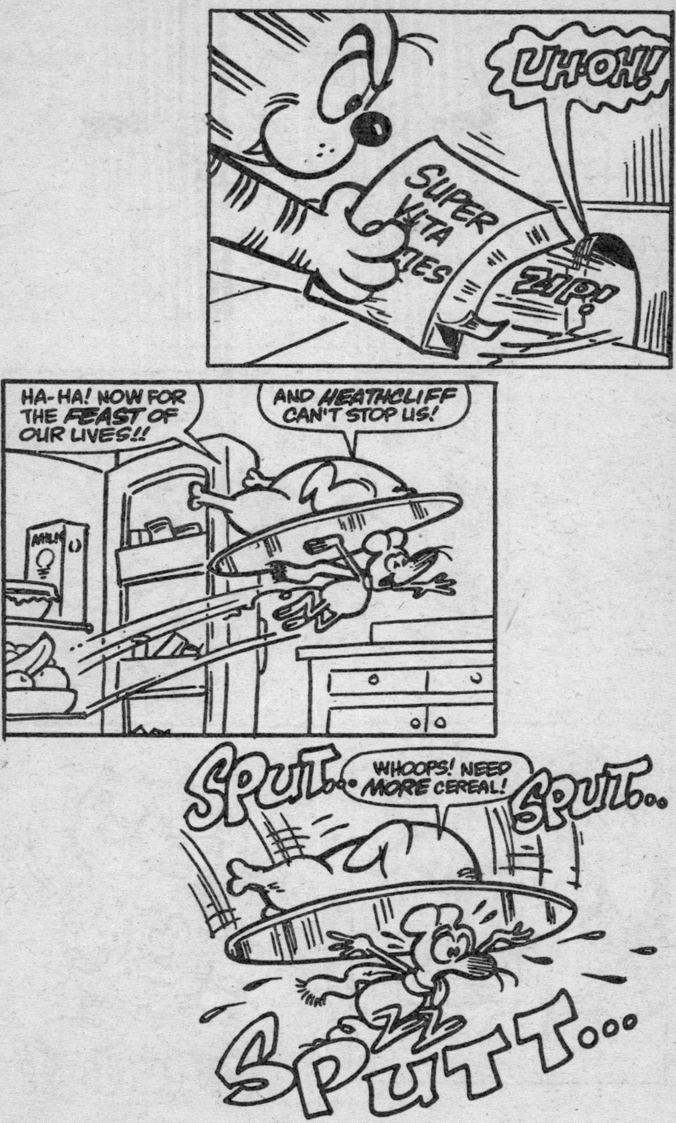
UH-OH!!
SUPER
VITA
IES
ZIP!
HA-HA! NOW FOR THE FEAST OF OUR LIVES!!
AND HEATHCLIFF CAN'T STOP US!
SPUT..
WHOOPS! NEED MORE CEREAL!
SPUT..
SPUTT...

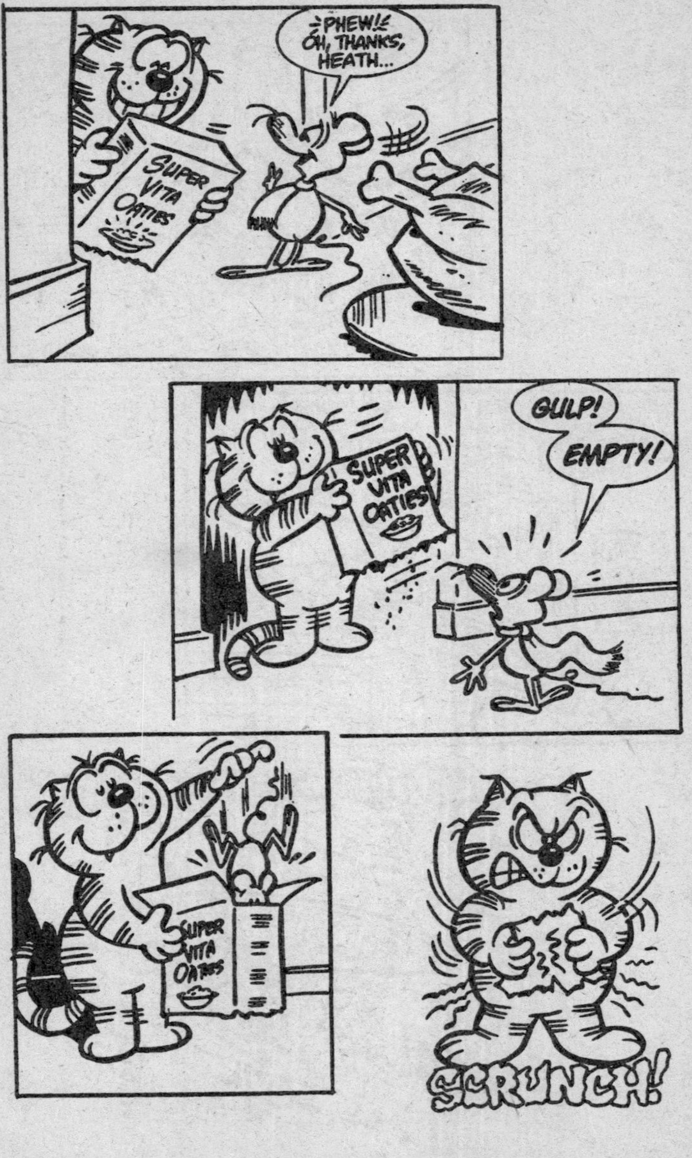
PHEW! OH, THANKS, HEATH...
SUPER VITA OATIES
SUPER VITA OATIES
GULP!
EMPTY!
SUPER VITA OATIES
SCRUNCH!

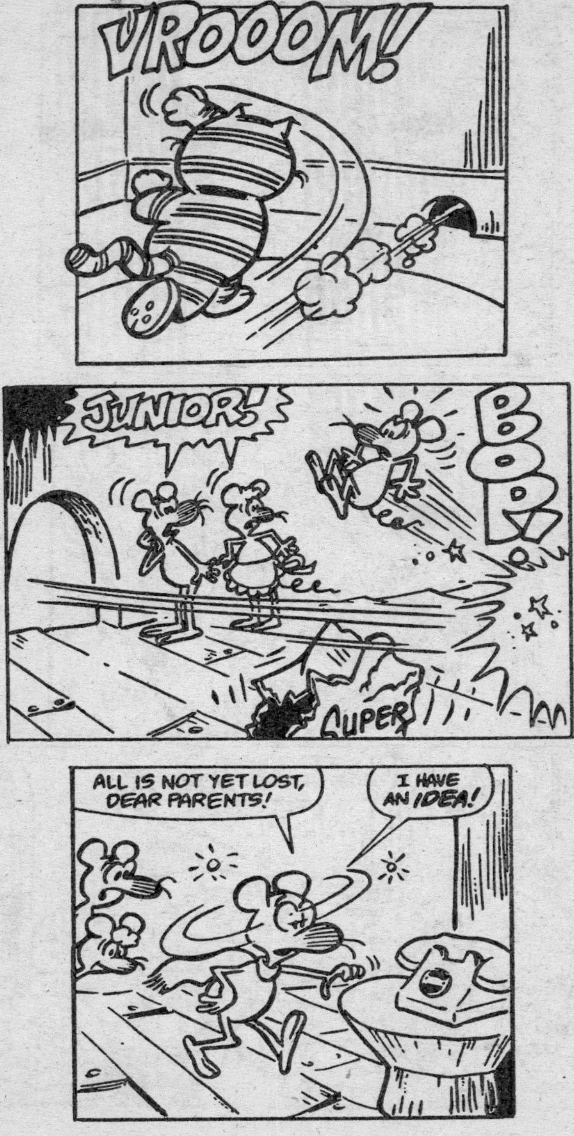
VROOOM!
JUNIOR!
BOP!
SUPER
ALL IS NOT YET LOST, DEAR PARENTS!
I HAVE AN IDEA!

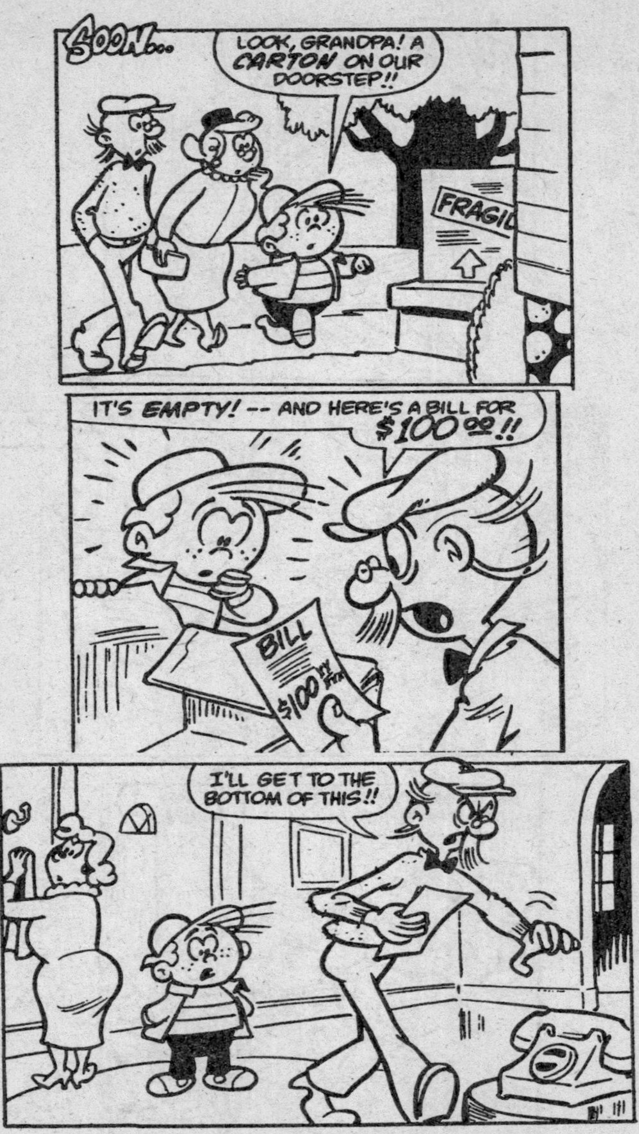
SOON...
LOOK, GRANDPA! A CARTON ON OUR DOORSTEP!!
FRAGIL
IT'S EMPTY! -- AND HERE'S A BILL FOR $100.00!!
BILL
$100
I'LL GET TO THE BOTTOM OF THIS!!

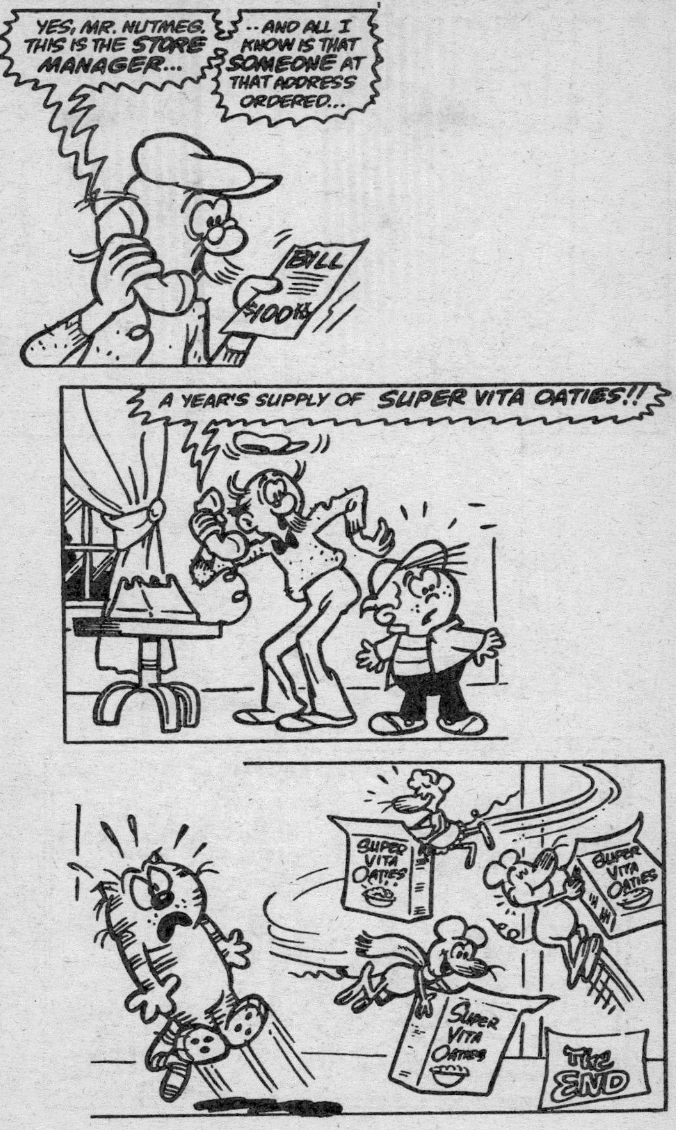
YES, MR. NUTMEG. THIS IS THE STORE MANAGER...
--AND ALL I KNOW IS THAT SOMEONE AT THAT ADDRESS ORDERED...
BILL
$100!!
A YEAR'S SUPPLY OF SUPER VITA OATIES!!
SUPER VITA OATIES
SUPER VITA OATIES
SUPER VITA OATIES
THE END

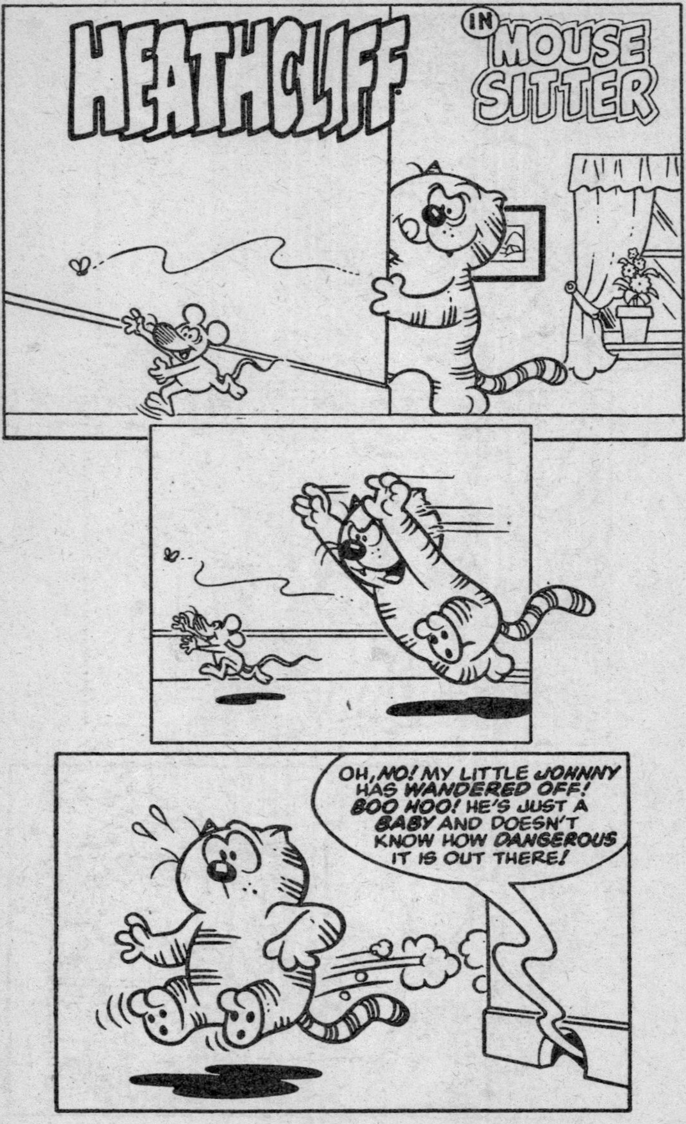
HEATHCLIFF
IN MOUSE SITTER
OH, NO! MY LITTLE JOHNNY HAS WANDERED OFF! BOO HOO! HE'S JUST A BABY AND DOESN'T KNOW HOW DANGEROUS IT IS OUT THERE!

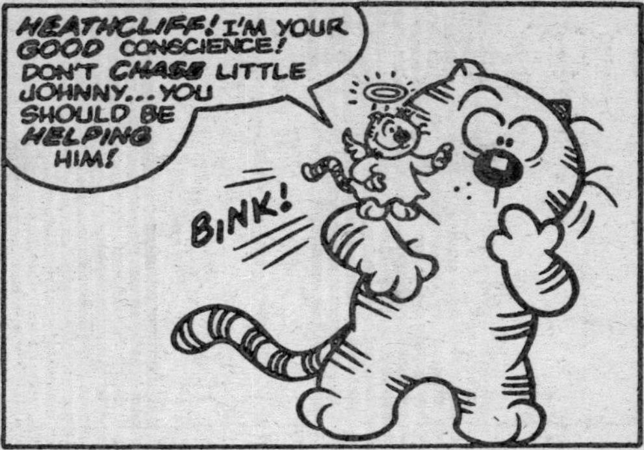
HEATHCLIFF! I'M YOUR GOOD CONSCIENCE! DON'T CHASE LITTLE JOHNNY...YOU SHOULD BE HELPING HIM!
BINK!

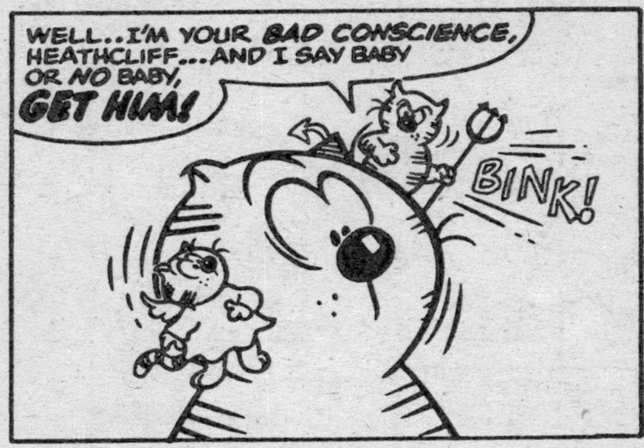
WELL..I'M YOUR BAD CONSCIENCE, HEATHCLIFF...AND I SAY BABY OR NO BABY, GET HIM!
BINK!

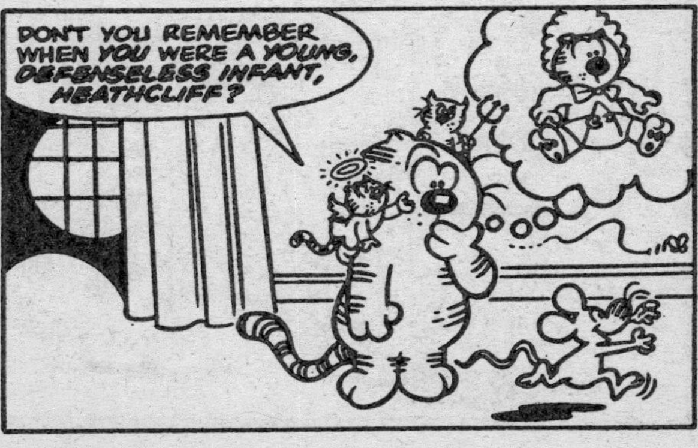
DON'T YOU REMEMBER WHEN YOU WERE A YOUNG, DEFENSELESS INFANT, HEATHCLIFF?

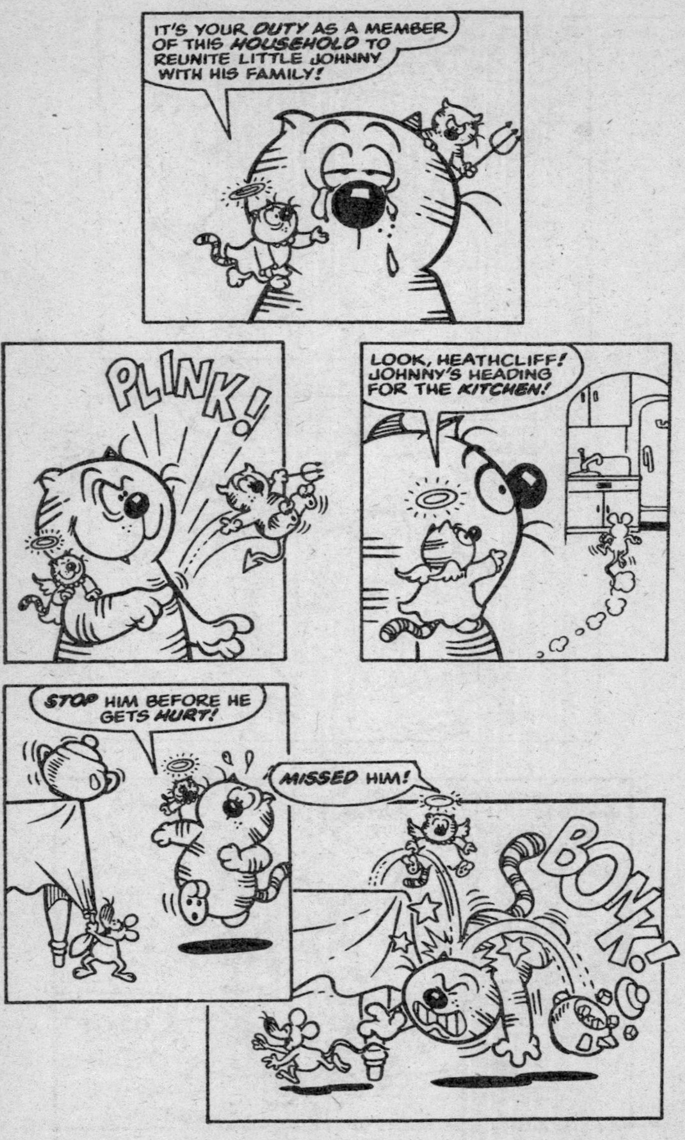
IT'S YOUR DUTY AS A MEMBER OF THIS HOUSEHOLD TO REUNITE LITTLE JOHNNY WITH HIS FAMILY!
PLINK!
LOOK, HEATHCLIFF! JOHNNY'S HEADING FOR THE KITCHEN!
STOP HIM BEFORE HE GETS HURT!
MISSED HIM!
BONK!

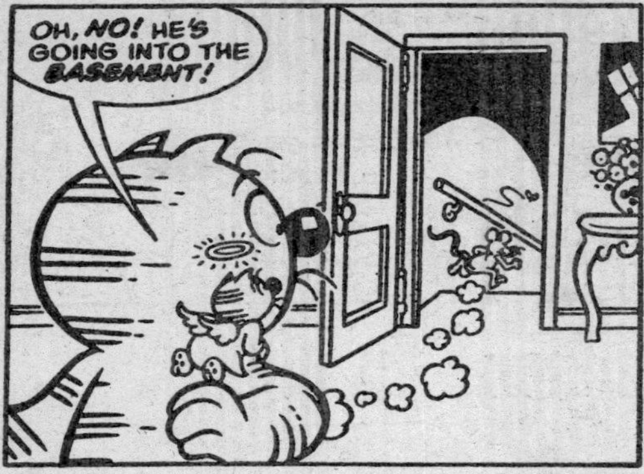
OH, NO! HE'S GOING INTO THE BASEMENT!

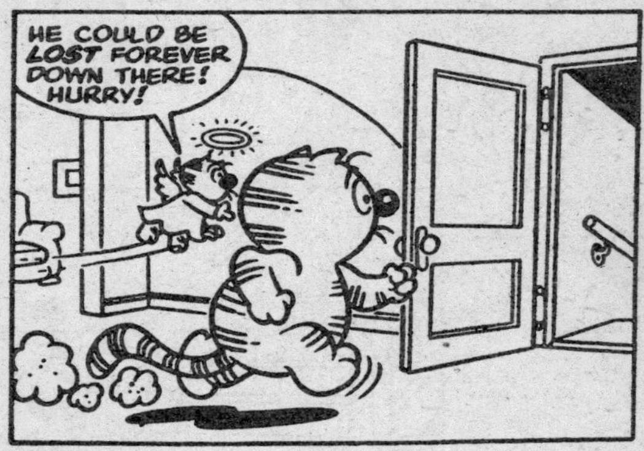
HE COULD BE LOST FOREVER DOWN THERE! HURRY!

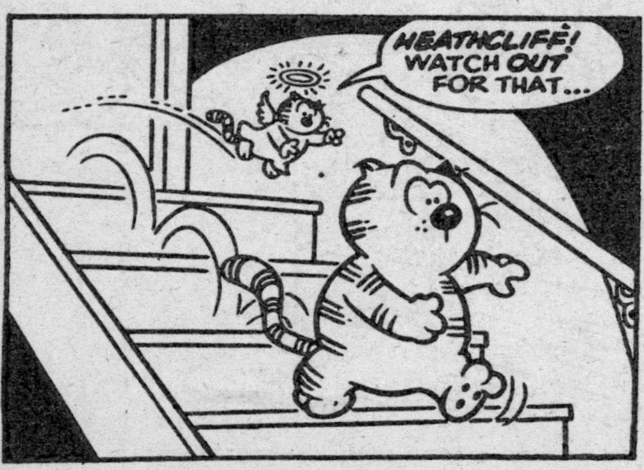
HEATHCLIFF! WATCH OUT FOR THAT...

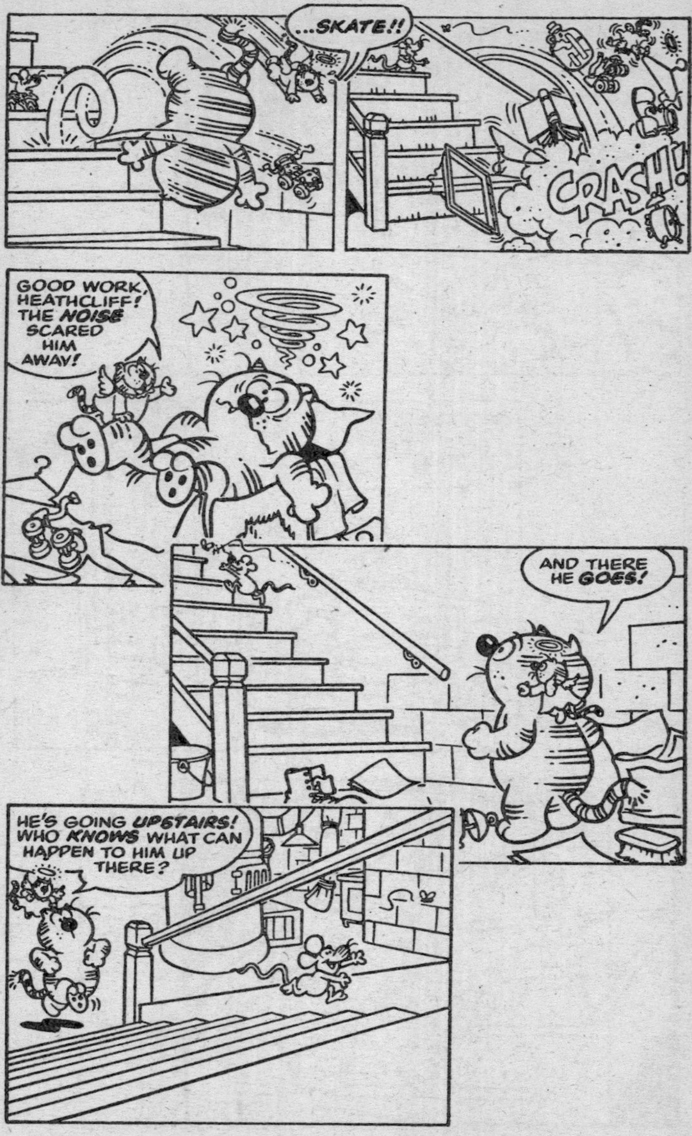

...SKATE!!
CRASH!
GOOD WORK, HEATHCLIFF! THE NOISE SCARED HIM AWAY!
AND THERE HE GOES!
HE'S GOING UPSTAIRS! WHO KNOWS WHAT CAN HAPPEN TO HIM UP THERE?

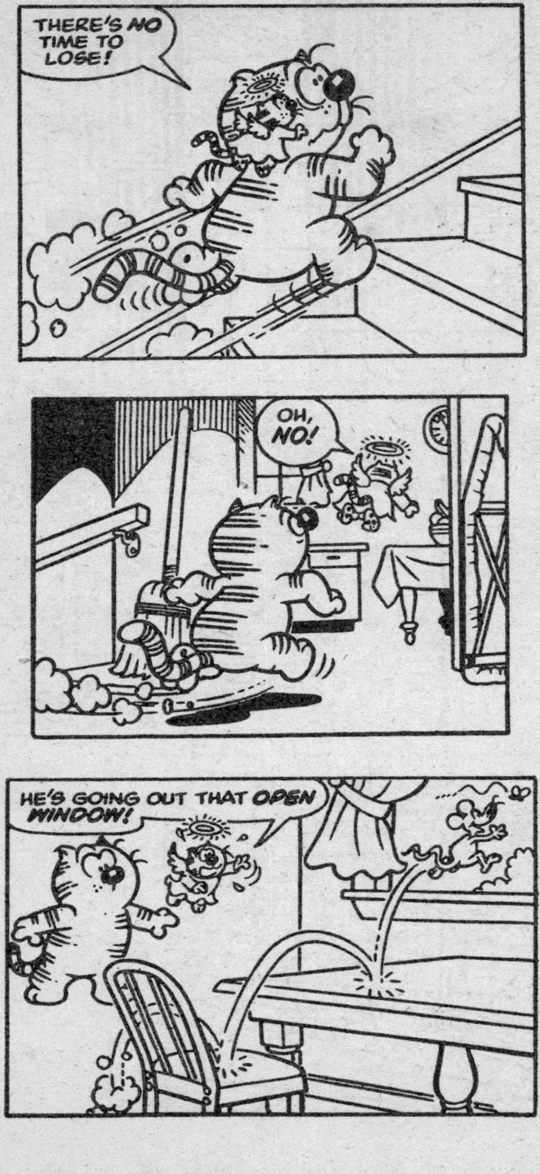
THERE'S NO TIME TO LOSE!
OH, NO!
HE'S GOING OUT THAT OPEN WINDOW!

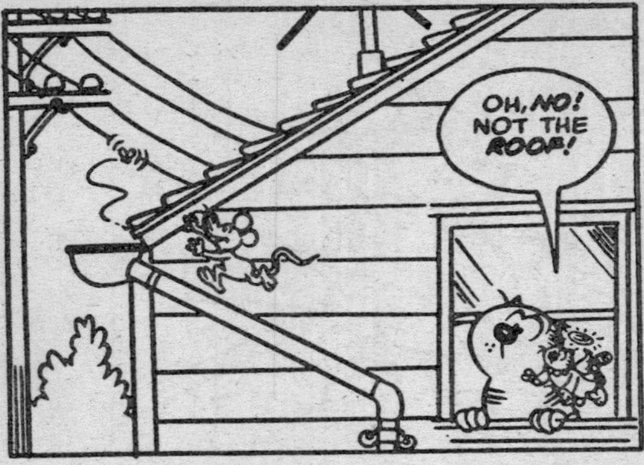
OH, NO! NOT THE ROOF!

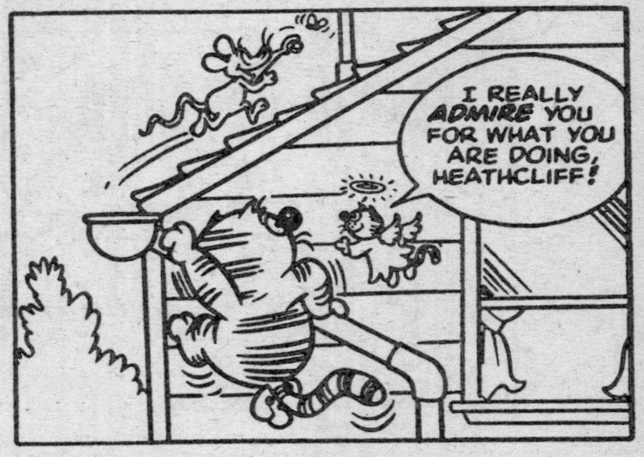
I REALLY ADMIRE YOU FOR WHAT YOU ARE DOING, HEATHCLIFF!

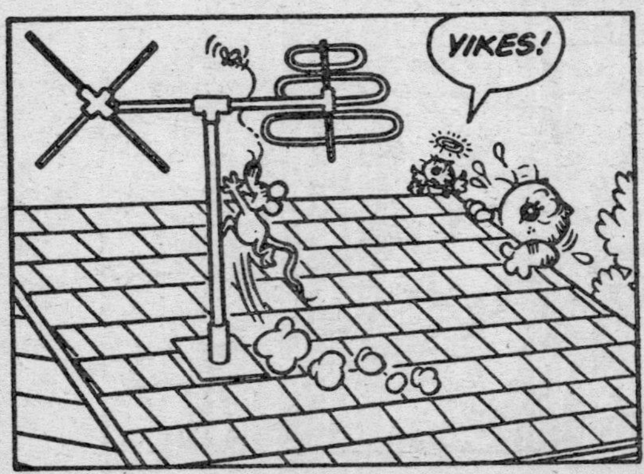
YIKES!

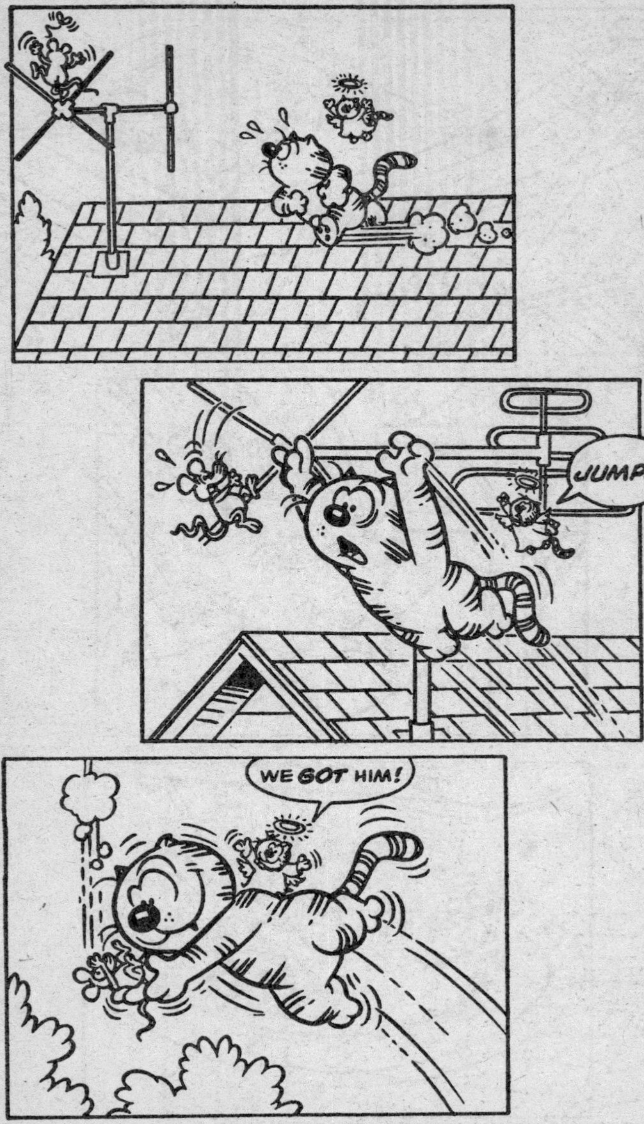
JUMP!
WE GOT HIM!

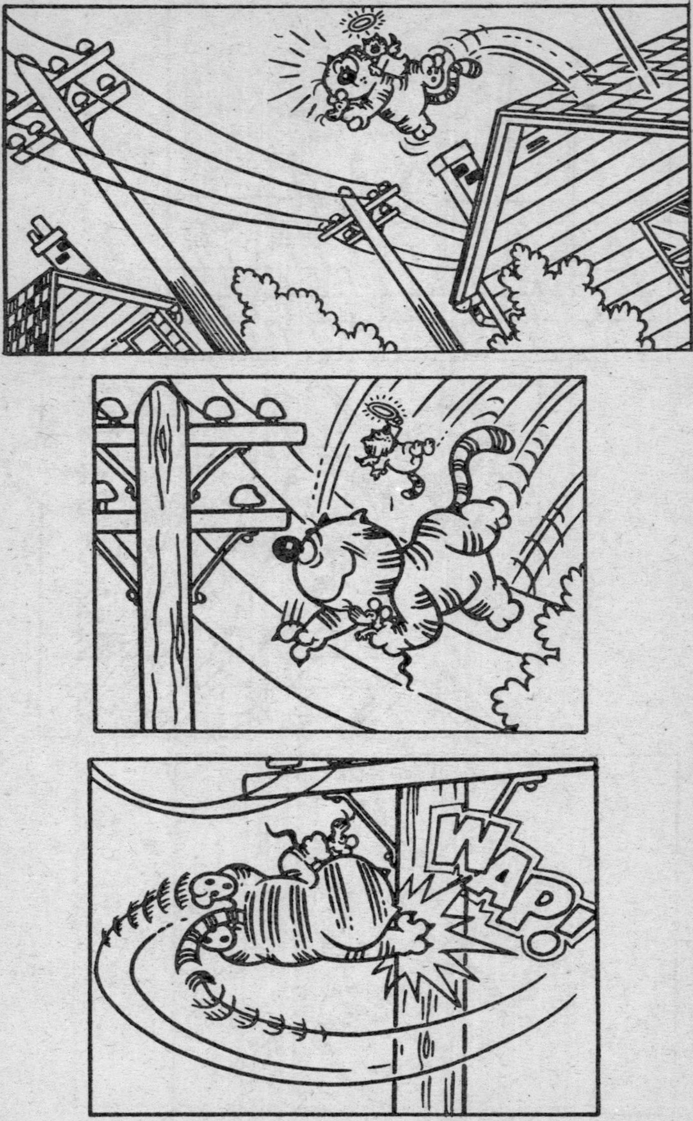
WAP!

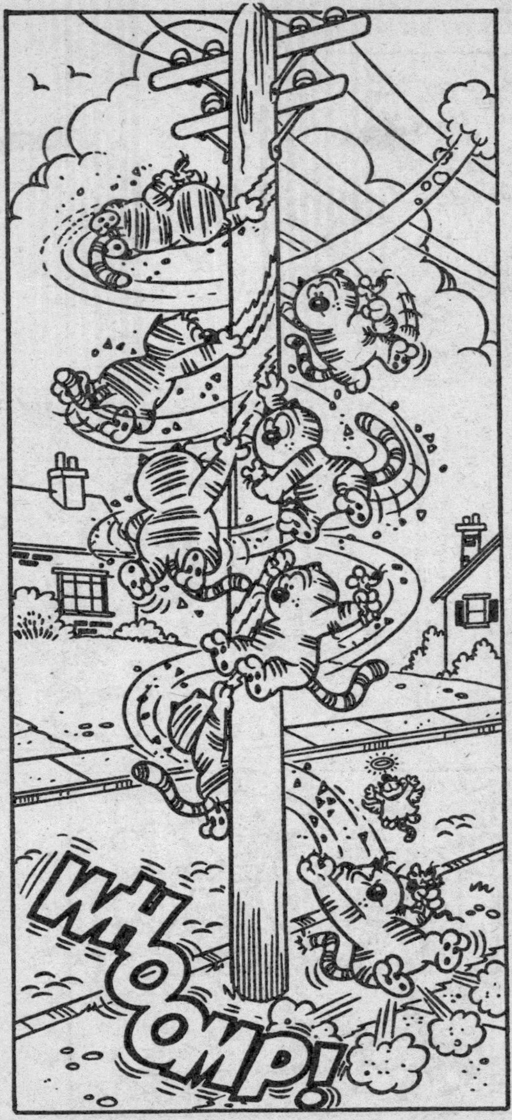
WHOOMP!

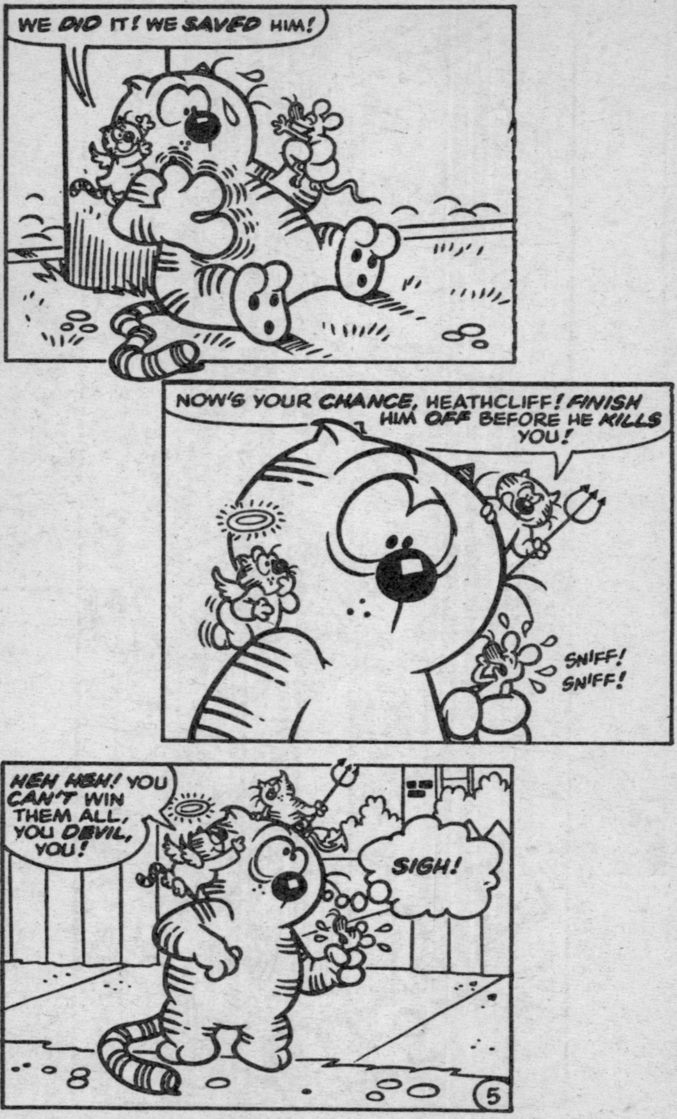
WE DID IT! WE SAVED HIM!
NOW'S YOUR CHANCE, HEATHCLIFF! FINISH HIM OFF BEFORE HE KILLS YOU!
SNIFF! SNIFF!
HEH HEH! YOU CAN'T WIN THEM ALL, YOU DEVIL, YOU!
SIGH!
5

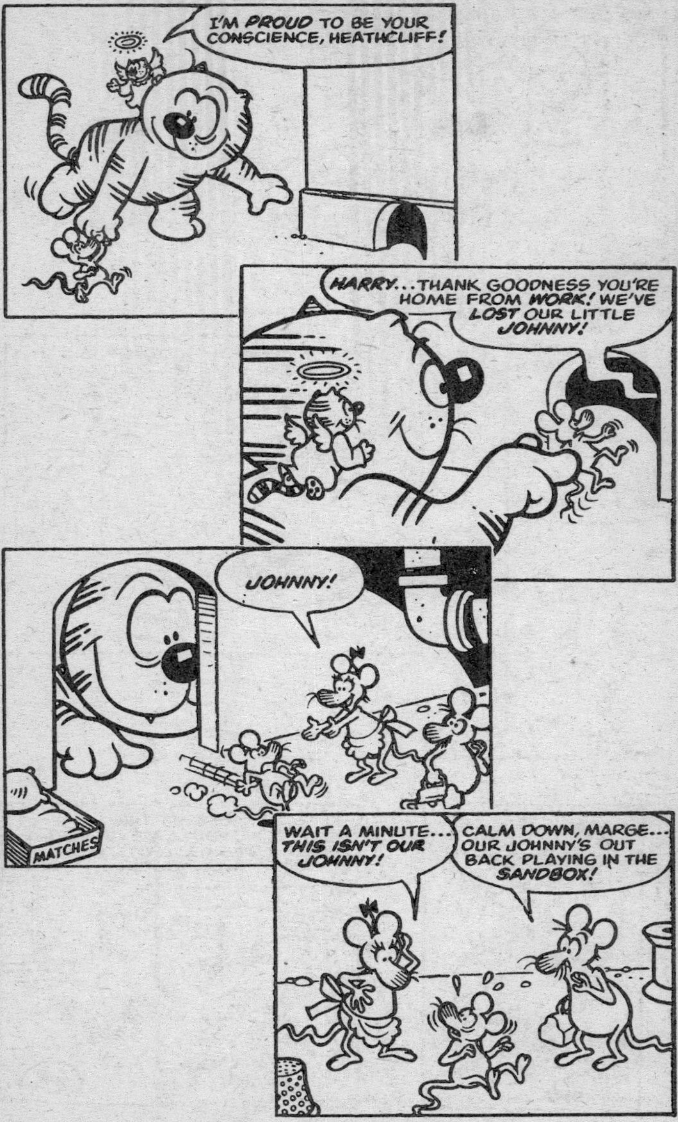
I'M PROUD TO BE YOUR CONSCIENCE, HEATHCLIFF!
HARRY...THANK GOODNESS YOU'RE HOME FROM WORK! WE'VE LOST OUR LITTLE JOHNNY!
JOHNNY!
MATCHES
WAIT A MINUTE... THIS ISN'T OUR JOHNNY!
CALM DOWN, MARGE... OUR JOHNNY'S OUT BACK PLAYING IN THE SANDBOX!

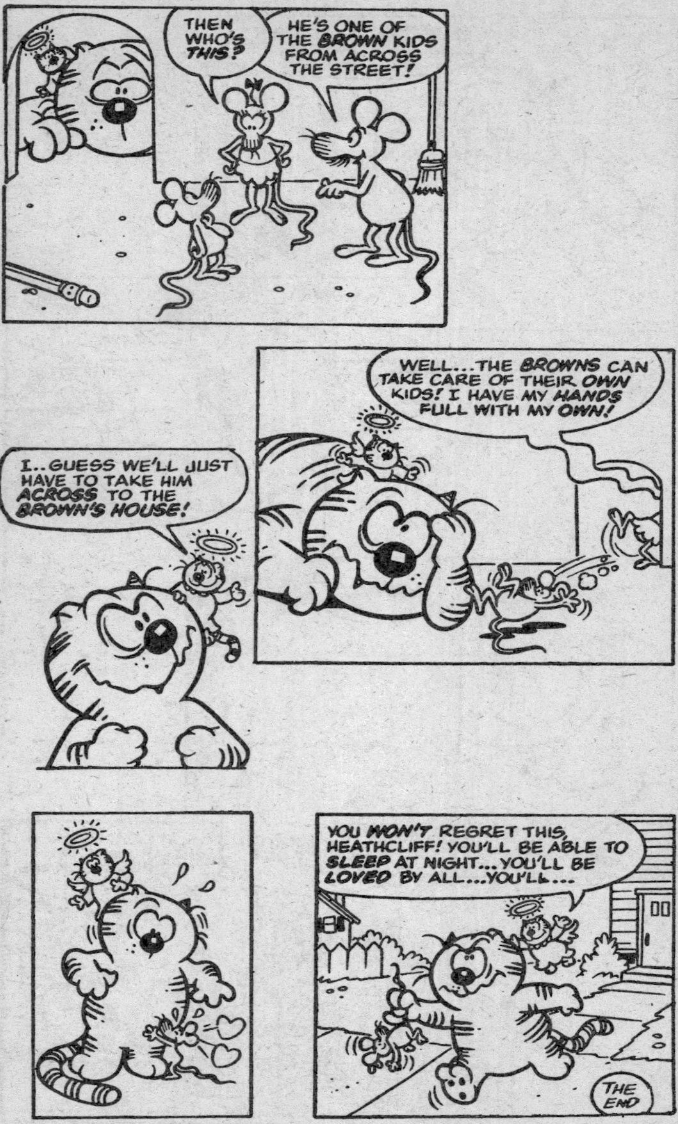
THEN WHO'S THIS?
HE'S ONE OF THE BROWN KIDS FROM ACROSS THE STREET!
I..GUESS WE'LL JUST HAVE TO TAKE HIM ACROSS TO THE BROWN'S HOUSE!
WELL...THE BROWNS CAN TAKE CARE OF THEIR OWN KIDS! I HAVE MY HANDS FULL WITH MY OWN!
YOU WON'T REGRET THIS, HEATHCLIFF! YOU'LL BE ABLE TO SLEEP AT NIGHT...YOU'LL BE LOVED BY ALL...YOU'LL...
THE END

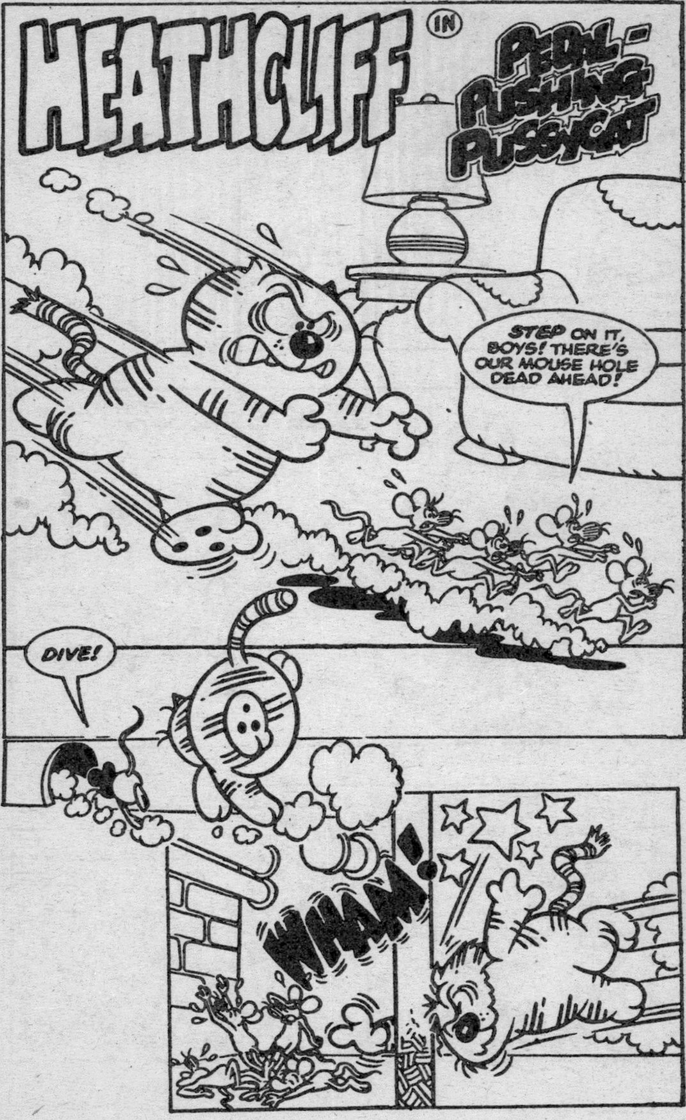
HEATHCLIFF IN
PEDAL-PUSHING PUSSYCAT
STEP ON IT, BOYS! THERE'S OUR MOUSE HOLE DEAD AHEAD!
DIVE!
WHAM!

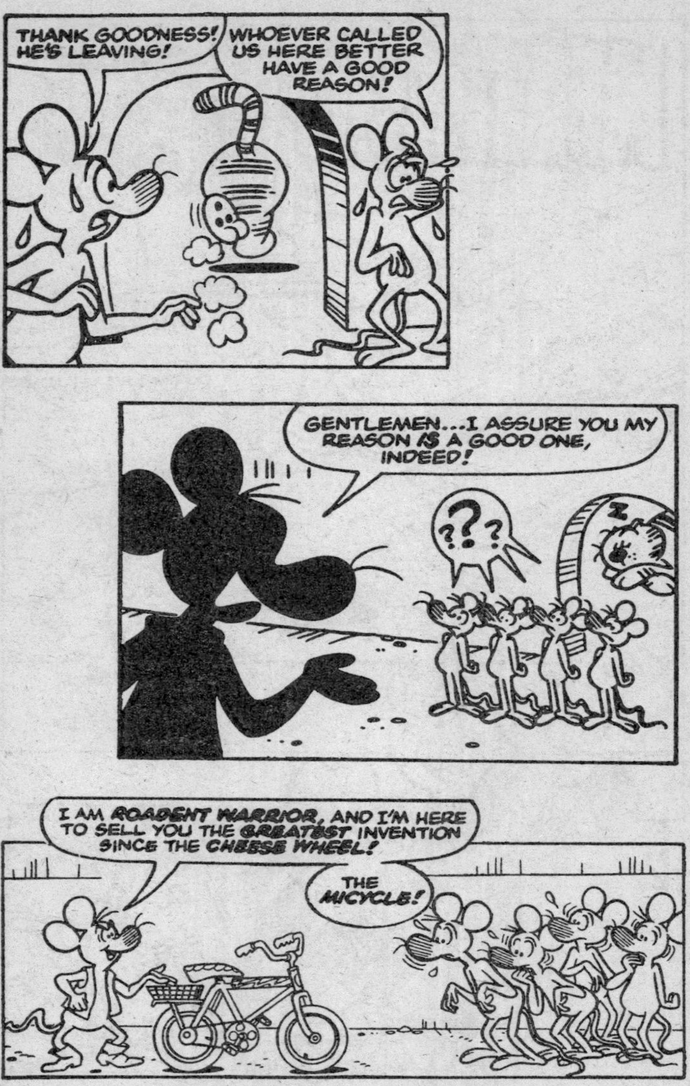
THANK GOODNESS! HE'S LEAVING!
WHOEVER CALLED US HERE BETTER HAVE A GOOD REASON!
GENTLEMEN...I ASSURE YOU MY REASON IS A GOOD ONE, INDEED!
???
I AM ROADENT WARRIOR, AND I'M HERE TO SELL YOU THE GREATEST INVENTION SINCE THE CHEESE WHEEL!
THE MICYCLE!

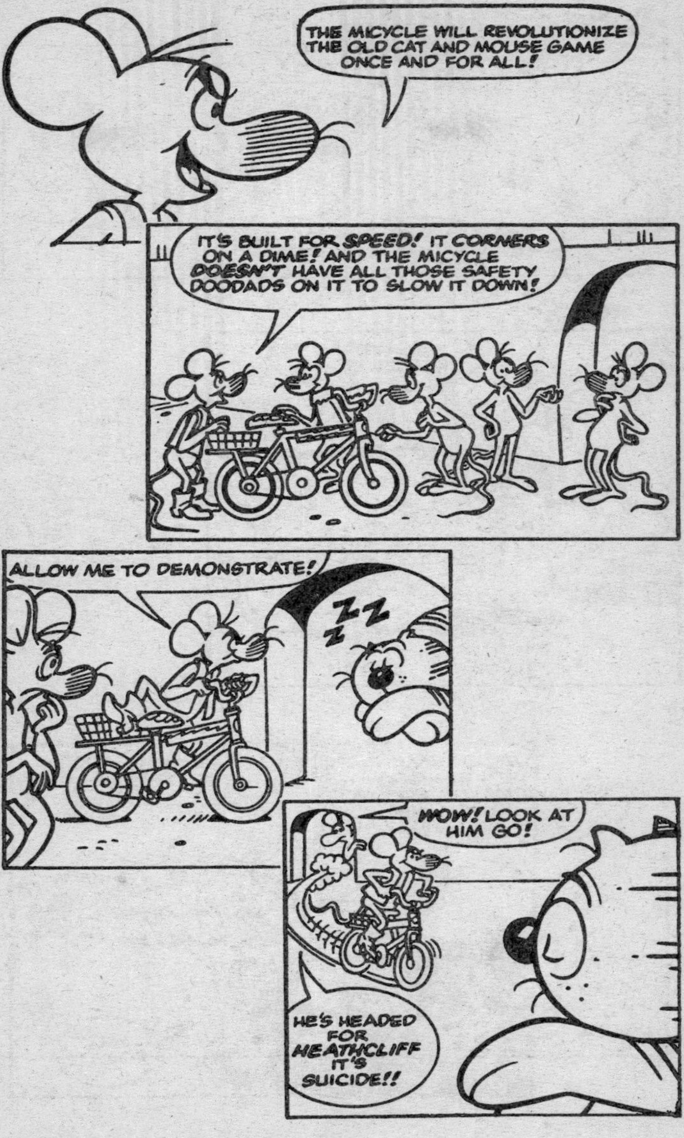
THE MICYCLE WILL REVOLUTIONIZE THE OLD CAT AND MOUSE GAME ONCE AND FOR ALL!
IT'S BUILT FOR SPEED! IT CORNERS ON A DIME! AND THE MICYCLE DOESN'T HAVE ALL THOSE SAFETY DOODADS ON IT TO SLOW IT DOWN!
ALLOW ME TO DEMONSTRATE!
ZZZ
WOW! LOOK AT HIM GO!
HE'S HEADED FOR HEATHCLIFF IT'S SUICIDE!!

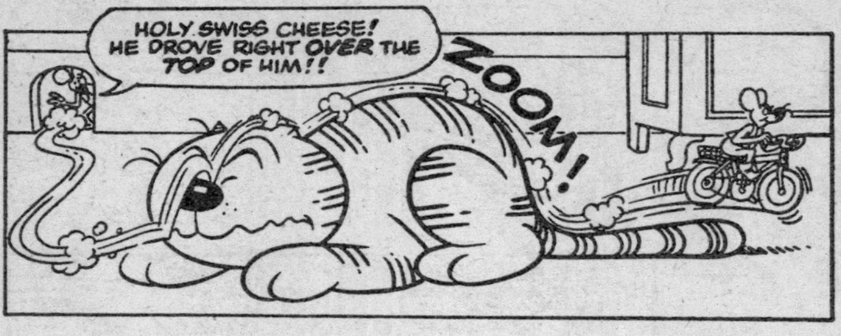
HOLY SWISS CHEESE! HE DROVE RIGHT OVER THE TOP OF HIM!!
ZOOM!

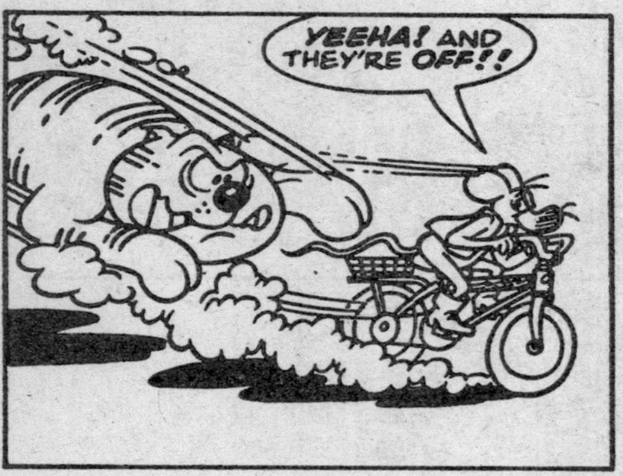
YEEHA! AND THEY'RE OFF!!

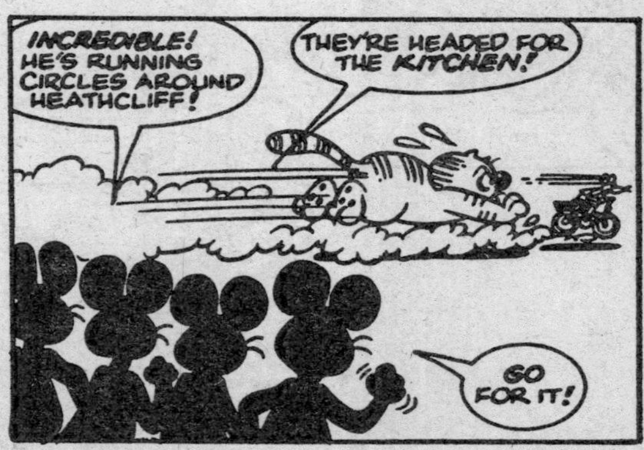
INCREDIBLE! HE'S RUNNING CIRCLES AROUND HEATHCLIFF!
THEY'RE HEADED FOR THE KITCHEN!
GO FOR IT!

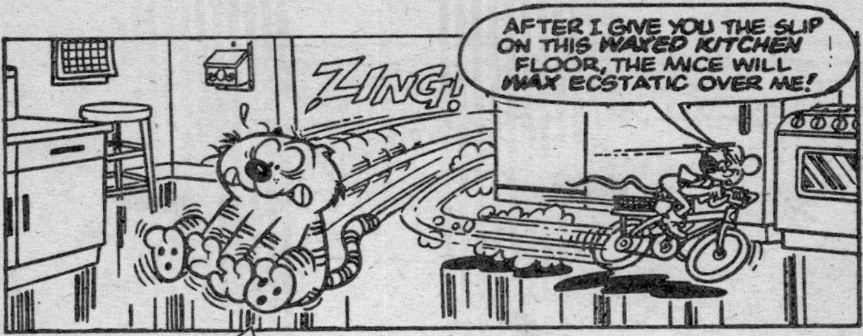
ZING!
AFTER I GIVE YOU THE SLIP ON THIS WAXED KITCHEN FLOOR, THE MICE WILL WAX ECSTATIC OVER ME!

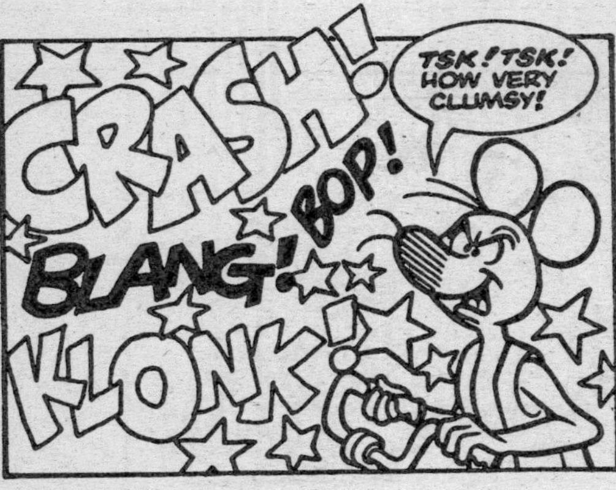
CRASH!
BOP!
BLANG!
KLONK!
TSK! TSK! HOW VERY CLUMSY!

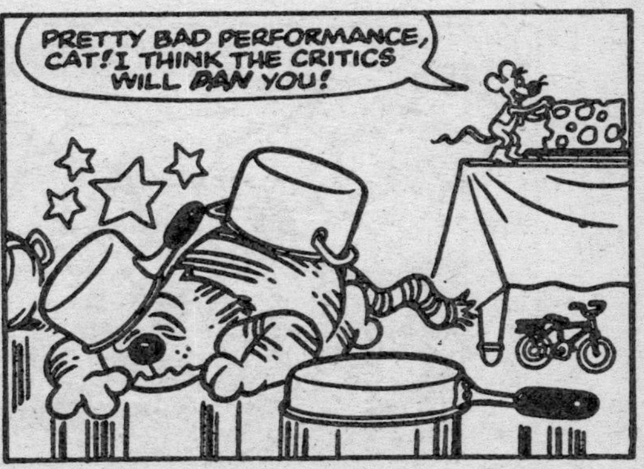
PRETTY BAD PERFORMANCE, CAT! I THINK THE CRITICS WILL PAN YOU!

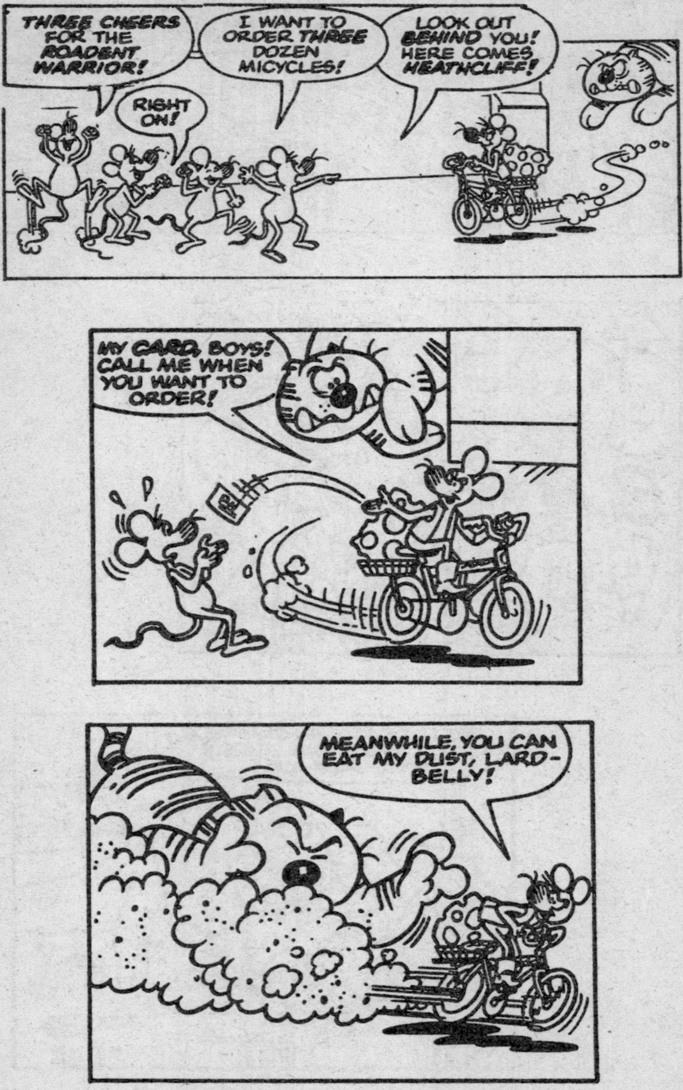
THREE CHEERS FOR THE ROADENT WARRIOR!
RIGHT ON!
I WANT TO ORDER THREE DOZEN MICYCLES!
LOOK OUT BEHIND YOU! HERE COMES HEATHCLIFF!
MY CARD, BOYS! CALL ME WHEN YOU WANT TO ORDER!
MEANWHILE, YOU CAN EAT MY DUST, LARD-BELLY!

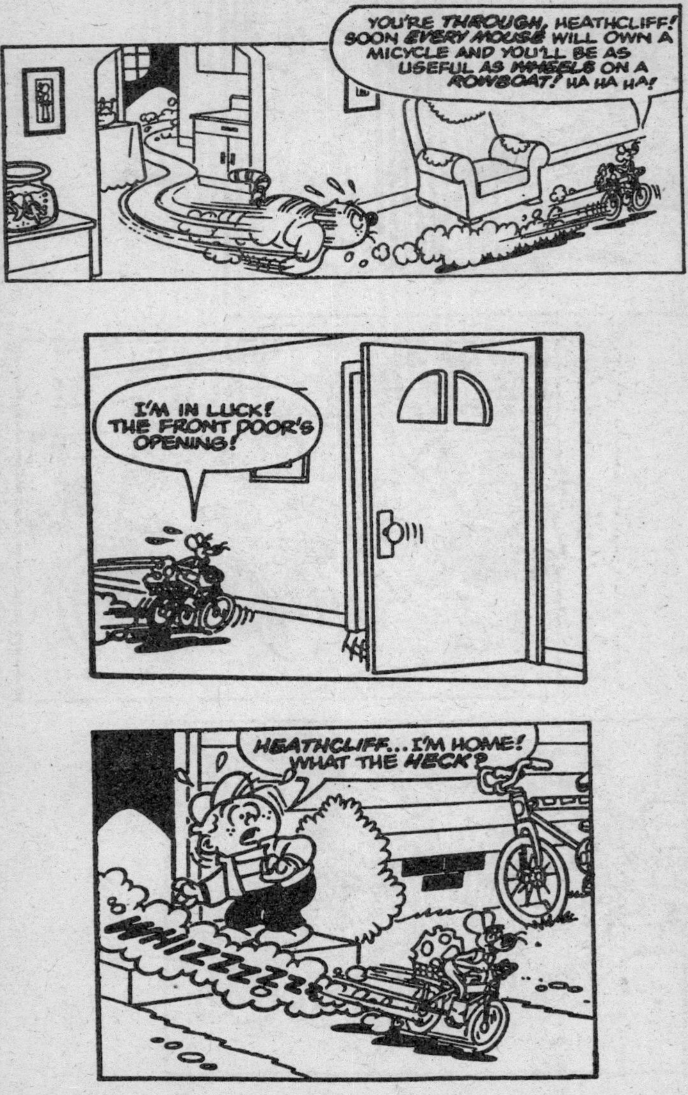
YOU'RE THROUGH, HEATHCLIFF! SOON EVERY MOUSE WILL OWN A MICYCLE AND YOU'LL BE AS USEFUL AS WHEELS ON A ROWBOAT! HA HA HA!
I'M IN LUCK! THE FRONT DOOR'S OPENING!
HEATHCLIFF... I'M HOME! WHAT THE HECK?
WHIZZZZZ

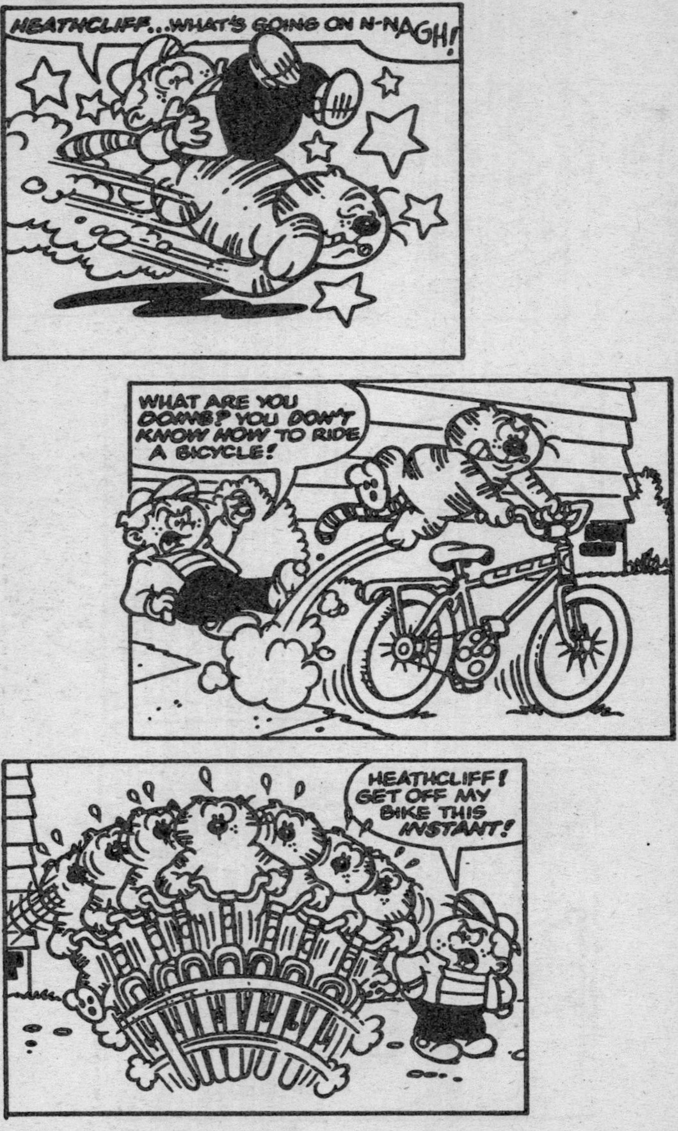
HEATHCLIFF...WHAT'S GOING ON N-NAGH!
WHAT ARE YOU DOING? YOU DON'T KNOW HOW TO RIDE A BICYCLE!
HEATHCLIFF! GET OFF MY BIKE THIS INSTANT!

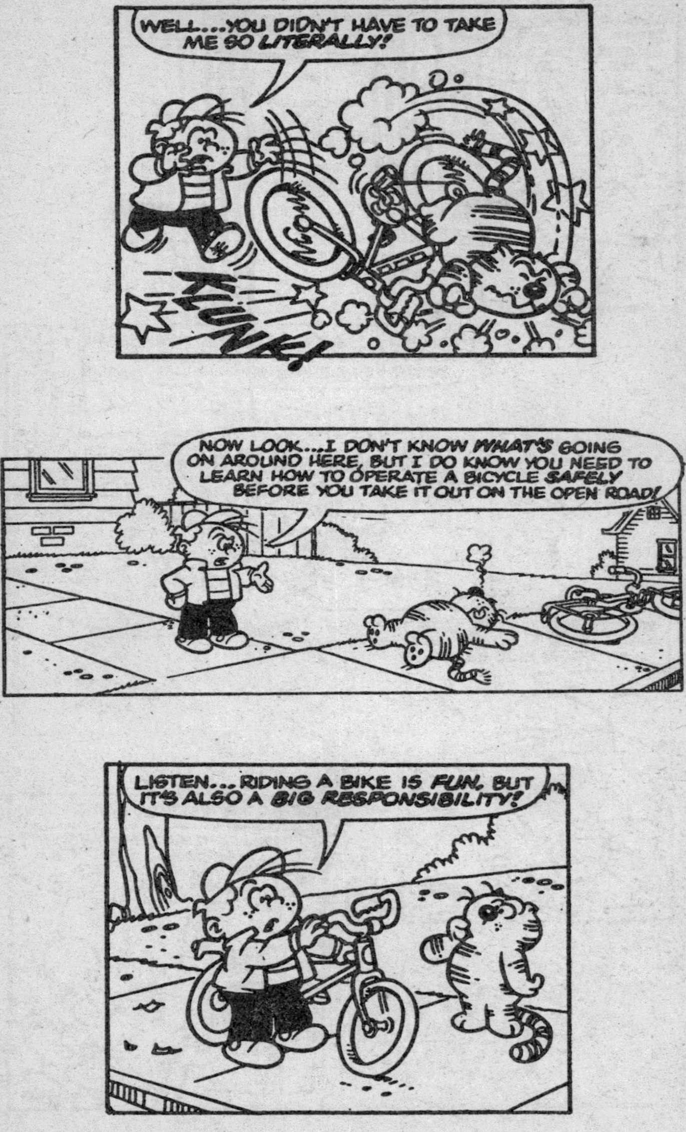
WELL...YOU DIDN'T HAVE TO TAKE ME SO *LITERALLY!*
KLUNK!
NOW LOOK...I DON'T KNOW *WHAT'S* GOING ON AROUND HERE, BUT I DO KNOW YOU NEED TO LEARN HOW TO OPERATE A BICYCLE *SAFELY* BEFORE YOU TAKE IT OUT ON THE OPEN ROAD!
LISTEN... RIDING A BIKE IS *FUN*, BUT IT'S ALSO A *BIG RESPONSIBILITY!*

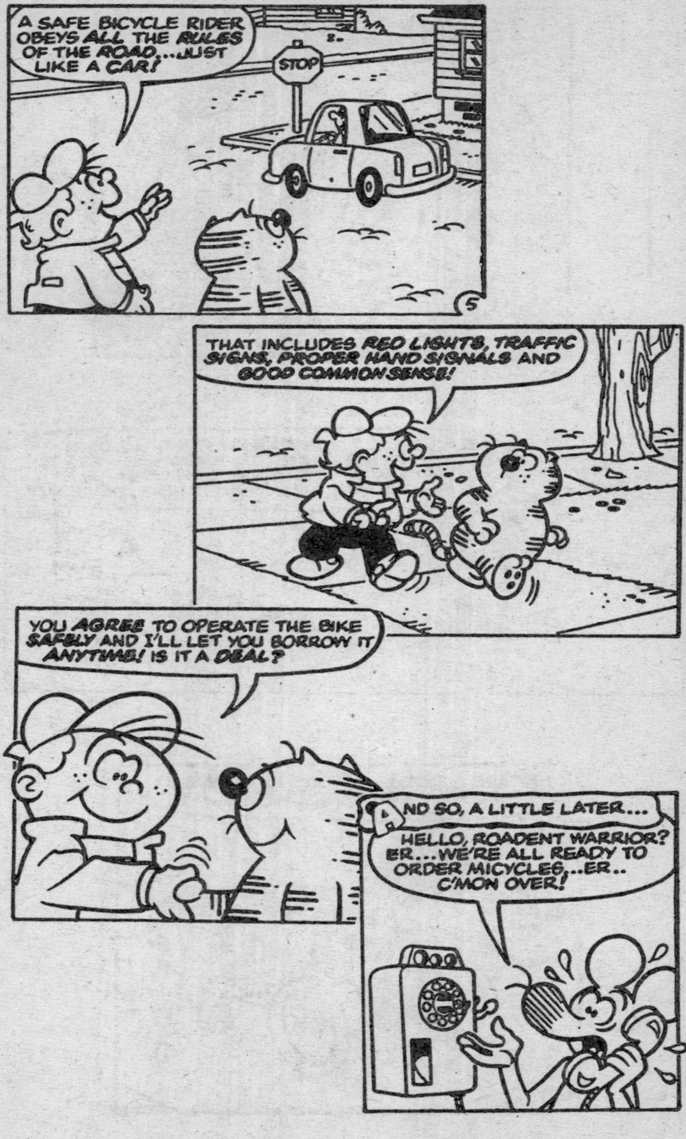
A SAFE BICYCLE RIDER OBEYS ALL THE RULES OF THE ROAD...JUST LIKE A CAR!
STOP
5
THAT INCLUDES RED LIGHTS, TRAFFIC SIGNS, PROPER HAND SIGNALS AND GOOD COMMON SENSE!
YOU AGREE TO OPERATE THE BIKE SAFELY AND I'LL LET YOU BORROW IT ANYTIME! IS IT A DEAL?
AND SO, A LITTLE LATER...
HELLO, ROADENT WARRIOR? ER...WE'RE ALL READY TO ORDER MICYCLES...ER.. C'MON OVER!

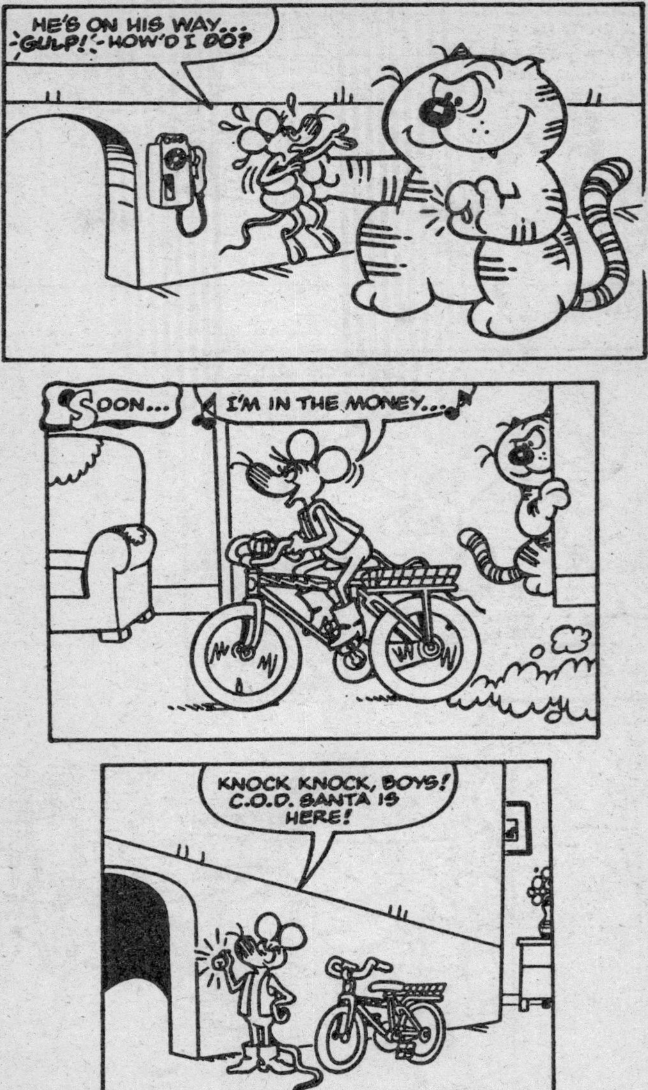
HE'S ON HIS WAY... -GULP!- HOW'D I DO?
SOON...
I'M IN THE MONEY...
KNOCK KNOCK, BOYS! C.O.D. SANTA IS HERE!

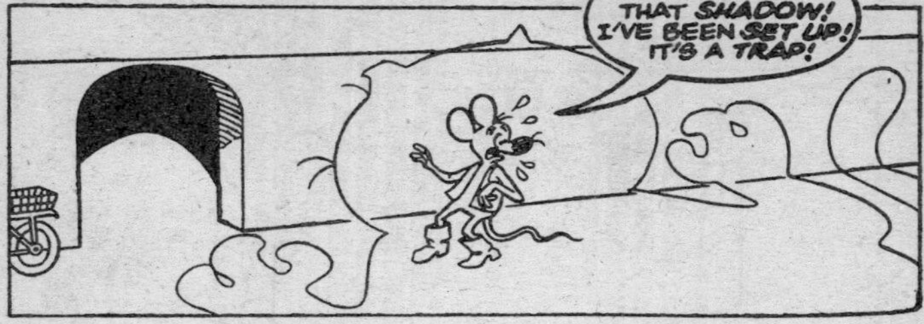
THAT *SHADOW*! I'VE BEEN *SET UP*! IT'S A *TRAP*!

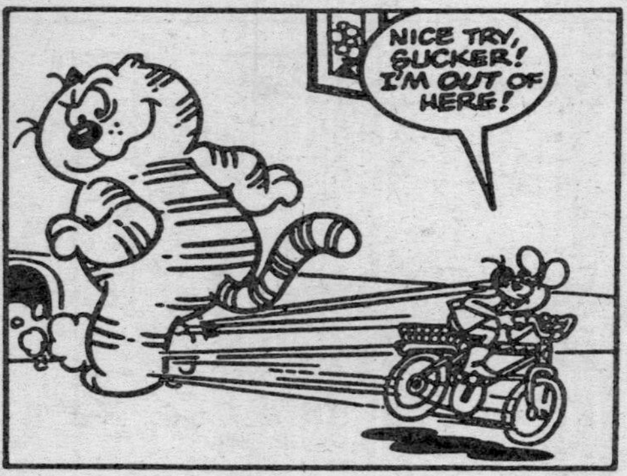
NICE TRY, SUCKER! I'M *OUT* OF HERE!

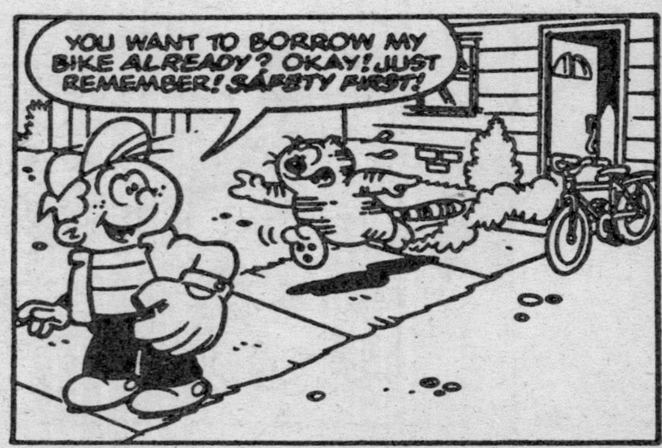
YOU WANT TO BORROW MY BIKE *ALREADY*? OKAY! JUST REMEMBER! *SAFETY FIRST!*

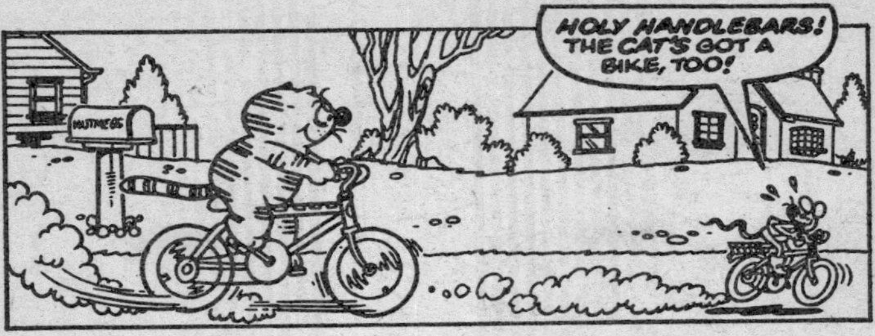
HOLY HANDLEBARS! THE CAT'S GOT A BIKE, TOO!

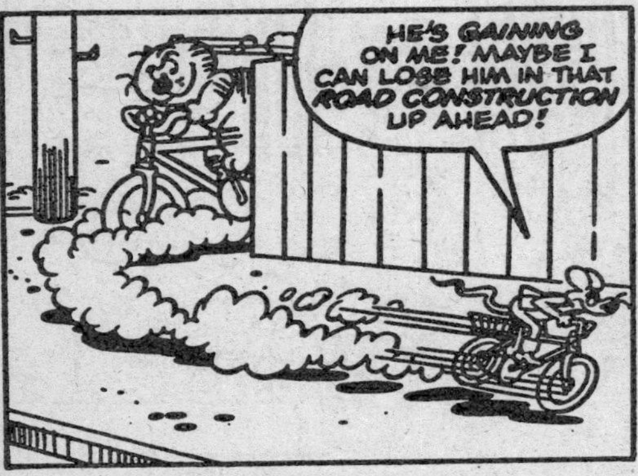
HE'S GAINING ON ME! MAYBE I CAN LOSE HIM IN THAT ROAD CONSTRUCTION UP AHEAD!

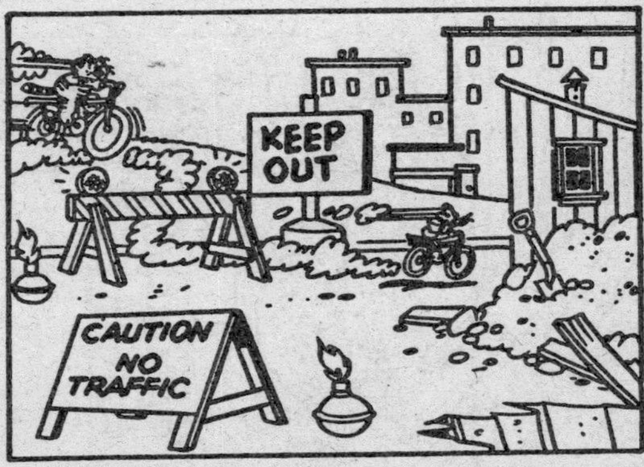
KEEP OUT
CAUTION NO TRAFFIC

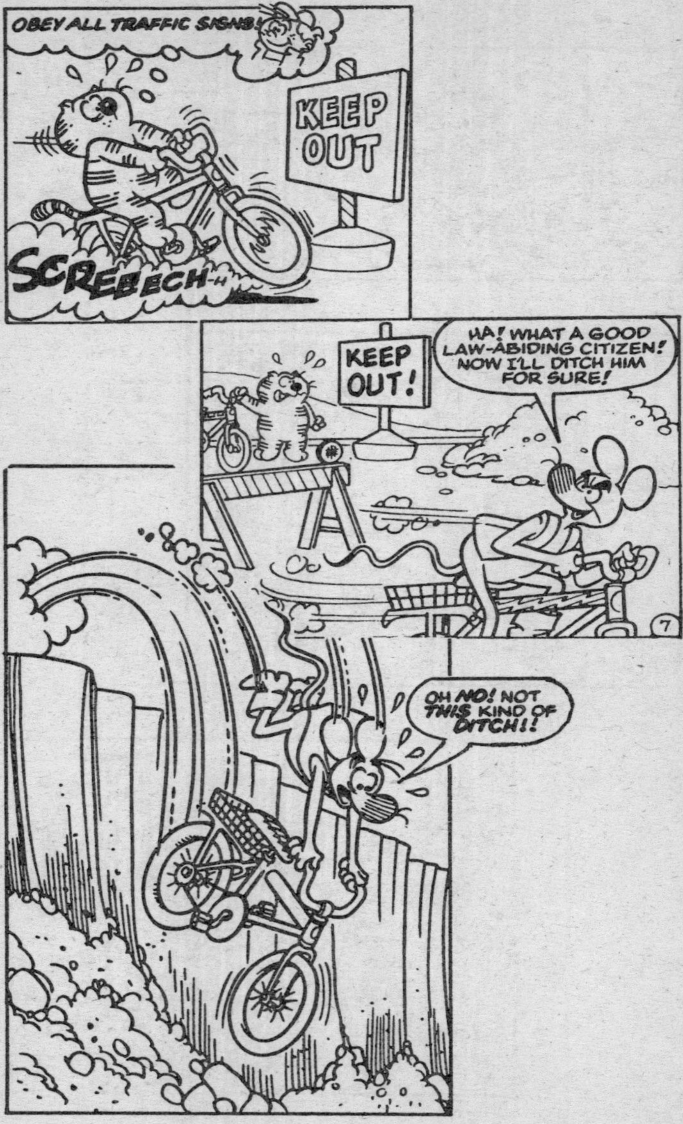
OBEY ALL TRAFFIC SIGNS!
KEEP OUT
SCREEECH-H
KEEP OUT!
HA! WHAT A GOOD LAW-ABIDING CITIZEN! NOW I'LL DITCH HIM FOR SURE!
7
OH NO! NOT THIS KIND OF DITCH!!

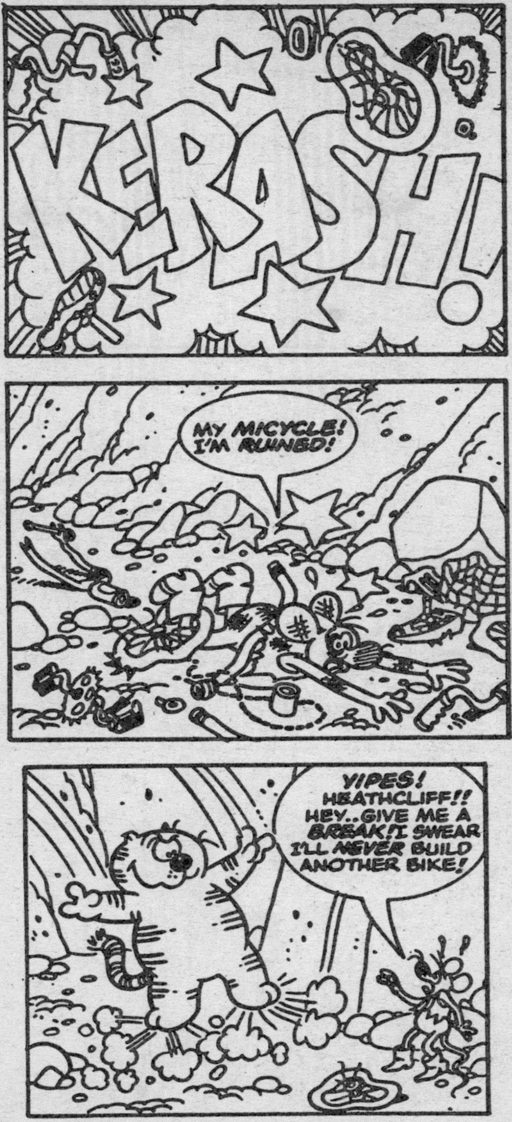
KERASH!
MY MICYCLE! I'M RUINED!
YIPES! HEATHCLIFF!! HEY..GIVE ME A BREAK! I SWEAR I'LL NEVER BUILD ANOTHER BIKE!

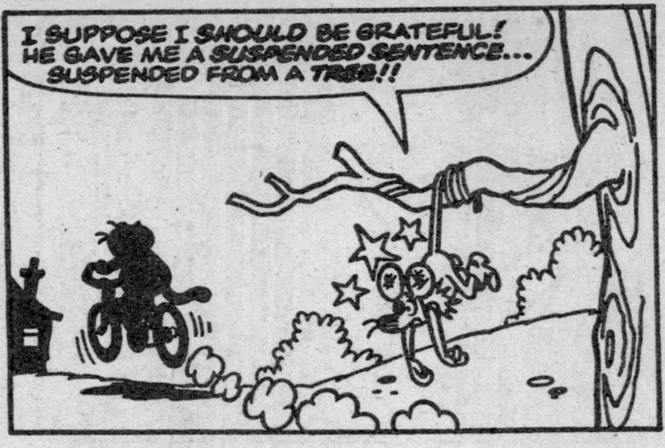
I SUPPOSE I SHOULD BE GRATEFUL! HE GAVE ME A SUSPENDED SENTENCE... SUSPENDED FROM A TREE!!

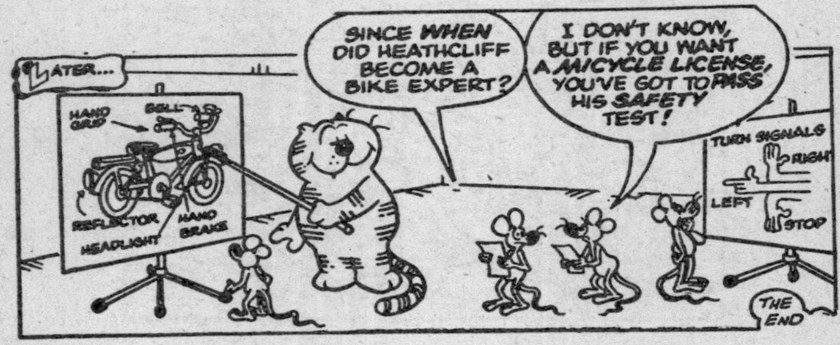
LATER...
SINCE WHEN DID HEATHCLIFF BECOME A BIKE EXPERT?
I DON'T KNOW, BUT IF YOU WANT A MICYCLE LICENSE, YOU'VE GOT TO PASS HIS SAFETY TEST!
HAND GRIP
BELL
REFLECTOR
HAND BRAKE
HEADLIGHT
TURN SIGNALS
RIGHT
LEFT
STOP
THE END

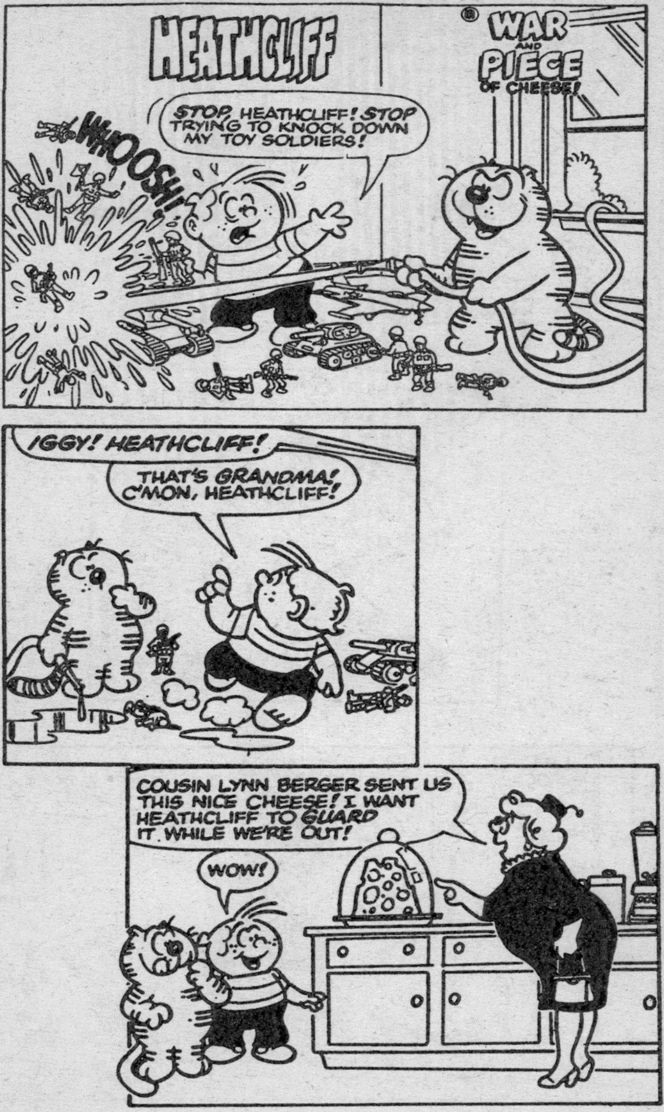
HEATHCLIFF
WAR AND PIECE OF CHEESE!
WHOOSH!
STOP, HEATHCLIFF! STOP TRYING TO KNOCK DOWN MY TOY SOLDIERS!
IGGY! HEATHCLIFF!
THAT'S GRANDMA! C'MON, HEATHCLIFF!
COUSIN LYNN BERGER SENT US THIS NICE CHEESE! I WANT HEATHCLIFF TO GUARD IT WHILE WE'RE OUT!
WOW!

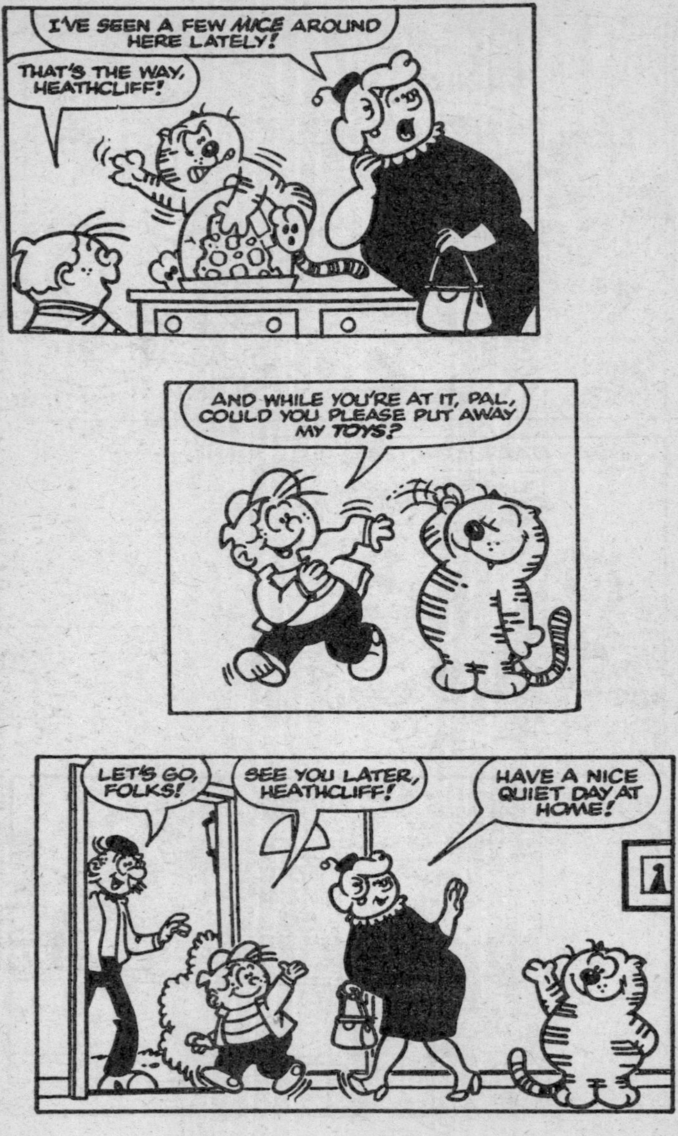
I'VE SEEN A FEW MICE AROUND HERE LATELY!
THAT'S THE WAY, HEATHCLIFF!
AND WHILE YOU'RE AT IT, PAL, COULD YOU PLEASE PUT AWAY MY TOYS?
LET'S GO, FOLKS!
SEE YOU LATER, HEATHCLIFF!
HAVE A NICE QUIET DAY AT HOME!

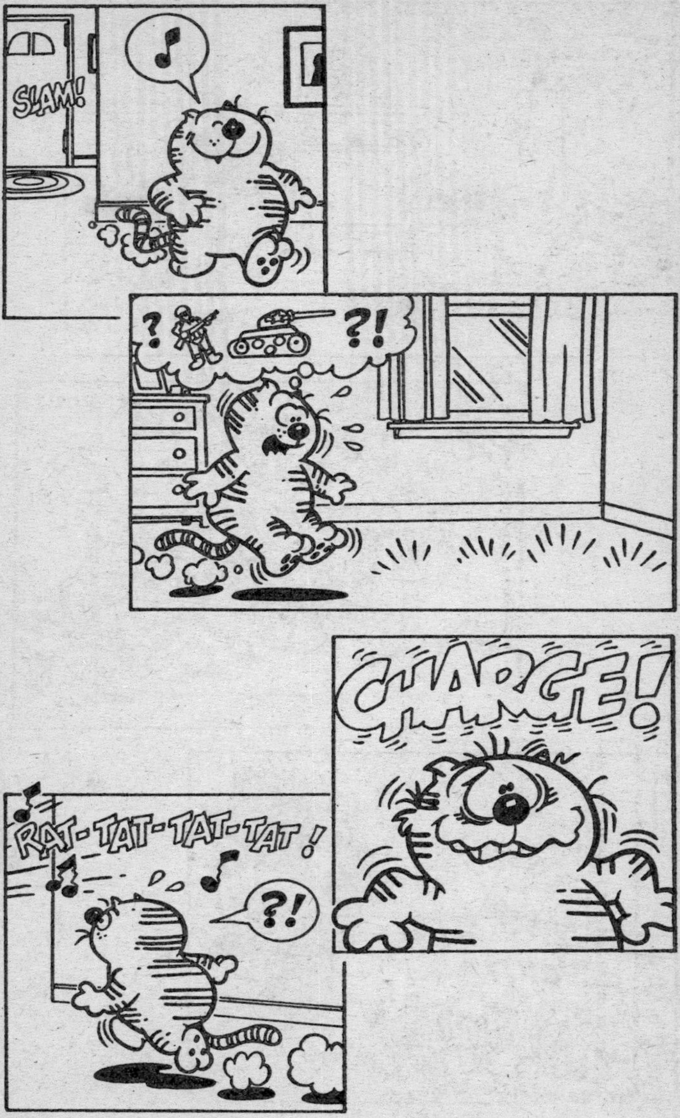
SLAM!
?!
?!
CHARGE!
RAT-TAT-TAT-TAT!
?!

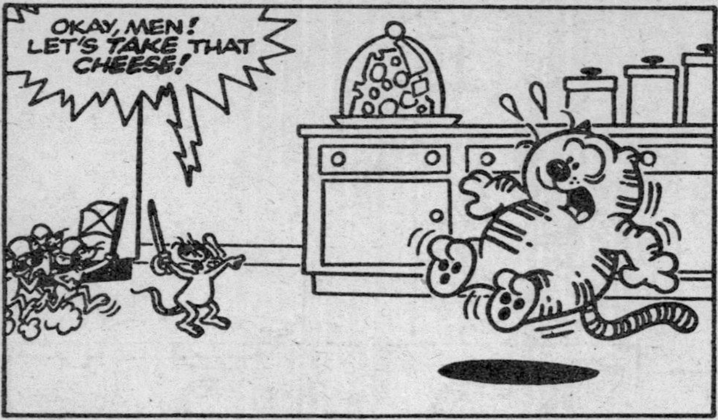
OKAY, MEN! LET'S TAKE THAT CHEESE!

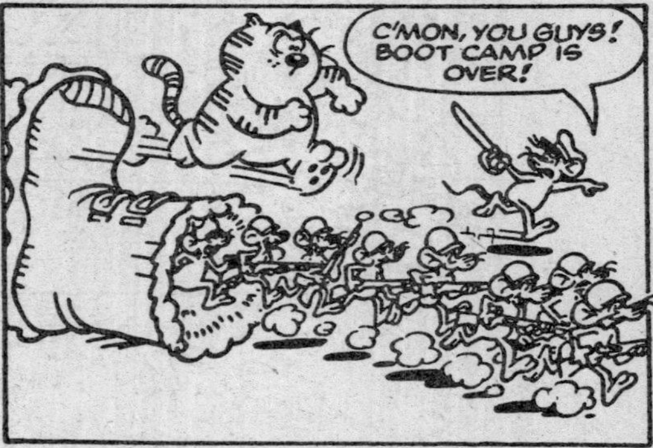
C'MON, YOU GUYS! BOOT CAMP IS OVER!

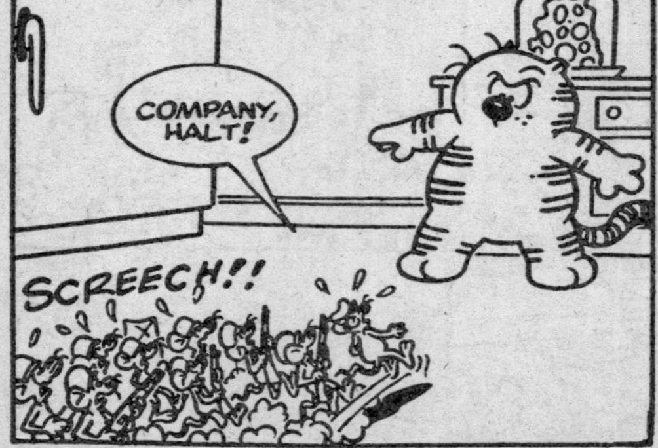
COMPANY, HALT!
SCREECH!!

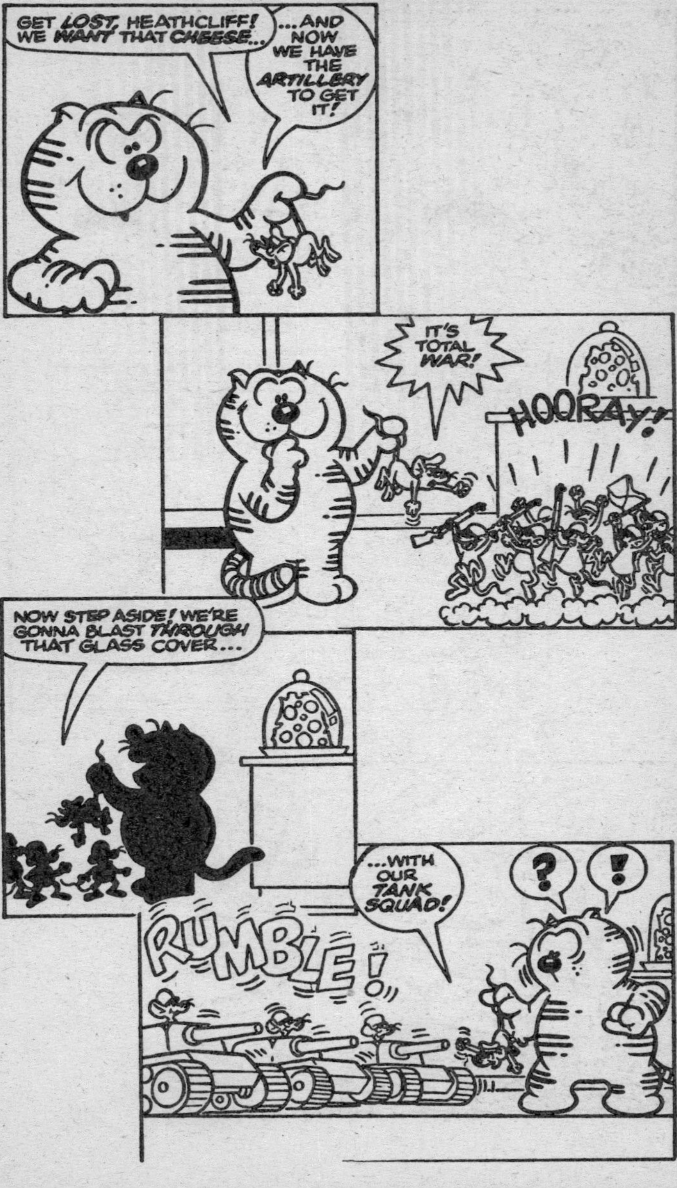
GET LOST, HEATHCLIFF! WE WANT THAT CHEESE...
...AND NOW WE HAVE THE ARTILLERY TO GET IT!
IT'S TOTAL WAR!
HOORAY!
NOW STEP ASIDE! WE'RE GONNA BLAST THROUGH THAT GLASS COVER...
RUMBLE!
...WITH OUR TANK SQUAD!
?
!

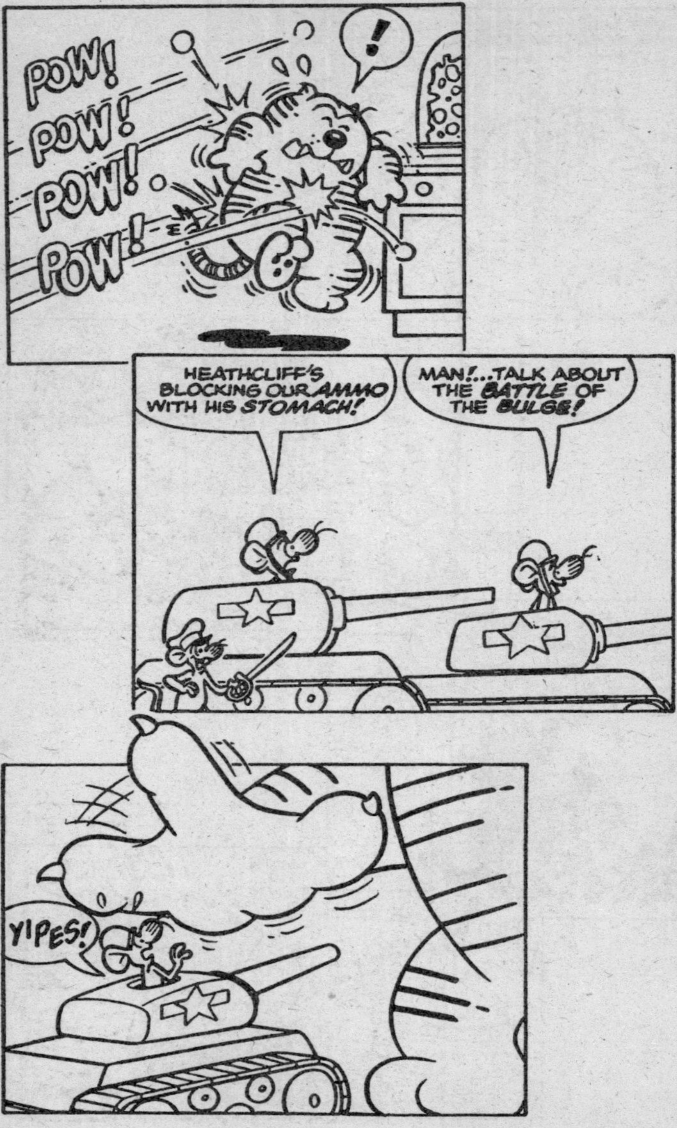
POW! POW! POW! POW!
!
HEATHCLIFF'S BLOCKING OUR AMMO WITH HIS STOMACH!
MAN!...TALK ABOUT THE BATTLE OF THE BULGE!
YIPES!

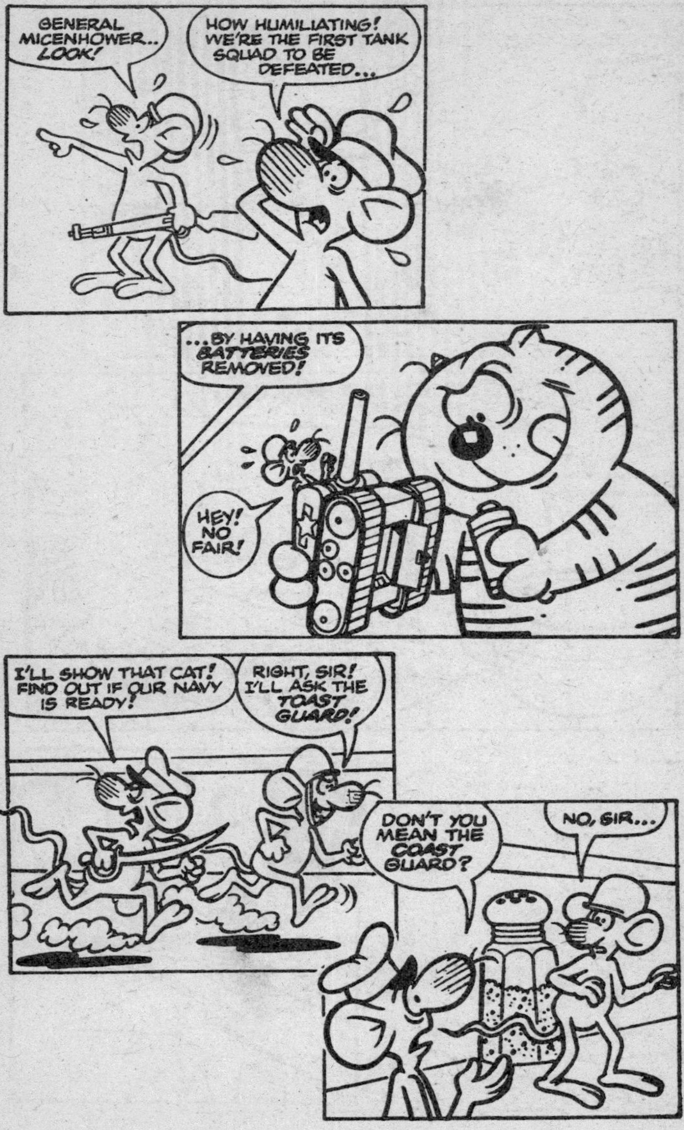
GENERAL MICENHOWER.. LOOK!
HOW HUMILIATING! WE'RE THE FIRST TANK SQUAD TO BE DEFEATED...
...BY HAVING ITS BATTERIES REMOVED!
HEY! NO FAIR!
I'LL SHOW THAT CAT! FIND OUT IF OUR NAVY IS READY!
RIGHT, SIR! I'LL ASK THE TOAST GUARD!
DON'T YOU MEAN THE COAST GUARD?
NO, SIR...

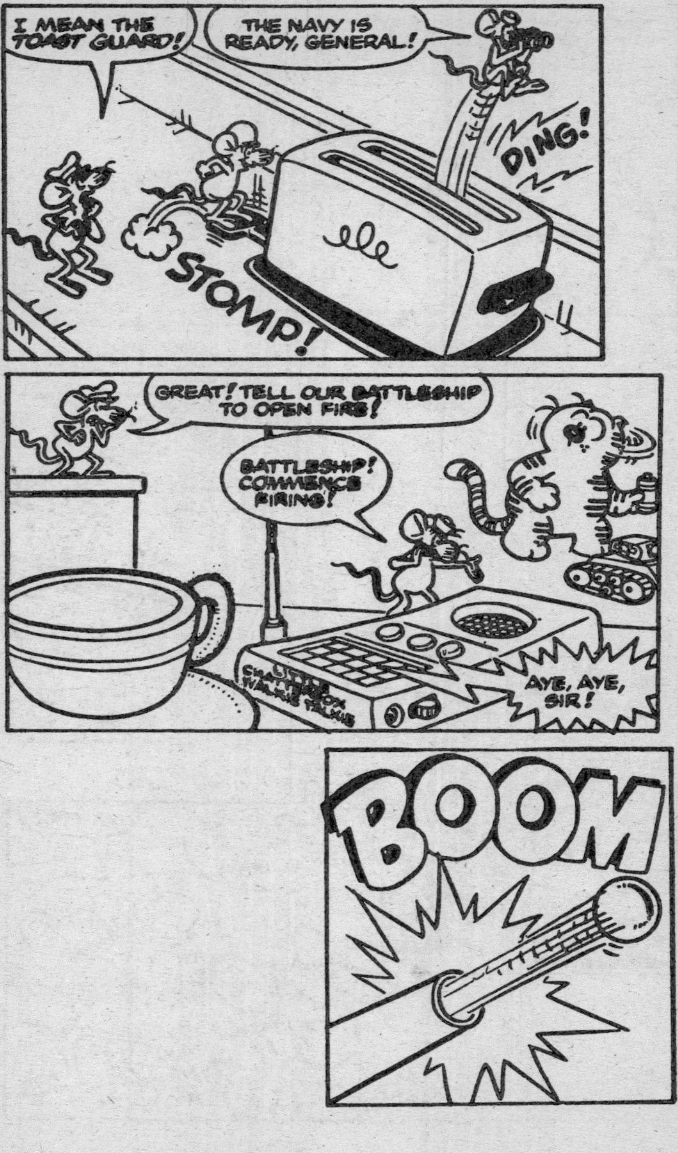
I MEAN THE TOAST GUARD!
THE NAVY IS READY, GENERAL!
DING!
STOMP!
GREAT! TELL OUR BATTLESHIP TO OPEN FIRE!
BATTLESHIP! COMMENCE FIRING!
AYE, AYE, SIR!
BOOM

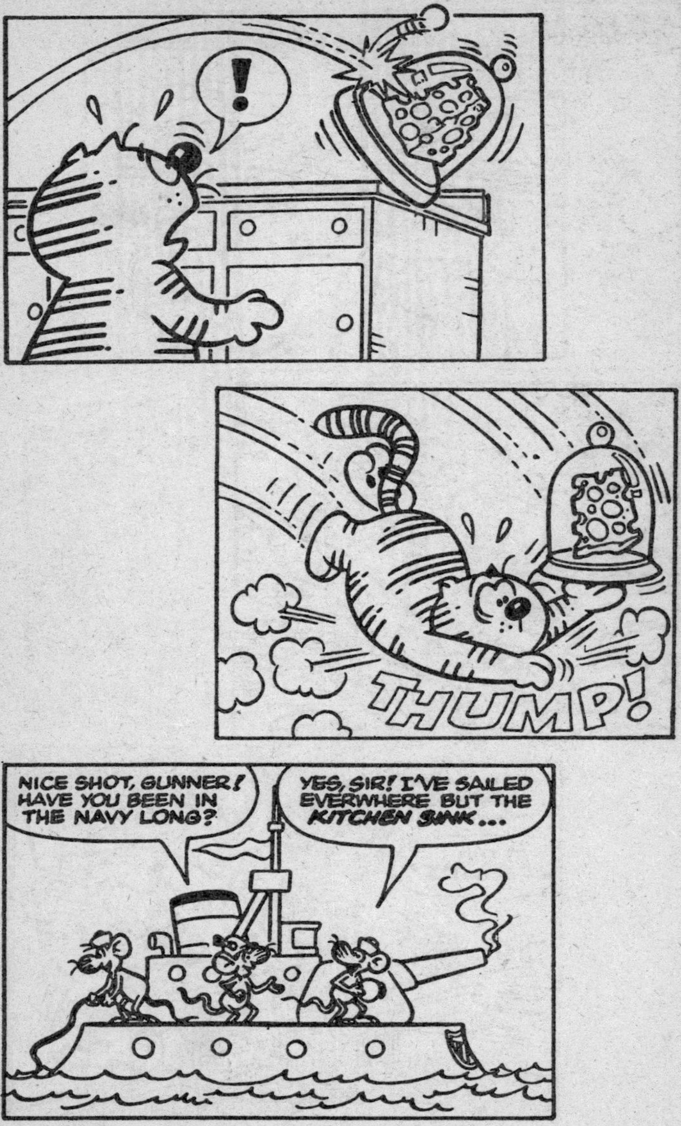
!
THUMP!
NICE SHOT, GUNNER! HAVE YOU BEEN IN THE NAVY LONG?
YES, SIR! I'VE SAILED EVERWHERE BUT THE *KITCHEN SINK*...

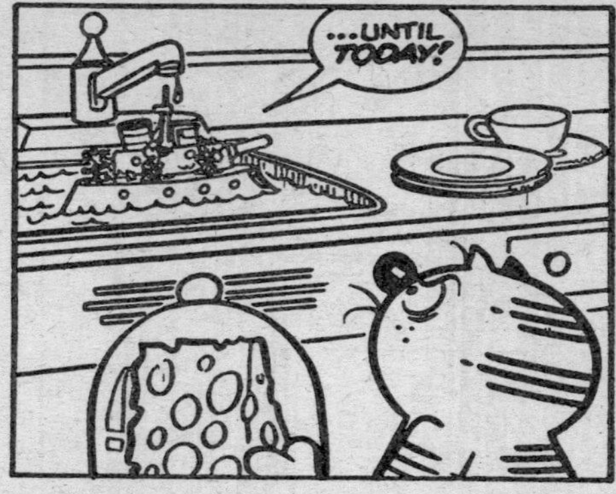
...UNTIL
TODAY!

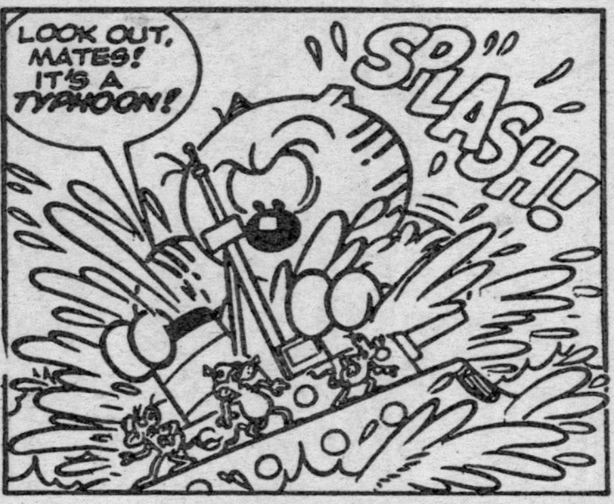
LOOK OUT, MATES! IT'S A TYPHOON!
SPLASH!

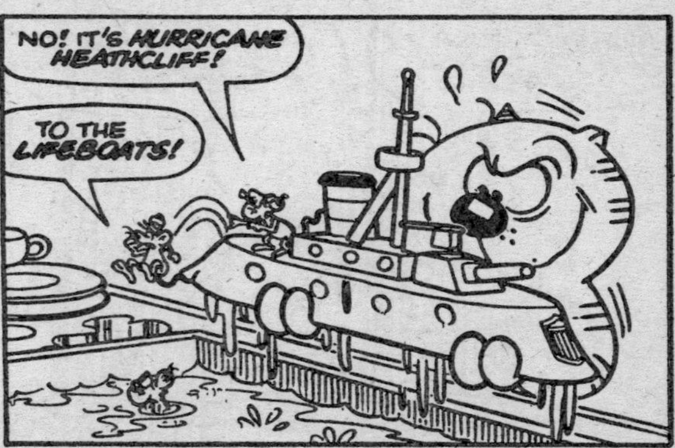
NO! IT'S HURRICANE HEATHCLIFF!
TO THE LIFEBOATS!

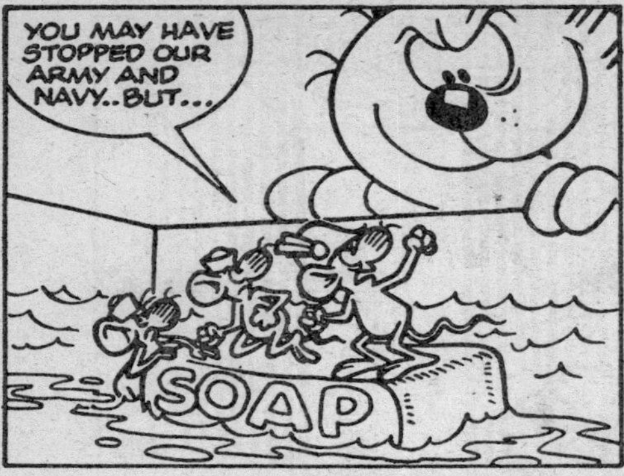
YOU MAY HAVE STOPPED OUR ARMY AND NAVY..BUT...
SOAP

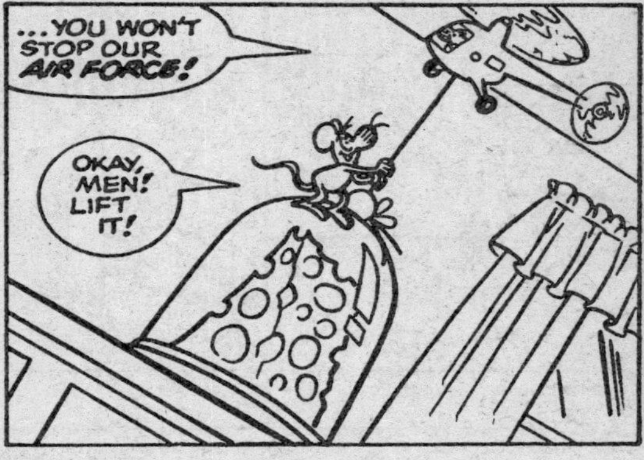
...YOU WON'T STOP OUR *AIR FORCE!*
OKAY, MEN! LIFT IT!

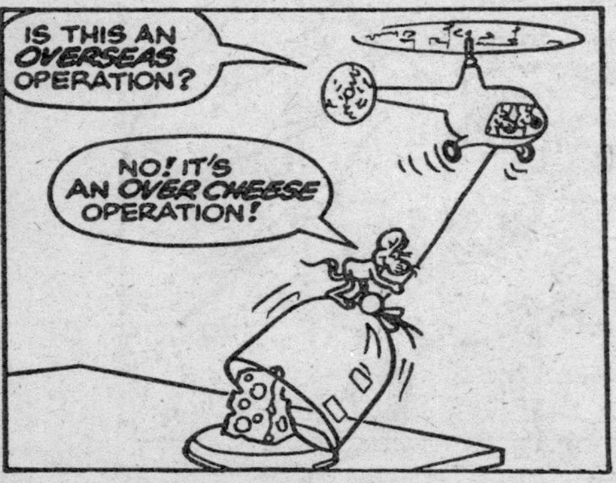
IS THIS AN *OVERSEAS* OPERATION?
NO! IT'S AN *OVER CHEESE* OPERATION!

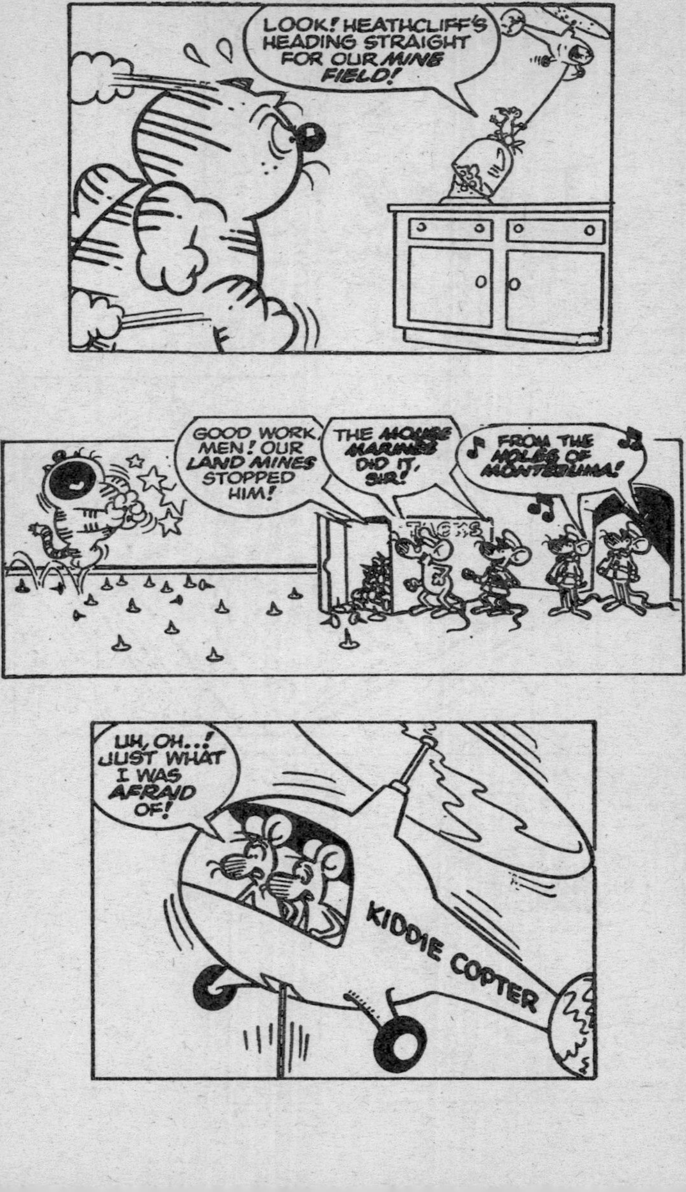
LOOK! HEATHCLIFF'S HEADING STRAIGHT FOR OUR MINE FIELD!
GOOD WORK, MEN! OUR LAND MINES STOPPED HIM!
THE MOUSE MARINES DID IT, SIR!
FROM THE HOLES OF MONTEZUMA!
TACKS
UH, OH..! JUST WHAT I WAS AFRAID OF!
KIDDIE COPTER

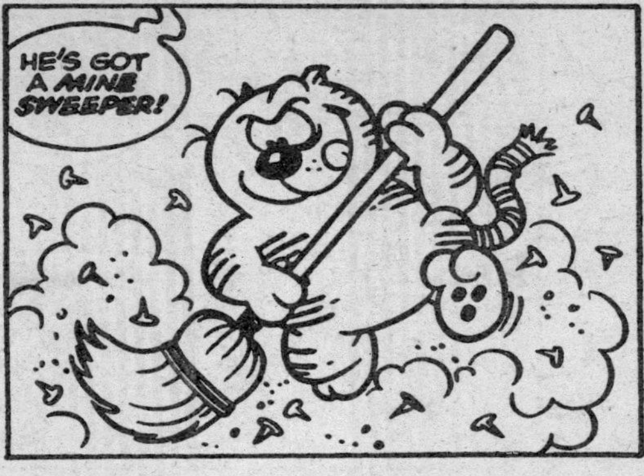
HE'S GOT A MINE SWEEPER!

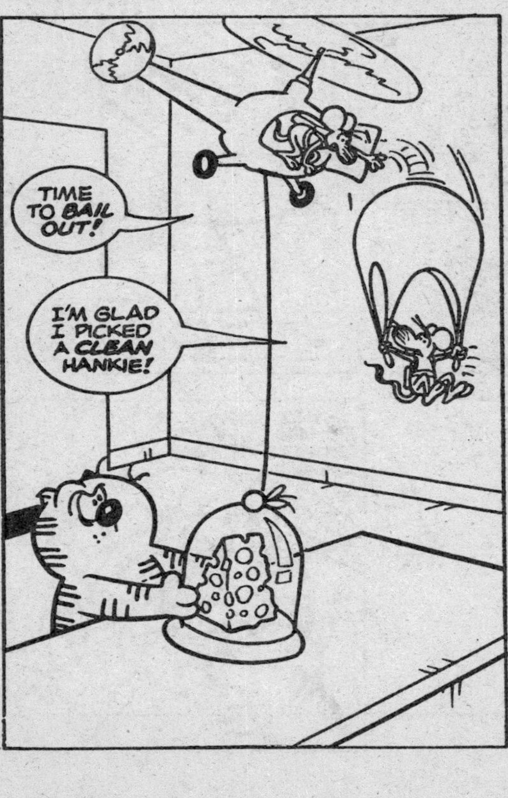
TIME TO BAIL OUT!
I'M GLAD I PICKED A CLEAN HANKIE!

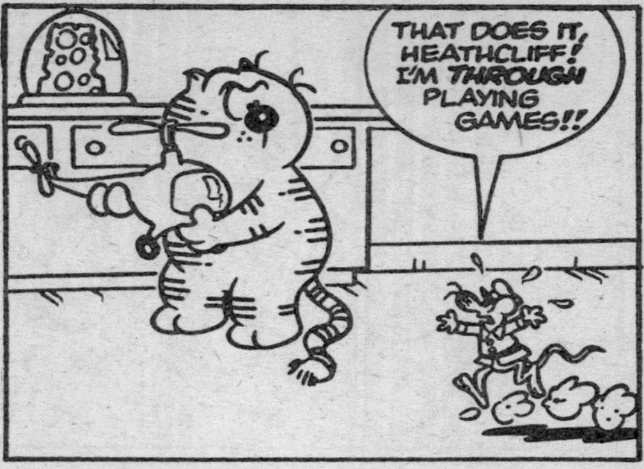
THAT DOES IT, HEATHCLIFF! I'M THROUGH PLAYING GAMES!!

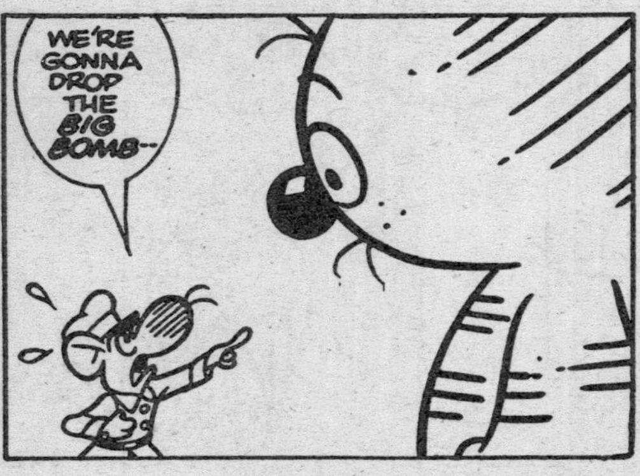
WE'RE GONNA DROP THE BIG BOMB--

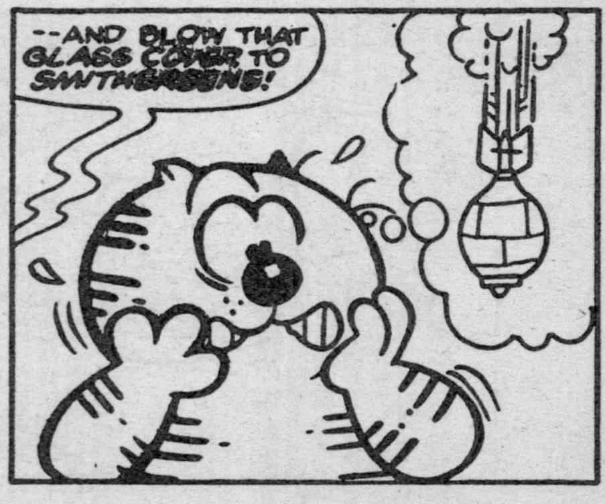
--AND BLOW THAT GLASS COVER TO SMITHEREENS!

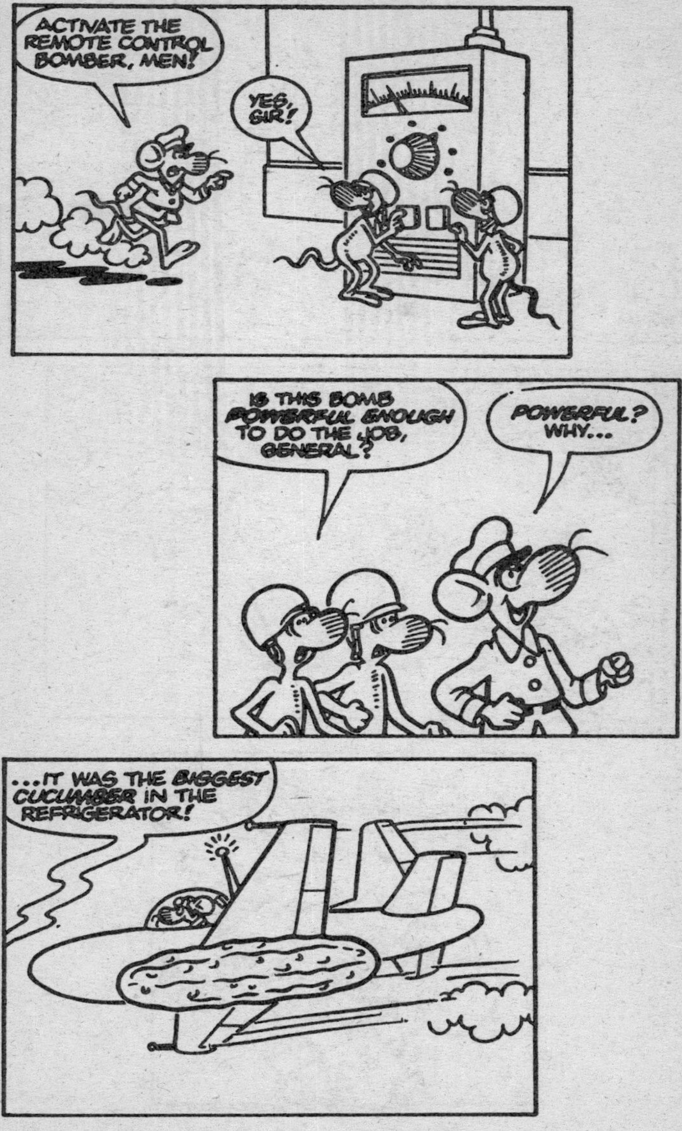
ACTIVATE THE REMOTE CONTROL BOMBER, MEN!
YES, SIR!
IS THIS BOMB *POWERFUL ENOUGH* TO DO THE JOB, GENERAL?
POWERFUL? WHY...
...IT WAS THE *BIGGEST CUCUMBER* IN THE REFRIGERATOR!

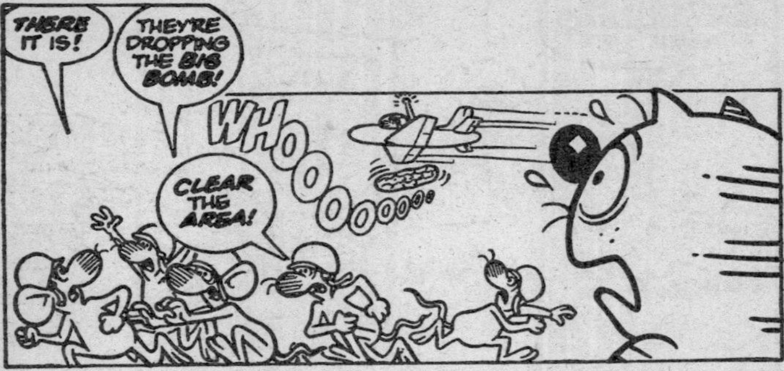
THERE IT IS!
THEY'RE DROPPING THE BIG BOMB!
WHOOOOOOOO
CLEAR THE AREA!

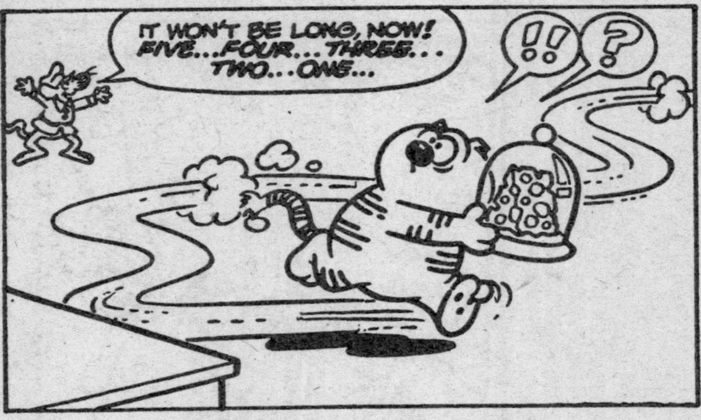
IT WON'T BE LONG, NOW! FIVE...FOUR...THREE... TWO...ONE...
!!
?

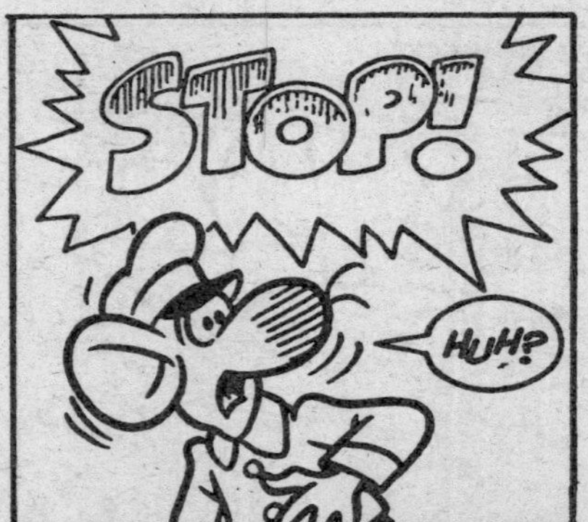
STOP!
HUH?

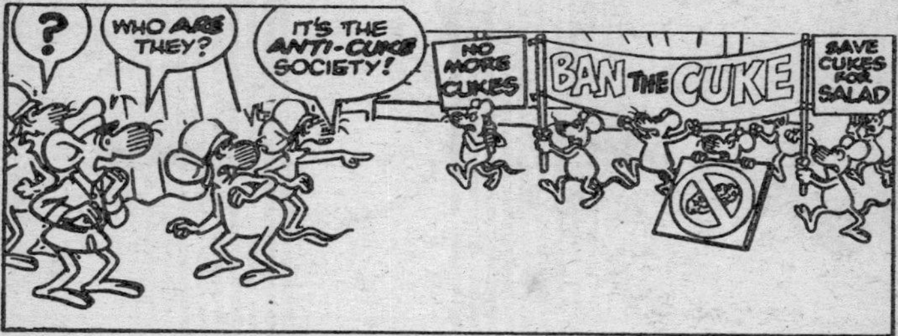
?
WHO ARE THEY?
IT'S THE ANTI-CUKE SOCIETY!
NO MORE CUKES
BAN THE CUKE
SAVE CUKES FOR SALAD

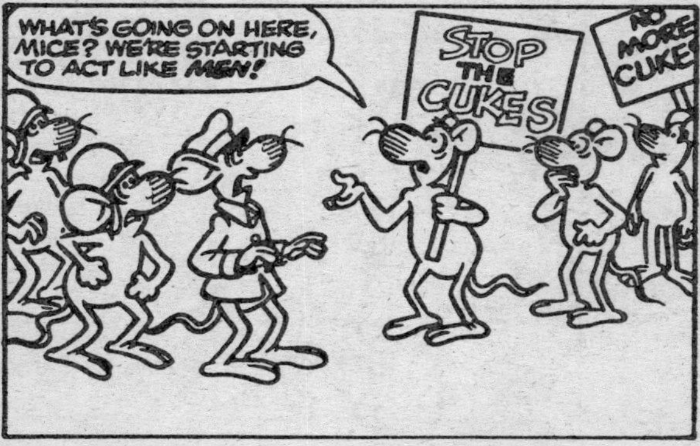
WHAT'S GOING ON HERE, MICE? WE'RE STARTING TO ACT LIKE MEN!
STOP THE CUKES
NO MORE CUKE

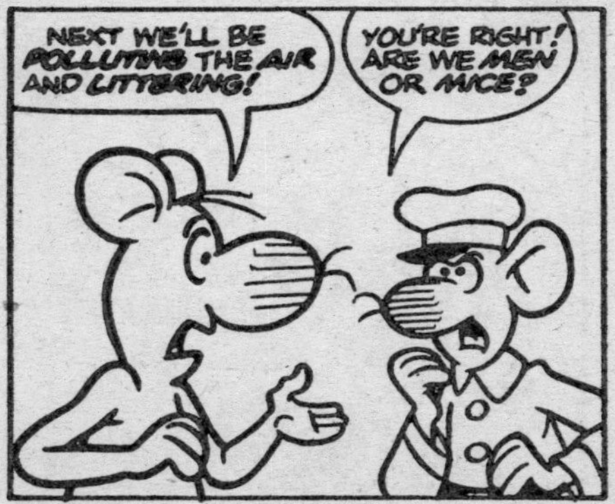
NEXT WE'LL BE POLLUTING THE AIR AND LITTERING!
YOU'RE RIGHT! ARE WE MEN OR MICE?

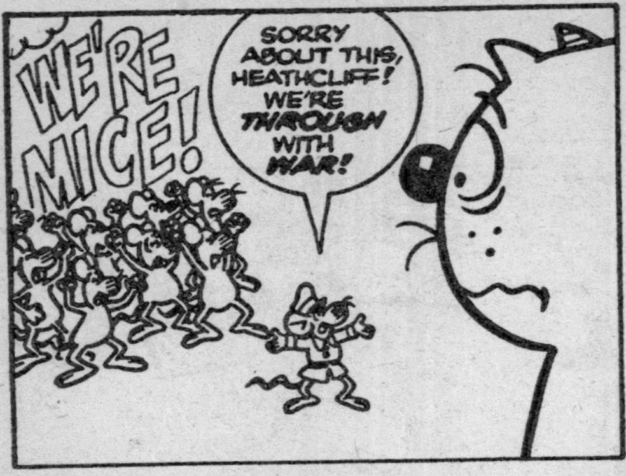
WE'RE MICE!
SORRY ABOUT THIS, HEATHCLIFF! WE'RE THROUGH WITH WAR!

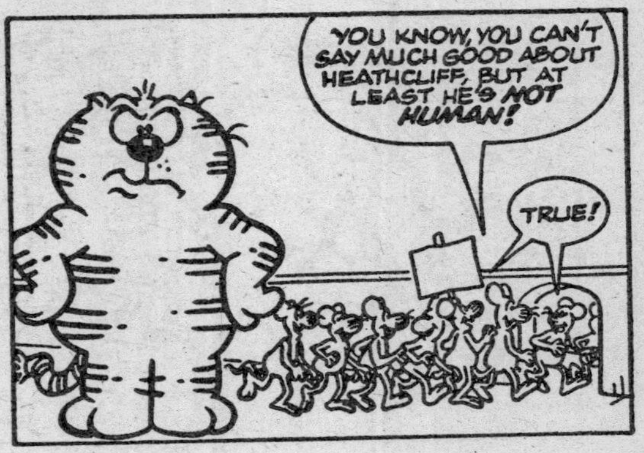
YOU KNOW, YOU CAN'T SAY MUCH GOOD ABOUT HEATHCLIFF, BUT AT LEAST HE'S NOT HUMAN!
TRUE!

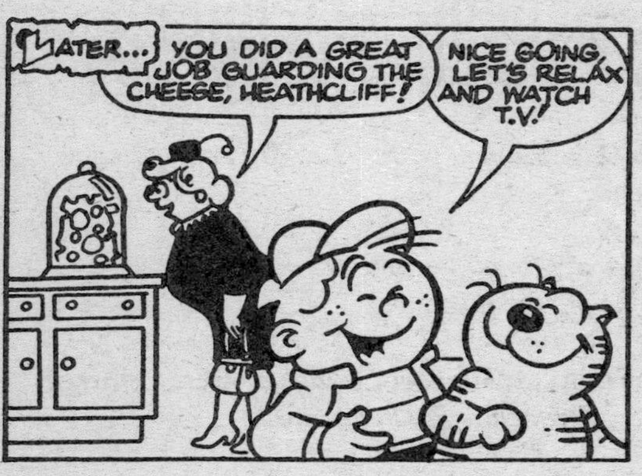
LATER...
YOU DID A GREAT JOB GUARDING THE CHEESE, HEATHCLIFF!
NICE GOING. LET'S RELAX AND WATCH T.V.!

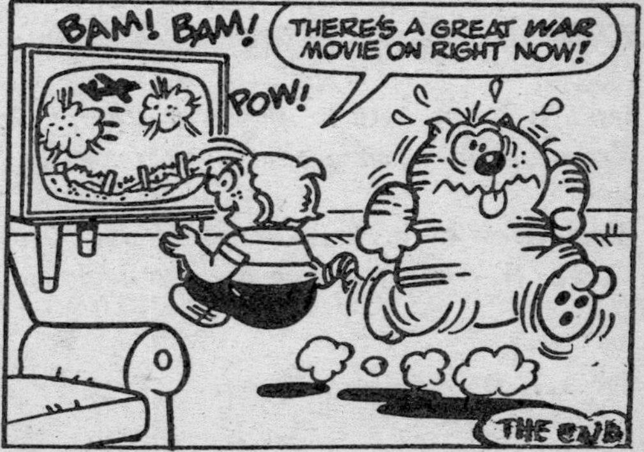
BAM! BAM!
THERE'S A GREAT WAR MOVIE ON RIGHT NOW!
POW!
THE END

Acting Up: *Angelo DeCesare, writer; Warren Kremer, penciler; Jacqueline Roettcher, inker.*

Vice Mice: *Michael Gallagher, writer; Warren Kremer, penciler; Jacqueline Roettcher, inker.*

Track Star: *Tony Franco, writer; Warren Kremer, penciler; Roberta Edelman, inker.*

Mousecapades: *Dave Manak, writer; Warren Kremer, penciler; Jacqueline Roettcher, inker.*

Muscle Mouse: *Dave Manak, writer; Howard Post, penciler; Ruth Leon, inker.*

Mouse Sitter: *Dave Manak, writer; Warren Kremer, penciler; Jacqueline Roettcher, inker.*

Pedal Pushing Pussycat: *Michael Gallagher, writer; Warren Kremer, penciler; Jacqueline Roettcher, inker.*

War and Piece of Cheese: *Angelo DeCesare, writer; Warren Kremer, penciler; Jacqueline Roettcher, inker.*

Isn't It Romousetic?: *Angelo DeCesare, writer; Warren Kremer, penciler; Jacqueline Roettcher, inker.*

Take Meow to the Ball Game!: *Michael Gallagher, writer; George Wildman, penciler; Roberta Edelman, inker.*